A white supremacy group is spreading its tendrils of hate through the bucolic hills of Middle Tennessee, holding target practice in Laurel Hill wildlife area and stockpiling explosives in preparation for a race war.

It's up to Savannah's husband Rafe to find and eliminate them... with a little help from Columbia chief of police Tamara Grimaldi, the joint sheriffs of Lawrence, Lewis, Giles, and Maury counties, and an undercover agent from the Tennessee Bureau of Investigation - an undercover agent Rafe trained, and one he wants to keep alive.

But it isn't Clayton in the cross-hairs when the members of the group discover they're under investigation. It's Rafe who goes down from a bullet to the chest, and Savannah who must sideline her worry to lend a hand in taking down the people responsible, before they can put their evil plans into action and affect damage that far supersedes the shooting of one man.

OTHER BOOKS IN THIS SERIES

A Cutthroat Business

Hot Property

Contract Pending

Close to Home

A Done Deal

Change of Heart

Kickout Clause

Past Due

Dirty Deeds

Unfinished Business

Adverse Possession

Uncertain Terms

Scared Money

Bad Debt

Home Stretch

Wrongful Termination

Conflict of Interest

Right of Redemption

COLLATERAL DAMAGE

Savannah Martin Mystery #19

JENNA BENNETT

COLLATERAL DAMAGE

Savannah Martin Mystery #19

Interior design and formatting: B. Gallagher
Cover Design: Dar Albert, Wicked Smart Designs

One

"Dear me," Mother said. She stuck her hand through the crook of my elbow and turned me a hundred and eighty degrees, so I was facing in the opposite direction. "Let's go this way instead."

It was a Saturday morning in early March, and spring had finally sprung in Middle Tennessee. There were leaves sprouting on the trees in Laurel Hill Wildlife Area, and the dry winter-grass was starting to turn green. Here and there, a brave dandelion opened its yellow face to the sun. It was hot enough that I had a trickle of sweat running down my back underneath the slightly too-warm jacket I couldn't take off because I had the baby strapped to my chest, and I could feel myself developing freckles from the UV rays.

None of that was what had prompted Mother's outburst. As I twitched my arm out of her grip, I tried to imagine what might have. A group of men with automatic weapons? A group of men with skull-masks covering the lower halves of their faces? A group of men doing the Nazi salute while goose-stepping?

That's what we were here looking for. Or rather, that was what my husband, and Mother's boyfriend, Bob Satterfield, the sheriff of Maury County, were here looking for. Mother and I were looking for them. In a very circumspect and roundabout way.

Rafe and his boss, police chief Tamara Grimaldi, along with Sheriff Satterfield and his colleagues in Lawrence, Lewis, and

Giles counties, plus any spare personnel they could rustle up from their respective departments, had been staking out Laurel Hill on the weekends for the past month. They were looking for a group of neo-Nazis who were rumored to be holding target practice, or maybe pep rallies, in the park. So far, they'd been down here three or four weekends running, without seeing anything out of the ordinary, so this weekend, Mother and I had invited ourselves along.

We didn't tell them that, naturally. They're both of the alpha-male/clap-the-women-and-children-behind-the-barricade type of man. Neither of them would have been happy about us walking into a potentially dangerous situation. So it was possible that Mother had simply seen Rafe or Bob, or someone else we knew who was part of the same taskforce, and she wanted to hustle us out of sight before they could recognize us.

And I was all about doing that. Rafe would not be happy about the fact that I'd put myself in what he'd consider danger by coming here, and he'd be even less happy about the fact that our almost four-month-old daughter was strapped to my chest while I was doing it. But even so, I couldn't keep myself from throwing a glance over my shoulder as Mother tried to hustle us away. I'm crazy about my husband, and any opportunity to look at him is a good one.

Although when I saw him, I stopped in my tracks. "What the hell… um… heck?"

"Shhh!" Mother hissed, still tugging on my arm. "Come on, darling. This isn't the time to cause a scene."

No, it wasn't. Now was the very last time I should draw any kind of attention to either of us.

Besides, if my husband had his arm around some other women's shoulders, and was smiling down at her while she beamed up at him, it was just part of his cover while he was here. Just a local guy and his girlfriend enjoying a nice hike in the park on their day off. Not keeping an eye out for neo-Nazis at all.

I might have wished the woman he was smiling down at—the woman gazing adoringly up at him—was his boss, or maybe cute, little Lupe Vasquez. Someone who had no romantic interest whatsoever in my husband. But I suppose that'd be too much to ask.

"That's Officer Robinson," I told my mother, and I'm pleased to say that my voice was perfectly even and calm. No jealousy here; no, ma'am. "She works for the Columbia PD."

And she probably had a first name in addition to the title, but I didn't know what it was. Officer Robinson didn't like me, and the feeling was mutual, so first names hadn't come up.

"Grimaldi must have put them together so they'd look like they have a reason for being here. Instead of having Rafe just wandering around on his own."

And Officer Robinson, too. She was young and pretty—and black—and might present a tempting target for a group of local skinheads.

Rafe isn't all that young anymore—almost thirty-two now—and doesn't look like an easy target for anyone. If there were enough of them, they might take him on in spite of that, but we had no idea whether the group was big or small, and he's tall enough and muscular enough that you can tell it wouldn't be easy, even if you had a crowd behind you. And after ten years deep undercover, working his way into one of the biggest South American Theft Gangs in the southeastern United States, he gives off a vibe that's as effective as a warning sign.

Not that it seemed to be having any effect on Officer Robinson. And I'll admit that seeing him with his arm around another woman was annoying.

Not because I have any reason to suspect my husband of infidelity, or even of harboring so much as a secret fondness for Officer Robinson.

No, he loves me, and he adores our baby. He even likes my

mother, and has no desire to get on the wrong side of her by making eyes at anyone else. The fact that he was grinning down at Officer Robinson with every sign of enjoying her company, was just part of the job. And besides, he probably did enjoy her company. Why wouldn't he, when she so visibly enjoyed his?

"Let's just get out of here before they see us."

Mother nodded, and as we hustled off down a path to the left, I congratulated myself on getting away without being seen.

I should have known better, of course.

When Rafe came home, it was late afternoon, and I was sitting at the island in the kitchen, in view of the back door—the one closest to the carriage-house-turned-garage—doing some work on my laptop.

We were living in Mother's house, while she was shacked up with the sheriff. The Martin mansion is a big antebellum plantation home that sits on a little knoll on the road between Sweetwater and Columbia, and in spite of the almost five thousand square feet and plethora of rooms to choose from, I often found myself hanging out in the kitchen. I'd grown up here, in what Rafe used to call the mausoleum on the hill, and in spite of having run and played in these rooms all my life, with just the two of us here—plus the baby and the dog—the size of the place was just a little daunting.

Pearl the pitbull lifted her head when she heard Rafe approach the door. I knew he was coming, of course, since I'd heard the car come up the driveway and around the back. Pearl may not have, not until he came closer. She gave a short, sharp yip when he inserted the key in the lock. By the time he'd pushed the door open and she could see him, her little stub of a tail was slapping against the pillow, and her jaws were split in a doggy grin.

"Yes," he told her, "that's a good girl. Good girl, Pearl." He bent to give her a scratch between her small, furled ears before shutting the door behind him and straightening to fix me with a look.

"What?" I said. And I might have sounded a little defensive. Maybe.

"Got something you wanna tell me?"

"No," I said.

He arched a brow.

"Fine." I huffed out an exasperated breath. It wasn't like I didn't know what he was doing, after all. He'd seen us earlier, and wanted to hear me admit it. And in case you're thinking that I gave in too quickly, there was no sense in dragging it out, since he already knew, anyway. "We were curious, OK? It's been a month, and you've gone down to Laurel Hill every weekend, and so far you haven't seen anything worthwhile. We figured it would be safe for us to take a walk in the woods ourselves."

He folded his arms across his chest. They're nice arms, and it's a nice chest, and under other circumstances my eyes may have lingered. At the moment, I just went on.

"The place was crawling with law enforcement, so it wasn't like we were in danger. And anyway, nothing was going on. All we saw were people fishing and riding horses and hiking. Did you see anything more than that?"

"I saw you," Rafe said.

"Other than me."

He shook his head.

I leaned back. "So that's four weekends in a row now with nothing going on. Do you think the reports were wrong?"

"They weren't wrong." He stepped away from the door and came over to lean on the island across from me. The head of the viper tattooed around one upper arm peeked out from under the short sleeve of the black T-shirt. "When we did the first search, we found spent bullet casings and masks. They'd been there."

But they hadn't been back since, or not as far as we knew.

"Maybe they don't meet at the same place every time they want to practice goose-stepping," I said. "That would be smart, wouldn't it? Even just a few young men with semi-automatic weapons and swastikas tattooed on their scalps aren't easy to overlook."

Which was how Rafe and the rest of law enforcement knew that they met—or had met—in the wildlife area for target practice before. Someone had seen them, and reported it. "Maybe they switch things up and go to different places every time. To make it harder to track them down."

"It's starting to look that way," Rafe agreed.

"What about Rodney and Kyle? You've got somebody sitting on them, right?"

Rodney Clark and Kyle Scoggins were two young men in the Columbia area, who had come to my attention—and thus Rafe's attention—during a murder investigation earlier in the year. Neither of them had been guilty, or for that matter much of a suspect, but one of them had a swastika tattooed on his head, and I'd heard them use racial slurs against Cletus Johnson's five-year-old daughter, which argued a high degree of probability that if there was a neo-Nazi group meeting in the area, they'd be part of it. Most people, decent people, don't call cute little African-American girls ugly names.

Rafe shook his head. "There ain't enough money in the budget to keep'em both under surveillance twenty-four/seven. The one week I did watch, they never did nothing to justify keeping'em covered like that."

"What about this weekend?"

I mean, if the Columbia PD couldn't justify paying six officers to keep an eye on Rodney and Kyle around the clock—and I quite understood why they couldn't—shouldn't there at least be enough money in the budget to watch them on the weekends to see if they traveled somewhere to meet their goose-stepping brethren?

"We did have somebody on'em this weekend," Rafe said. "They didn't go nowhere. Rodney worked this morning."

So clearly this hadn't been a weekend when the neo-Nazis met for target practice.

Either that, or we were wrong about Rodney and Kyle, and they weren't part of the group, swastikas and racial slurs to the contrary.

"Do you think they noticed that someone noticed them?" I asked. "The group, I mean. Back in February, when the park rangers let law enforcement know what was going on, do you think they noticed that they'd been noticed, and now they've stopped getting together?"

He shrugged. It set off a nice chain reaction of muscles under the tight T-shirt. "Might be. Or maybe they're just hanging out somewhere else."

"Or they don't meet every week, Or even every month."

Rafe nodded. "We'll try again next weekend, I guess. Although at the rate we're going, I don't see us being able to keep this up indefinitely. Maybe we'll just have to wait for the park rangers to give us another heads up next time it happens."

He dismissed the conversation to look around the kitchen. "Where's the baby?"

"Having her last nap of the day." Upstairs in her crib. "You can go check on her if you want."

He glanced at the doorway to the hall, and then looked back at me. "Maybe I'll just stay down here."

My lips curved up when he started to move around the island toward me. "That's fine with me."

"You don't mind?"

He plucked me off the stool and boosted me up on top of the island, where he nudged my thighs apart so he could step between them.

"Why would I mind?" I wanted to know, my voice

breathless.

"No reason I can imagine." He bent his head to nuzzle below my ear. I arched my neck to give him better access while I wrapped my arms around his shoulders. Down on the pillow, Pearl closed her eyes with an almost human-sounding sigh.

Rafe's lips curved against my skin. "Prob'ly thinking, *'not this again!'*"

Probably. "I'm not thinking, *'not this again,'*" I pointed out.

"No." He chuckled. "Good thing, too."

It was. A very good thing. I put the dog out of my mind and concentrated on the moment.

With one thing and another, it was at least an hour before we got back to the conversation. By then the baby was awake, and we had moved from the kitchen to the parlor. Pearl had curled up on another pillow—we kept them in several of the rooms where we spent a lot of time—and Rafe and I were sitting on the peach velvet loveseat while I was feeding Carrie.

"So if you saw us," I told Rafe, referring back to Laurel Hill and this morning, "you must have realized that we saw you, too…"

A corner of his mouth turned up. "Yeah. Your mama all right?"

"Fine," I said. "A little shocked when she first saw you, I think. Maybe a touch inclined to think the worst."

"I hope you set her straight, darlin'. Not sure I can afford having your mama think the worst of me."

"There's not much chance that that would happen," I told him. "My mother's crazy about you. She wouldn't believe that you'd misbehave until she had incontrovertible evidence that you were cheating, and even then, she'd probably try to make it my fault. Not giving you enough attention, or something."

"I get plenty of attention," Rafe said, with a gleam of remembered 'attention' in the curve of his lips. "Besides, your mama would never blame you if I screwed up. She'd have me tarred and feathered and run outta town on the point of a pitchfork, but she wouldn't blame you."

Maybe not. "So are you going back tomorrow? To Laurel Hill?"

He shook his head. "I gotta drive up to Nashville tomorrow. The contractor called while I was trying to keep Felicia's mind on the job."

I put the idea of Felicia Robinson aside for the more important matter. "Something wrong?" We had a house under reconstruction in Nashville, and the contractor didn't usually call. Or if he did, Rafe hadn't mentioned it before.

"Nothing too bad. There's a problem with something—the wiring, I think—and now he wants more money."

Of course he did. Home renovation always takes longer and costs more than you think it will.

We'd suffered a fire in early January—arson—and had moved to the mansion in Sweetwater while repairs were being made to house. The fire had been confined to just the front foyer and living room, but it had taken out part of the staircase, and we couldn't get up to the bedrooms on the second level. And it's an old Victorian, so there were historical considerations to take into account. You can't replace original wood windows with vinyl replacements, for example, or the Historical Commission will have a fit. Besides, it's not like hundred-and-forty-year-old wood windows come in standard sizes, so we'd spent a fortune on special-order materials so far.

I wrinkled my nose. "I'd offer to come with you, but I have an open house scheduled at the house on Fulton."

On the topic of renovations: Over the past couple of months, my friend Charlotte and I, with some help from my sister Darcy, who had put up the money, had bought and renovated a little house on Fulton Street in Columbia. We had hired professionals to do the complicated things, like wiring and plumbing and anything else we thought might actually hurt us if we fouled it up, but we'd gotten a crash course in painting and hanging tile and operating a floor sander. Even the murder that had taken place in the house a week or so after we bought it, hadn't stopped us for long enough to matter.

And now the house was ready for the market, and I would be over there from two to four tomorrow afternoon, greeting visitors.

"I guess I'll have to ask Mother or Catherine to mind the baby," I added. "I thought you'd be here to take care of her. Unless... will you be back by one-thirty?"

He shook his head. "Sorry, darlin'."

"No problem," I said. "I'll go to the Wayside Inn for lunch with the family after church, and see who I might inveigle into taking her home with them. Worst case scenario, she'll just have to come with me. Chances are nobody will really mind if there's a baby in the house when they walk through. As long as she isn't crying."

Rafe nodded, his lips twitching.

"It's no problem," I told him.

The twitching turned into a smile. "I didn't think it was, darlin'."

Good. "So about Felicia Robinson..." I said, and Rafe chuckled.

Two

The next morning, he rolled out of bed and got dressed in faded jeans and boots and a T-shirt and his black leather jacket. While I was still wiping the drool off my chin, he gave me a wink and sauntered out the door and down the stairs. A minute later, I heard the big, black Harley-Davidson start up with a roar and take off down the driveway toward the Columbia Road. Carrie, next to me in bed—because Rafe had given her to me before he got dressed—made a kind of inquiring noise, and I nodded. "Daddy's gone for the day, baby. From now on, it's just you and me."

And Pearl, of course. Rafe had let her out, but I fed her and took care of her, and then I bundled Carrie and myself into the Volvo and headed to church in time to hear the end of the sermon. And after that, I went to meet the rest of the Martins and assorted friends and hangers-on for the weekly family brunch at the Wayside Inn.

It's Mother's favorite restaurant, and exactly what it sounds like: a two-hundred-year-old log cabin on the road between Pulaski and Columbia. A German chef took it over a few years ago, so the food is excellent, and Mother enjoys the ambience and the white cloth napkins and sparkling stemware.

There are quite a few of us when we're all together, although of course Rafe was missing today. My sister-in-law, Sheila, had died more than a year ago now, and Dix hadn't officially replaced her yet, so we were down one member there, too. On the other hand, Bob Satterfield was squiring Mother, although his son Todd and Todd's fiancée Marley were absent. And there was my sister Catherine, her husband Jonathan, and their three kids, plus Dix's two, and now Carrie.

"Hello, darling." Mother aimed a kiss at my cheek and her eyes over my shoulder. "Where is Rafael?"

"He had to run up to Nashville for something," I said, and pulled out a chair while Mother made a moue. "I have an open house over on Fulton at two, so I couldn't go with him."

Mother nodded and devoted herself to the next best thing, which was Carrie. I run a distant third behind my daughter and her father in Mother's affections.

Dix nodded to me across the table. "Sis."

"Bro," I answered, and made him grin. "Small crowd today."

He nodded. "Audrey and Darcy went back to Audrey's house with Mrs. Jenkins. Marley isn't feeling great, so Todd took her home."

Marley was pregnant, so I wasn't surprised.

"I'm looking for a babysitter for Carrie," I said, "so I don't have to bring her to the open house."

Dix shook his head. "Don't look at me. We've got a birthday party to go to after this."

"Us, too," Catherine said from farther down the table.

I turned to Mother, who looked up from where she was tickling Carrie's toes. "Sorry, darling. Bob and I are driving up to Nashville for a concert. We'll be leaving before you're finished with your open house."

I sighed.

"Maybe you can ask Charlotte," Dix suggested.

I shook my head. "She'll be there, too. And I can't ask Mrs. Albertson to take my daughter as well as Charlotte's two kids. I guess Carrie will just have to come with me."

"If you plan to keep your real estate license now that the

baby's born," Mother said, "she should probably get used to it, don't you think?"

I supposed she should. Not that I make a whole lot of money from my real estate license, but I didn't want Carrie to grow up thinking she didn't have to work for a living. I'd been brought up to think that all I needed was a man to take care of me, and look where that had gotten me.

I mean, yes, it had gotten me Rafe. Eventually. But not before I'd wasted my virginity and two years of my life—and my first "I do,"—on Bradley Ferguson.

"I guess it won't matter." Not to Carrie, certainly. She'd be in her car seat, or bouncy seat, or on a blanket on the floor, wherever we were. The surroundings didn't matter to her. I didn't want to appear unprofessional, though.

"Nobody will care," Mother said firmly. "Besides, who could resist this little face?"

She tickled Carrie's cheek. Carrie gurgled. Mother beamed.

A year and a half ago or so, when I'd first gotten my license, I'd hosted a lot of open houses. They're common practice in real estate, and although I'd never had a lot of listings of my own—I just wasn't that successful—I'd volunteered to sit a fair few for other agents in my brokerage. I'd even picked up a buyer client or three that way.

After a few not so good experiences—one of which had found me tied to a bed in my underwear by a murderer (and being rescued by Rafe)—I had volunteered for less, though. And then I'd gotten attached to Rafe and had wanted to spend my weekends with him instead. So it had been quite a while since last time.

Carrie had fallen asleep on the drive from Sweetwater to Columbia, so when I arrived at the house on Fulton, I tucked her away in a corner of the living room before wandering through the house fluffing pillows and picking up specks of dust. We'd decided to have the place staged, at the additional cost of a couple thousand dollars of Darcy's money, to make it look lived in—some people have a hard time with empty rooms—and the staging did, if I do say so myself, look good.

We'd done a halfway decent job on the renovations, too, if you ask me. The tile backsplash in the kitchen looked practically professional, and the new cabinet doors—Shaker style, to replace the old slab-fronts that had been there—updated the look of the whole house.

It was the same thing in the bathroom, where the tile—again, practically professional—made everything look so much better than it had with the old plastic insert. The hardwood floors gleamed, the bulbs in the light figures shone, and everything smelled fresh and new, if a little like paint.

Charlotte walked in at a couple of minutes to two, in a green silk dress that was probably a leftover from her marriage to Doctor Dick, the cosmetic surgeon. She stopped just inside the door and looked around. "Looks good."

I nodded. "I think it was worth the money for the staging. Houses look so much better when they're lived in. And they echo less. Besides, we wouldn't have had anything to sit on."

"What do you want me to do?"

"For now," I said, "we can just hang out here together. But when people start arriving, one of us should go into the back of the house—the master suite—and be available for questions." And just so no one decided to stick a staging item into their pocket and walk off with it. I didn't want to have to pay Michelle the stager for any replacements. "One of us needs to stay here to greet the people who come in."

Charlotte nodded. "You do that. I'll go to the back. That way you don't have to leave the baby."

Another reason why I wanted someone in the living room. Carrie would wake up if I kept moving her around—she might wake up anyway, when people started coming in—and besides,

I wanted to make sure no one had the bright idea to walk off with her. That probably wasn't likely to happen, but why take chances?

"Do you think we'll get an offer today?" Charlotte wanted to know, taking a seat on the sofa with her legs tucked to one side, folding her hands in her lap like a proper lady.

"I'm not sure," I admitted. "It could happen, but it probably won't. Most houses take a little longer than that to sell. Although I think we're priced pretty well."

I'd checked the competing properties in the area, and priced ours below some of the more expensive ones, so we'd look like good deal in comparison. And the spring market was warming up, although how that would play out in a small town like Columbia—small in comparison to Nashville, at least—I had no idea. Maybe the spring wasn't any busier here than the rest of the year.

"And we look good," Charlotte said, looking around.

I nodded, and cut my eyes to the window at the sound of a car door slamming outside. "Looks like the first visitors are here. Let's get this show on the road."

Charlotte got to her feet, smoothing down the skirt of her green dress. "Good luck," she told me.

"Same to you." She needed the money we'd get for the house more than I did, actually. It would make me happy to contribute to Rafe's and my household expenses, but we were living rent-free, both here in Sweetwater and in Nashville, and Rafe had a job that paid well enough that we were scraping by with a little extra to spare. Charlotte, on the other hand, was in the process of getting back on her feet after leaving her husband, and as he was currently in prison facing kidnapping charges, there wasn't likely to be much money left for settlement after everything was said and done.

"If we get an offer," I told her, "I'm going to squeeze every penny I can out of it."

She smiled, and headed off to the back of the house, her heels clicking on the newly-sanded oak floors. I squared my shoulders and marched toward the front door to greet the visitors.

They kept coming for the next two hours after that. A few of the neighbors stopped by, out of curiosity and to see what we'd done to the place, and a handful of potential buyers walked in and out, commenting on the finishes and the abundance, or lack thereof, of closet space.

"The two bedrooms at the end of the hall are part of the original house," I explained. "It's from the nineteen-forties, and people didn't need huge closets then. But we created the master suite in the back, and we added a walk-in closet and a big bathroom in there. Unfortunately, there was nothing we could do about the size of the closets that were already here."

Toward the end of the open house, Mrs. Allen from down the street came in, followed by her husband and—of all people—Rodney Clark, one of the guys Rafe and I suspected was part of the neo-Nazi group Rafe was hunting.

Rodney had been dating the Allen's daughter Natalie when she'd been murdered three or four years ago. Nancy Allen wasn't all that fond of him, but I knew he had a habit of stopping by their house once in a while. Now he gave me a smirk, while Nancy Allen grabbed me in a hug. "Savannah!"

She and I, with some help from her husband, had taken out Natalie's murderer last month. I guess we'd bonded, at least a little.

I squeezed her back. "How are you?"

"Better now." She let me go and stepped back to give me a smile. "No bail. Did you hear?"

I nodded. Natalie's murderer was languishing in prison, and was likely to stay there, since if he was let out, he'd be off and running so fast we'd only see the dust. The trial was set for

June, but we were all hoping he'd just enter a guilty plea before then and save us all the trouble. There was no chance at all he'd get off, at least not in my opinion.

"We wanted to see what you'd done with the place," Gary Allen said, and shook my hand. "Looks good."

He glanced around the living room. Nancy and Rodney did the same. Nancy was admiring the sofa—chartreuse velvet; I could see her eyes snag on it—but Rodney zeroed in on Carrie, cooing in the car seat. "That your baby?"

I nodded, and zeroed in on her, too.

In case I haven't mentioned it, she's gorgeous. And yes, I know that most babies are pretty. It's even possible I might be a little biased, since she looks a lot like her daddy, and he's gorgeous, too. But she really is a very pretty baby. Dusky skin, black curls, winged brows, and clear, blue eyes. She got those from me, and everything else from Rafe. I keep expecting them to turn brown, because sometimes that happens to babies born with blue eyes, but so far they've stayed blue.

"She's beautiful," Nancy Allen said. Gary Allen nodded.

Rodney said nothing, and after a second, I gave them all a polite smile. "Feel free to look around. The setup is much the same as in your house." Most of the houses on Fulton had been built from the same architectural drawing. Small tract houses from WWII. "We turned the garage into a master suite. It was already a rec room by the time we bought the house; we just took it one step further."

"That's where Morris got it," Rodney said, "wasn't it?"

Where Morris got…?

"Yes," I said. "It was."

The previous owner of the house, the recently-acquitted-but-still-suspected murderer of Natalie Allen, had been killed in what had then been the rec room. It wasn't something I particularly wanted to dwell on, though. Or something I wanted anyone else to dwell on, either; especially at my open house. Murders tend to be turnoffs for most home buyers, even if Rodney seemed more excited than anything else.

He headed in the direction of the kitchen. Gary gave me an apologetic smile and wandered after, while Nancy made a face. "Sorry. He's young."

He was. Although not young enough that a bloody murder should appeal to him. Natalie had been his girlfriend, though, and Morris had still been the obvious suspect when he was killed, so maybe I could just chalk Rodney's ghoulish interest up to that.

And if not, maybe I could chalk it up to the fact that Morris had been black and Rodney was a racist. That made for an acceptable explanation, too.

At any rate, they disappeared into the back of the house, where they became Charlotte's problem. I turned back to the door and greeted the next couple to come through.

We stayed busy until almost four-thirty. The Allens and Rodney left again, and so did several other people. But at a couple of minutes to four, just as we were thinking it might be time to take down the Open house sign and lock the door, a lady and gentleman around fifty walked in. The guy looked a little familiar, and I thought he might be someone I should recognize. But I didn't, and by then Carrie had woken up and I had to deal with her, so I just greeted them in the friendliest manner I could manage, and let them pass by me and into the kitchen.

And then I listened as they proceeded to pick apart the renovation Charlotte and I had done, in excruciating detail and with many unflattering words.

"Look at these cabinets, Eddie. They're not even new. These are the old cabinets with new doors. If they're going to ask this much money for an old house, they could at least put in all new cabinets!"

Eddie muttered something I couldn't hear.

"And these appliances are hardly top of the line. This fridge doesn't even have an ice-maker!"

Eddie muttered again.

"And look at this tile. The grout lines look like calligraphy. Whoever tiled this backsplash must have been drunk or blind or both!"

I felt my cheeks flush. I had tiled that backsplash, and I hadn't been either. What I had been, up until right now, was proud of myself. It had been my first backsplash, and I thought I'd done a pretty good job.

They moved into the hall bath, after disparaging the stain color we'd chosen for the hardwood floors, and I heard the lady raise her voice in blatant disbelief than anyone could have such bad taste as to paint the ceiling blue.

Charlotte came scurrying into the living room. "What a witch," she whispered.

I would have used a different word, one that rhymed but started with a B, but I nodded.

"You know who it is, don't you?"

I had no idea who it was, and shook my head.

Charlotte lowered her voice another degree. "That's one of the guys from the auction. Not the one who kept bidding against us just to increase the price we had to pay, but one of the others. I think he dropped out at around fifty thousand."

"I don't remember him," I admitted, "but I'll take your word for it."

That explained the attitude of the lady, anyway. The guy's wife, probably. Someone who had hoped to benefit from this flip, until we'd intervened and bought the place.

"People are such bastards," Charlotte said, scowling at the doorway.

"Go ahead and go home," I told her. "Relieve your mother of babysitting duties. I'll stay and lock up."

Rafe wasn't back from Nashville yet anyway. Or at least I

assumed not. I hadn't heard from him.

"Are you sure?" She looked from me to the door and back.

"There's no reason we both have to be here. And I have to put the key back into the lockbox in case another agent wants to show the property this week. You can't do that. But I also don't need you for me to do it."

She hesitated. "Are you going to be safe?"

Of course I was going to be safe. It was broad daylight on a friendly street in a good neighborhood, and whatever else I might think about the guy from the auction—whom I now vaguely remembered—I was positive he and his wife weren't going to kill me.

"This isn't my first rodeo," I told Charlotte. "I used to sit open houses all the time in Nashville. In neighborhoods that were a lot worse than this one." And once or twice I had gotten in trouble. But I really didn't think that was likely to happen today. "Just take the Open house sign and put it in the trunk of my car so anyone else doesn't think we're still open, and go home to your kids."

She hesitated.

"I'll be fine.," I said. "They're not going to be here much longer." It was a small house; they'd run out of things to criticize soon. "And if it'll make you feel better, I'll text you when they're gone, so you know I'm still alive."

She hesitated.

"I have pepper spray and a knife in my purse," I said. Charlotte's eyes widened. "They're disguised as lipstick tubes, but I've had to use them before. They work."

She blinked.

"I'll take you up to Nashville and show you where I got them, if you want to get your own set." And she might want to. She'd been kidnapped at gunpoint a month ago, by the person who had promised to love and cherish her, and while that wasn't likely to happen again, I wouldn't blame her for feeling a little jumpy.

"Sure," Charlotte said, her eyes still wide.

"But for right now you can go home. I've got this."

She nodded. And grabbed her coat and headed for the door, her eyes still a little wider than usual.

"Don't forget the sign," I called after her. She nodded, and shut the door behind her.

The guy from the auction and his wife stayed another ten minutes after Charlotte drove away. I'm sure they would have stayed longer if Charlotte had been in the back where she could hear them, but since they'd lost the audience for their grousing, I guess they decided there was no point in hanging around. I gave them a polite smile (but with sharp teeth) when they walked through the living room, and wished them a lovely evening as I held the door open for them.

"Good to see you both," I lied as I edged the door closed before they could say anything. "Thanks for stopping by."

I shut the door with a soft but decisive click, and turned the bolt. Mother would have been appalled at my lack of manners, but as I listened to the couple on the stoop take stock for a second—probably staring at the door before staring at each other—and then stepping down to the walkway, I couldn't find it in myself to feel too bad. Considering the way that woman had talked about my taste and my handiwork, I could have been a lot more rude than I'd been.

I waited for them to get in their car—a small and ladylike SUV—with the wife driving, before I walked through the house to make sure that all the windows and doors were secure. Finally, I got my coat, my purse, and my baby, and headed out. Charlotte had put the Open house sign in the back of my car, as requested, and before I reversed down the driveway, I sent her a text. *They're gone. I'm headed home.*

Ten seconds later, my phone rang. I rolled my eyes as I

answered it. "Hi."

"It's you," Charlotte said.

"Of course it's me." But I guess it was nice of her to check that I hadn't been left for dead on the living room floor and someone else wasn't using my phone. "I'm fine. Going home with Carrie. I'll let you know if I hear from anyone tonight."

Or tomorrow morning. Or any time. Any time was a good time for someone to call and say they wanted to buy our house.

Charlotte said thank you, and hung up. I dialed Darcy and left a brief message about the open house on her voicemail—she was probably out with Patrick Nolan, or maybe in Sweetwater with her mother and great-aunt—and then I put the phone down and kept both hands on the wheel until we made it back to Sweetwater and the mansion.

Three

I heard the Harley come up the driveway just before six. By then I was back in the kitchen, making dinner—fish tacos with cabbage slaw and a side of beans and rice—and keeping an eye peeled for Rafe's return.

He'd been gone a long time, much longer than I'd expected him to be gone. It shouldn't take nine hours to drive to Nashville, meet with the contractor, meet with Wendell, and drive back. Not when Nashville is only an hour away, at least the way Rafe drives. It takes a little longer for me, admittedly, but at nine on a Sunday morning, with the roads mostly empty, he'd have made good time between here and there.

When I'd gotten home and he hadn't been there, I'd sent him a text on the pretext of letting him know that I was home and safe. Not that I thought he was worried. But it was a gentle nudge, and a (silent) request for reassurance back.

Which I got. *Home by 6,* the text said. I went upstairs, changed my clothes, gave Carrie thirty minutes of tummy time on the blanket in the parlor, and then I went to the kitchen and started dinner. And that's what I was doing when the Harley drove into the garage and when Rafe crossed the grass to the back door and let himself in.

He scented the air. "Smells good."

"Hopefully it'll taste good, too." I stirred the beans. "You have ten minutes, if you want to take a shower before we eat."

He shook his head. "All I've been doing today is talk.

Nothing I need to shower off."

"You must have been doing a lot of talking. You've been gone almost nine hours."

He shrugged.

"Everything all right?"

"Fine." He took a seat at the island and folded his arms on the granite top. "How'd your open house go?"

"Rodney Clark showed up," I said, and abandoned the beans in favor of leaning on the island across from him. "With the Allens. Nancy and Gary."

"He say or do anything?"

I shook my head. "Just walked through the house. They were only there for ten minutes or so, before they left again. We had a few more neighbors show up, a couple and a single guy who were both actually in the market to buy a house, although they already had real estate agents—and just before we closed, one of the guys who also tried to buy the house at auction showed up with his wife."

Rafe arched a brow.

"She spent fifteen minutes pointing out—to her husband, but loud enough that both Charlotte and I could hear her—everything that was wrong with the place. The floor stain. The tile. The way the tile was laid. The kitchen cabinets. I tuned her out when they disappeared down the hallway to the master suite."

"Sounds like she's jealous," Rafe said.

"The guy dropped out of the bidding at fifty thousand, I think. He wasn't the one who kept driving the price up. That was someone else. So I don't think he would have gotten the house even if we hadn't been there. But I'm sure he wanted it."

He didn't say anything else, and I added, "You don't think my tiling is ugly, do you? Or the wood floors too light? Or that my bathroom light fixture looks cheap?"

His lips quirked. "No, darlin'. The floors are great. So is the tiling. And the light cost more than a hundred bucks, didn't it?"

It had. Not that that's a big sum in the scheme of things, but I'd passed up cheaper lights because they *did* look cheap. So it wasn't like I would put just anything into the house. I'd done my best to balance cost and impact, since I was spending my sister's money and since I didn't want to waste any of it. Up until today, I'd thought I'd done a good job.

"Don't let one jealous cow ruin all your hard work, darlin'," Rafe told me. "Wasn't there somebody else who told you how much they liked the place?"

There had been, actually. "Nancy Allen admired the kitchen backsplash. And someone else commented on the original wood floors. There were people there who liked the house."

"Then ignore the old witch," Rafe said, using the B-word Charlotte and I couldn't bring ourselves to utter. "You did a good job. The house looks great. And now that it's on the market, you'll get an offer soon, and the three of you can cash out."

"From your lips to God's ears," I said, and turned back to the stove to finalize the preparations for dinner.

We were sitting in the parlor, talking about Rafe's day, when my phone rang. I excused myself to pick it up. The number was unfamiliar, and I put it to my ear with a pleasant, "This is Savannah. How can I help you?"

"Miz Martin?" a voice said. It wasn't familiar, either, or at least I didn't think so. "This is Arlene Woods with Exit Realty. I'm calling about your house on Fulton Street."

"Yes!" It wasn't quite a triumphant shout, but it came close. Rafe grinned and Ms. Woods hesitated a moment.

"My clients walked through the place during the open house this afternoon. I was wondering whether I could take them through for a second look tomorrow morning?"

"Of course," I said brightly. "The house is unoccupied. The

furniture is all staging. Go any time you want. Lock box on the front porch." I gave her the code.

"Can you tell me anything about the home? Or the renovation?"

"Everything," I said expansively, and then reeled myself in a little. "The house belongs to my sister. We bought it at auction a couple of months ago. I did some of the cosmetic repairs, but we had licensed plumbers and electricians in for the renovations that required it. What would you like to know?"

We talked renovations for a few minutes while Rafe watched me with a pleased curve to his lips and while I threw everything I had into making the house sound as great as I possibly could, and Darcy sound as easygoing as anyone could wish for. Not a tall order, since she isn't difficult to deal with at all.

Arlene hesitated. "I understand there was a murder in the house last month?"

And there it was. The stigma.

"Yes," I admitted, "but it had nothing to do with the house." A small, white lie, that. The dead guy had been the previous owner. But he didn't own the house when he died in it. "Someone broke in through the back door. Everything's been replaced, though. The floors. The drywall. The door." Or at least the window pane that had been broken. "As far as I know, he doesn't walk."

Rafe smothered a snort.

Arlene, on the other hand, didn't sound like she thought it was funny. "We'll take a look," she told me. "But don't be surprised if you don't hear back. That kind of thing isn't going to do you any favors."

Believe me, I knew that. "By the time it happened," I told her, "we'd already bought the place and started working on it. It's not like we can forget we own it just because something bad happened there."

Although we had discussed the fact that if we couldn't sell again within a reasonable amount of time, we might have to rent it out for a while, to let the crime recede in people's minds. Darcy would get her money back more slowly, and Charlotte and I would have done all that work for nothing, but it wasn't like we wouldn't all be OK.

Arlene made a non-committal sort of noise.

"Just let your clients make up their own minds," I told her. "And if it doesn't work out, it doesn't work out. Their loss. We'll sell it to someone eventually."

I kept my fingers crossed and hoped I wouldn't have to eat those words.

"We'll see," Arlene said darkly, and hung up.

I turned to Rafe with a shrug. "Not like I didn't expect it."

He shook his head. "Might not be a problem. Not everybody minds a house where somebody died."

No. And speaking of… "How did it go in Nashville? Does the place look OK?"

"The place looks great," Rafe said. "It's slow going, though. They're not just replacing the stairs, you know. They're replicating them. And that kind of handiwork takes time."

Of course it did. Everything is mass-produced today. But the stairs in Mrs. Jenkins's house dated from the eighteen-eighties, and had been hand-carved. Not only did someone have to replace them, they had to re-create them from old pictures and from what was left.

"But it's looking all right?"

He nodded. "Most of the woodwork is done. They're still working on trying to match the stain to what was there originally. Same with the floors."

"So it's going to take a while longer."

"Another month. But it's gonna look good as new when they're finished."

Part of me wanted to ask whether he'd want to move back

to Nashville when the house was ready, or whether he'd want to stay here. I didn't, partly because I wasn't sure I was going to like the answer.

"It's good that it's going to look nice," I said instead. "You were gone a long time."

"I told you I was meeting Wendell. We had some stuff to work out."

Rafe was still officially working for the Tennessee Bureau of Investigations. On loan to the Columbia PD at the moment. Wendell Craig, who had been Rafe's handler during his undercover years, and his boss during the eleven months he'd been a trainer for other undercover agents, was currently doing both his own new job, and his old job, which was now supposed to be Rafe's job. It's a long story. The bottom line, I guess, is that Rafe is still sort of working undercover, as a detective for Tamara Grimaldi's police department, but under his own name and in his own home town, where everyone knows who he is and remembers his past.

"Everything all right?"

"Fine," Rafe said. "Just some personnel matters."

Personnel? "Is everything all right with the boys?"

The boys are the three young men Rafe spent the best part of a year training. There were four of them originally, but Manny Ortega was killed early last year. The three that were left were José Garcia, currently working undercover in Memphis, Jamal Atkins, working with Wendell in Nashville, and Clayton Norris, who'd been shipped off to Chattanooga.

Rafe nodded. "Memphis says that José's working his way into the distribution chain of a Mexican drug cartel. He's doing fine. And Jamal's working with Wendell, and I guess getting ready to be a daddy."

I grimaced. I was still feeling a bit guilty about that one.

Jamal—and José and Clayton and of course Wendell—had been invited to Rafe's and my wedding, right here in the garden of the mansion, last June. So had my young friend Alexandra Puckett, whose mother Brenda had been murdered in Mrs. Jenkins's house in Nashville on the day I first met Rafe—or met him again, twelve years after he left Columbia High.

Unbeknownst to us, Jamal and Alexandra had hooked up, and now Alexandra was expecting Jamal's baby. She was seventeen, he was twenty or twenty-one, or maybe twenty-two by now. Better than seventeen, but not really in a position to be a good daddy. Especially not with the work he was getting into.

"I haven't spoken to her for a while," I admitted. "She calls or texts now and then. But I haven't seen her since we left Nashville."

"Maybe you should take a drive up there one day and take her to lunch."

Maybe I should. Now that the house on Fulton was finished, I didn't have to stick around Maury County every day anymore. A trip to Nashville might be nice. I could bring Charlotte, and take her to Sally's Security for pepper spray.

I texted Alexandra Puckett the next morning, and suggested that we meet for lunch the following Saturday. She was in her last year of high school, and as far as I knew, she still planned to try to graduate with the rest of her class in May. As long as she was healthy and able, I imagined she was in school.

She set me straight within the next thirty minutes. *How about tomorrow?*

Shouldn't you be in school? I texted back.

Spring break. I'll come to you.

Fine by me. If she wanted to make the drive, I wasn't going to stop her. Although—

Should you be driving on your own?

She had to be eight months along by now. And it was a first baby and she was quite young. I hated the idea of her going into labor on the side of Interstate 65 between Nashville and Sweetwater.

Yes.

OK, then.

See you tomorrow, I told her, and started thinking about where I'd be able to take her that she'd enjoy, and where she wouldn't get dirty looks for being a young—a very young—woman with a baby on the way.

I was still thinking an hour later when my phone rang. I checked the number and saw that it was Arlene Woods calling back.

It was only fifteen minutes into their appointment time, so that was either good news or bad, depending. They'd looked at the house again and decided that they loved it enough that they needed to make an offer right now. Or they'd looked at the house again and rejected it as soon as they walked into the master bedroom, because of the specter of Steven Morris.

Not literally, of course. He didn't haunt the place.

Either way, they probably hadn't had enough time to make a well-reasoned decision. Unless they'd been early. Maybe they'd been excited enough about the prospect of buying our house—Darcy's house—that they'd shown up thirty minutes early. They knew the house was unoccupied, so they might have.

I put the phone to my ear with a sense of cautious optimism. "Arlene?"

"Yes," Arlene's voice said grimly. My optimism took a nose dive. "I hate to be the bearer of bad news, but I think you ought to come over here."

"To the house on Fulton?"

"Yes," Arlene said. I mean, it was obvious. I guess I was just trying to put off the inevitable for another few seconds.

"What happened?"

She hesitated. "I think I'd rather just let you see for yourself."

That didn't sound good. "I'll be there in thirty minutes," I said.

"I'll wait for you."

There was a beat before she added, "You may want to call the police now. That way you won't have to wait for them to get here."

My mouth opened. I'm not sure whether my jaw dropped or whether I planned to ask her, again, what had happened. Either way, I told her, "I'll do that," before I hung up.

And did that.

Four

Rafe was already on-scene when I arrived. The Chevy he drives to work was parked at the curb outside the house, behind Arlene's much more elegant Mercedes. I guess real estate in mostly-rural Maury County could pay off, too, if you knew what you were doing.

I parked my less-elegant Volvo in the driveway, since no one else was there, and hauled Carrie and her seat across the grass and up on the stoop. The door stood open, so I walked in and raised my voice. "Rafe? I'm here. What—?... Oh, no!"

I stopped dead a couple of feet into the living room and looked around, my eyes wide. Steps on the kitchen floor heralded the appearance of my husband in the dining room. His face was grim as he came toward us. "Savannah."

He dropped a kiss on my mouth—quick and chaste—and took the car seat out of my hands.

I relinquished it without even looking down. My voice came out on a pained moan. "What happened?"

The mid-century sofa the stager had brought in—and charged us through the nose for—was a mess of ripped fabric, with stuffing spilling out, like internal organs from a bad wound, and over in the dining room area, every place setting on the table, plus the centerpiece, lay in broken pieces of ceramic on the floor. My beautiful pearl gray paint was destroyed, and so was the drywall below.

"The back door's busted," Rafe said.

Just as when Steven Morris had been killed. I felt myself turn pale. "Oh, my God. Rafe. Nobody's—?"

He shook his head, clearly understanding what I wasn't able to get out. "Nobody's here. Just a lot of damage."

A lot of—? "There's more?"

"Sorry, darlin'." He led the way to the kitchen, where the panes of glass in the newly installed cabinet doors lay in shards on the counters and floor.

"My feet are wet," I said stupidly.

Rafe nodded. "They turned the water on and hung the faucet attachment over the edge of the sink. The water went mostly that way—" He indicated the bedroom wing, "and down the AC vent."

So not only did we have the water to deal with, we'd have to have the air conditioning ducts cleaned, and maybe even some of the wood floors replaced. The water would make the planks cup, but maybe, if we gave it a few days, they'd settle back down as they dried out.

"What else?" The first flush of disbelief and tears had faded, and now I was getting angry.

Rafe didn't say anything, just pointed me down the hall.

The hall bath was intact, other than that the mirror was broken—seven years bad luck—and the light fixture that had gotten such a tongue-lashing yesterday had been ripped out of the wall and was dangling by the electrical wires.

"Remember what I told you last night," I asked Rafe, as we continued down the hallway past the two secondary bedrooms—slashed comforter in the room that had a bed, broken desk lamp in the one that was set up as an office, "about the guy who was at the auction and his wife—?"

He nodded. "We'll talk about it later."

That was probably best. In my shock and dismay I'd forgotten that Arlene was still here. And until we knew exactly what was going on, the less we said in front of anyone else, the better.

So I followed him to the end of the hall in silence, and into the master suite.

Arlene was there, in the master bedroom, standing in the middle of the floor. Instead of focusing on her, though, I did a quick overview of the damage first.

The back door was broken and hanging open, just as Rafe had said. Last time, someone had knocked out one of the windows in the fifteen-pane door, stuck their hand through, and unlocked the door from outside. This time, it looked like a simple kick, since the wood next to the lock was splintered.

Bedding was torn off the bed and tossed onto the floor along with throw-pillows and knick-knacks from the bedside tables. The watercolor above the bed—a seaside scene with sailboats—was torn at a diagonal. And in the bathroom, someone had taken a blunt instrument of some kind to the big panes of frameless, tempered glass surrounding the shower, which had exploded inward into a pile of small glass pieces that covered the tile floor of the shower. Some of them had probably gone down the drain, too, and would have to be gotten back up.

All that seen and internally logged, I turned my attention to Arlene Woods, who was standing in the middle of the master bedroom, looking up at the fan that was slowly revolving overhead.

The master suite is the old garage, so it was a big room, even after we had partitioned part of it off for the bathroom and closet. And after some discussion, we had decided to vault the ceiling, so it was a long way up. We had also covered it in stained beadboard, which made a nice contrast to the white walls. The ceiling fan we'd installed was huge, easily four feet across, and it looked like it belonged on the front of a propeller airplane: a real statement piece.

At the moment, it was sporting a noose fashioned out of one of the bed sheets, which was lazily floating through the air above Arlene's head.

"At least it's empty," fell out of my mouth.

They both looked at me like I'd lost my mind. After a second, the corner of Rafe's mouth curved up, but Arlene continued to look shocked.

"I've found dead bodies before," I told her, apologetically. "One right there, as a matter of fact." I pointed to the place where Steve Morris had breathed his last: not too many feet from where Arlene's suede half-boots were currently parked. "I'll take a crime scene without a dead body any day."

Rafe had gotten his expression under control, but there was still a little light of… maybe it was approval in his eyes. "If you wouldn't mind telling Savannah what you told me?" he prompted Arlene.

She shrugged. "We arrived a few minutes after ten. The front door was locked. Whoever did this must have come and gone through the back."

Obviously. Or at least it was obvious that they'd come in this way. If the front door had been locked from the inside, it was logical to assume they'd gone out this way, too. I would have. And I would have parked several blocks away, so nobody would have seen my car in the neighborhood.

"We saw the damage as soon as we came in," Arlene added. "We walked back out immediately. My clients left, and I called you. Your husband," she gave him a look, hard to decipher, "arrived and walked through the rest of the house. Then you came."

I nodded. That seemed straight-forward enough. "Thanks for calling me."

"I don't think I have any more questions," Rafe added, "but thanks for sticking around for Savannah."

"No problem." Arlene gave him a tight smile.

"It'll probably take us a week or two to fix the damage," I told her, "if your clients are still in the market for a house then."

She gave me a look. It didn't quite say '*I can't believe you're stupid enough to suggest that*,' but it was close. "I don't think so."

No, I didn't, either. "Thanks for trying," I told her.

She nodded. "Good luck."

She headed out, the heels of her boots clacking against the floors in the hallway.

I turned to Rafe, who took one look at my face and moved to put his free arm around my shoulders. "Sorry."

"I can't believe this," I told his leather jacket. "Why does this kind of stuff follow me around? What is this? The third of my places that's been vandalized? The fourth?"

"I'm gonna guess more than that." His voice was perfectly calm. "Look on the bright side, darlin'. Nobody's dead. The rest of this can be fixed."

Yes, it could. With more of Darcy's money.

"I have to contact my sister," I said. "And Charlotte." Who'd be just as devastated as I was.

And although I wanted to reject what he was saying, Rafe was right. In addition to having dealt with vandalism more than once, I'd also walked in on more than one dead body, and the fact that there wasn't one lying on the floor here, or worse, hanging from that noose revolving slowly above my head, was a blessing. Even if everything else about this situation made me feel violated and sick to my stomach.

"We need to take that down before Darcy sees it," I said.

Rafe nodded, eyeing the loop of fabric. It hung low enough that the bottom of the noose just missed brushing the top of his head on each circuit. As it passed overhead, it would cast a shadow across his face for a moment before it revolved away, and then it did it again on the next rotation. His jaw was tight and his eyes flat and hard.

"Do you think—" I began, and then stopped when he shook his head.

"I ain't gonna speculate. Could be something small and

stupid—the lady and gentleman who stopped by yesterday decided to mess up your hard work and make sure you can't get your house sold and your money out with spending more."

I nodded. That thought had crossed my mind, too. "Or it could be something else. Someone sending a message to me. Or to Darcy."

My half-sister, with her black hair, dark eyes, and *café au lait* skin.

"Like I said," Rafe said, with a last narrow-eyed glare at the noose, "I ain't gonna speculate. I'm hoping it's small and stupid."

I did, too. "Rodney Clark was here yesterday. Accompanying the Allens."

"I'm gonna have to talk to them." Rafe said. "And all the other neighbors. In case somebody heard or saw something."

I nodded. "What about Rodney? Are you going to talk to him, too?"

He contemplated me in silence for a second. "Not sure yet. On the one hand, it'd make for a handy excuse to have a conversation with him. On the other…"

He didn't complete the sentence, just trailed off, his eyes distant.

"I have a list," I told him. "Of everyone who was here for the Open house. I'm not sure everyone signed it—if somebody came here with the thought that they'd case the place to do damage to it later, they probably would have written down a fake name and email—but I spent most of the open house in the living room, and I'm pretty sure everyone wrote something."

"That'll be helpful."

"The list is at home. When I get there, I'll scan it to you."

"Thanks, darlin'." He gave me a quick look, and then a slower and more careful one. "You OK?"

"I'm angry," I said. "I feel violated. I'm pissed off that now I have to spend more of Darcy's money to fix what we already spent Darcy's money to do. And I'm really annoyed that we lost Arlene Woods's buyers, and we won't find any others for another few weeks, at least. Every month we have to hang on to this place, the carrying costs mount up. We may even be responsible for the furniture that was destroyed."

And that was something else I had to do: call Michelle the stager and tell her what had happened. She wasn't going to be happy, either. Hopefully she was insured.

"And on top of that, that thing—" I looked at the noose, "feels a little like a threat. Like this is going to happen again. Or something else will. Something worse."

We weren't strangers to nooses in these parts. The Ku Klux Klan was first formed just about thirty minutes south of here, in the town of Pulaski. And the lynching of Cordie Cheek, accused and arrested, but never indicted, of raping a white girl, took place just a mile or two from where we were standing. What happened to Cordie, and the fear that it would happen to someone else, was what started the Columbia Race Riots in 1946.

Rafe nodded, his face grim. In the car seat over his arm, Carrie was following the movement of the noose, her eyes wide. To her, it probably looked like another mobile, like the one with the zoo animals hanging above her bed at home. I wished to God I didn't have to bring my daughter up in a world where she'd encounter this kind of ugliness just because of the color of her skin, but there was no chance of that.

"What do you think?" I asked Rafe.

He hesitated. "I'd like to think that this was just somebody having some fun—in their way—and that..." He nodded to the noose, "was an afterthought they came up with once they got here and saw the sheets."

"If they'd planned to do it, they might have brought a rope," I said.

Rafe nodded. "Mighta. It ain't proof one way or the other."

No. It wasn't.

"I'll call somebody in to go over the place." He gave one last look around the bedroom before he headed for the doorway, still carrying the seat with Carrie in it. She'd been quiet, except for some cooing noises, this whole time. "I don't imagine whoever did this was stupid enough to leave fingerprints, but we gotta check."

I nodded, trailing him down the hallway toward the kitchen. Of course we did. It was more time and manpower wasted, but yes. He had to check.

"And I'll talk to Tammy. We'll decide whether we wanna keep the place shut down for a few days, or whether you can get back to work on it."

I groaned. "It's not that I don't understand what you're saying. But we've already spent two months on this house. It's going to take another couple of weeks to redo everything that's broken. At least. The sooner we can get started, the better."

"I get that, darlin'. For now, just let me talk it over with Tammy. And maybe Bob. He's been living here longer than either of us. It's Columbia's jurisdiction, not his, but he oughta know what's going on."

I nodded. He did. "I guess I'll drive to Sweetwater and give Charlotte and Darcy the bad news." And the stager. I wasn't looking forward to that. "Just let me know when we can get in here and start working. I'm sure Michelle will want to see the damage for herself, too."

"She can do that anytime," Rafe said, passing through the front door and out onto the stoop. "There'll be somebody here for the rest of the day. Just tell her not to start clearing stuff out until we're done."

I assured him I wouldn't dream of telling Michelle she could remove any of her property before the police was finished with it. Then he gave me Carrie, and I gave him a kiss, and we parted ways. Him to go back into the house to call in the crime scene crew and start talking to people, and me to drive back to Sweetwater to update my two partners in home renovation on what had happened.

Five

Michelle the stager was, as expected, livid. "My sofa? My beautiful sofa? That sofa cost me six grand!"

I'm sure it had. It was—or had been—a lovely sofa. "And your bedding," I said, helpfully. "And some pillows."

Although truthfully, our hit to the wallet—or Darcy's wallet—was probably worse than Michelle's. We had to replace doors, walls, paint, tile, shower glass, maybe even floors…

And if that noose meant something more than just a momentary attempt to upset us and make us feel afraid, we had bigger problems than the money, too.

Michelle was breathing loudly in and out through her nose. "I'm pulling the rest of my furniture out of there as soon as the police are done," she told me.

"Of course." I'd been prepared for that. I would have done the same thing.

"And I'm keeping the money you paid me to pay the deductible for the insurance."

I grimaced. I'd been prepared for that, too, but that didn't mean I liked it. "I understand."

"Let me know when the police are done so I can get a truck over there."

She hung up in my ear before I could respond. I dropped the phone with a wince and concentrated on driving.

It isn't a long trip from Columbia to Sweetwater, especially not when traffic is light, which it tends to be in the late morning. It was less than thirty minutes before I pulled up in front of Martin and McCall Law Offices on the town square, and turned off the engine.

Carrie had gone down for her morning nap, and didn't stir when I pulled the seat out of the car. I had just turned toward the door to the family law firm—Martin is my brother Dix, and our father and his father before him, while McCall is our brother-in-law Jonathan, as well as Catherine, now that she has taken her husband's name—when someone called my name.

It wasn't Charlotte. I had texted her on my way over, and asked her to meet me here, so I wouldn't have to go over the story more than once. She was either here already, or on her way, but this wasn't her voice.

I turned toward it, and greeted Audrey, Darcy's birth-mother. I guess that sort of made her a secondary mother to me too, if she was my sister's mother, although there was nothing new about that: Audrey and Mother had been best friends since Mother married Dad some thirty-three years ago.

I was twitching to get inside and get the story over with, but I mustered a gracious smile. "It's good to see you. We missed you at the Wayside Inn yesterday."

"Aunt Tondalia is under the weather," Audrey said.

She's a stunning woman, a year or so older than Mother, and a totally different type. Where Mother is soft and ladylike, Audrey is angular and dramatic. She's tall, taller than me by a couple of inches, and in her usual three inch heels with platforms, towered over me. Her cheekbones are to die for, and she had her black hair styled in her usual severe bob, with her usual blood red lipstick on.

"Oh, no." Tondalia Jenkins, Audrey's aunt and Rafe's grandmother, is in her seventies. She's small and scrawny and as wrinkled as a raisin, and physically she's the kind of desiccated little person who looks like she could live forever.

It's usually her mind that's the problem. Moving down here after Thanksgiving, and in with Audrey, had seemed to help a little. She had a home again, with her sister's daughter—or her sister, since Mrs. Jenkins wasn't always clear on exactly who Audrey was. She had the same problem with Rafe and me, and with Rafe's son David. But Mrs. J had been happy and had seemed healthy the past few months.

"She's running a fever," Audrey said. "She eats like a bird most of the time, so it's hard to say whether she has any loss of appetite, but I couldn't get any breakfast into her. I'm just here to put a sign on the door that the store will be closed, and then I'm going back home again."

"Don't let me keep you," I said. "I'm just going in to talk to Darcy." And there was no need to burden Audrey with the reason I had to talk to her daughter. Audrey had troubles of her own. "Have you tried ice cream?"

"Excuse me?"

"She likes ice cream. Whenever I've had to take care of her, I've always taken her for ice cream. If she won't eat anything else, she'll eat that. She likes the kid meals at Burger King, too."

"Of course she does," Audrey said.

I shrugged apologetically. "It's probably more important to get some food into her than making sure the food is nutritionally optimal, don't you think? And you don't want her to get dehydrated."

"No," Audrey said, "I don't. Thanks, Savannah."

"Don't mention it." I turned as a car door slammed halfway around the square. It was Mrs. Albertson's car, and Charlotte raised a hand as she headed our way.

I raised one back. "We should get inside."

Audrey nodded. "I'm just going to put that note on the door, and then I'll head back to Aunt Tondalia."

"Let us know how it goes," I told her. "If you need any help, I'll be happy to help out, you know. She isn't just your family.

She's mine, too."

"I know, Savannah. I'll keep you updated."

She hustled toward the door to Audrey's on the Square, the fashion boutique she runs, on her patent-leather heels, and I moved a few yards closer to the door to the law firm while I waited for Charlotte to catch up.

"Everything OK?" she wanted to know, a little out of breath, when she did.

"Rafe's grandmother's sick with a fever. Audrey's putting a note on the door of the shop and then going back to her."

That wasn't what Charlotte meant, of course, and I knew it, but I still didn't want to say anything before we had gathered up Darcy, as well. "Let's go in."

I headed for the door. Charlotte got there first, and held it open so I could maneuver the car seat inside. "Morning, Darcy."

"Savannah." She looked beyond me to where Charlotte was coming in and shutting the door behind her. A small wrinkle appeared between her eyes. "Charlotte. What's wrong?"

I hadn't texted Darcy on my way here, since I had assumed she'd be present and available to talk. Now I opened my mouth, and found the words hard to find.

"This doesn't look like good news," Darcy said dryly. "I guess we didn't get an offer on the house last night."

I shook my head. "Is there somewhere we can talk? Is the conference room empty?"

She nodded. "Go on down. I'll switch the phones over to Dix's extension and let him know I'm taking a break."

She's nothing if not efficient, my half-sister. Charlotte and I wandered down the hall and into the conference room on the left, and thirty seconds later Darcy joined us, and pulled the door shut. "What's going on?"

By that point I had deposited the car seat with Carrie on the floor and unwound my scarf. And since all the activity had woken the baby, who started to fuss, I unbuttoned my blouse and prepared to feed her while we were talking. "There's a problem over at the house."

"What kind of problem?" Darcy wanted to know, and sat down across from me. Charlotte dithered for a second before she sank into the chair on the other side of me.

"Someone broke in last night and tore the place up."

Charlotte gasped. Darcy's lips tightened. "Tore it up, how?"

"Every way it could be torn up," I said. "The back door's busted. Not just one of the windowpanes this time, but the whole door. It looks like someone kicked it in. The lock is shot, and so is the wood next to it. We'll need a new door. I suggest steel with tempered glass."

Darcy sighed. "How much is this going to set me back?"

"Quite a bit," I said honestly. "We'll need to replace the glass in some of the kitchen cabinets, and redo the backsplash. The shower glass is broken in the master bath, and that wasn't cheap. We'll need all new light fixtures throughout the house." Except for the airplane propeller in the master bedroom. That was still in perfect condition, and obviously functioned just fine, too. But considering the noose, maybe we'd want to replace it anyway. "New paint. New drywall. Hopefully, when the floor dries, we won't have to replace that, although there might be some places we'll have to feather in new hardwoods. If that happens we'll have to sand and stain everything again."

By this point, Charlotte had hidden her face in her hands and was moaning softly. Probably remembering all the hours we'd spend laying the tile and sanding the floors and painting the walls. Darcy was still staring at me, her eyes dark and angry. "Anything else?"

"Most of the staging is ruined. I called Michelle, and she's bringing in a van as soon as the police are done. We're out the money we spent on the staging, and of course we're out the staging itself, too."

Although, on the bright side, if this situation had a bright side, we would have had to move the staging furniture out in order to do the necessary repairs anyway. At least this way, someone else would do that job for us. A very slim silver lining in the middle of the gloom.

"Of course," Darcy said tightly. "Anything else?"

I hesitated, but figured I probably shouldn't hold anything back. She was my sister, and it was her house. She needed to know, even if I'd prefer to spare her this particular knowledge. "Someone hung a noose from the ceiling fan in the master bedroom. Made from the flat sheet Michelle put on the bed. It was spinning overhead when we walked in."

There was a moment of silence. Charlotte had looked up, and was gaping at me, her eyes wide in her now-pale face. Darcy's jaw was tight. "That doesn't sound good."

I shook my head. "I could tell it bothered Rafe."

"He was there?"

"We had a showing this morning," I said. "This real estate agent named Arlene Woods called me last night and said her clients had walked through the house yesterday afternoon, during the open house. They wanted a second look, so she set up a showing for this morning. When they got there around ten, they opened the front door and immediately saw the damage in the living room. She called me, and I called Rafe. We all met over there."

They both nodded, since that was clear enough.

"He's bringing in a crime scene crew," I added. "He doesn't think it's likely that whoever did this left any fingerprints—every wannabe burglar knows to wear gloves these days—but he said it had to be done."

"Maybe there'll be hair or other DNA," Charlotte said optimistically.

"Maybe. With as many people as walked through the house yesterday, it's going to be hard to narrow it down, though."

If one of Rodney Clark's brown hairs was found on scene, it wouldn't prove anything. He'd been there in the afternoon, so his hair had every right to be there.

"I don't think anything's going to come from that," I said. "DNA testing takes a long time. Months. Especially for something like this, where the only damage was to property. If somebody had been killed, it might be a different matter…"

"Thank God no one was killed," Darcy said.

I nodded. "We can fix this. It's going to take more time and more money, but it can be fixed. It could be worse."

We sat in silence a moment.

"What about that couple?" Charlotte wanted to know. "The guy from the auction and his wife?"

Darcy looked from me to her and back. "Who?"

"They showed up at the open house yesterday." I explained who they were. "The lady wasn't very complimentary about the work we'd done."

"Bless her heart," Charlotte added, "she had her nose so high in the air she would have drowned in a rainstorm."

Darcy's lips twitched, but she refrained from comment. "And you're thinking they might have had something to do with it?"

"I can't quite picture the lady kicking in the back door," I admitted, "not in the boots she had on yesterday, anyway, but most of the things that got destroyed were things she talked about. The kitchen backsplash, the cabinets, the floor stain. The bathroom light, that's ripped out of the wall. When she headed down the hallway to the master suite I stopped listening, but in the front of the house, she made a big deal out of pointing out all the things she didn't like, and they're all going to need replacing now."

"Did you tell Rafe about her?"

I nodded. "I'm sending him the sign-in list from the open house when I get back to the mansion. He'll have to track them all down and talk to them, I guess. Including the couple from the auction."

"I'd like to be there for that," Charlotte muttered.

So would I. Although I didn't see much chance of that happening. "He'll have to treat this like any other investigation. Mostly that means no civilians sitting in on the interviews."

Not that he—or we—hadn't broken that rule before. Although I didn't see it happening this time.

Charlotte nodded. "Well, I hope she confesses."

I hoped so, too. But I didn't see much chance of that, either. Whether she'd done it or not. "I guess I should get home so I can send him those names."

"Let's discuss what we're going to do first," Darcy said.

"Yes," Charlotte nodded, "what's going to happen now?"

Well... "I guess first of all the police have to release the crime scene, after the CSI crew is done. Then we'll have to let Michelle know that they're finished, so she can get her things out. Once that's done, we can take stock of what needs doing, clean up, and order new materials. It could be the end of the week before we can get going again." Or longer.

Charlotte moaned. Darcy sighed. "OK," she said. "Let me know if you hear from Rafe. In the meantime, I guess we can plan to meet over there after I get off work this afternoon. I'd like to see for myself what it looks like."

I couldn't blame her. I would have wanted that, too. "I'll meet you there at five-thirty."

Darcy nodded. "I should get back to work." She pushed up from the table.

"I'll just sit here until Carrie has had enough," I said. "I'll see you both later. I'll let you know if I hear anything."

They both walked out, Darcy only as far as the desk in the lobby and Charlotte, I assumed, all the way out to her car, while I focused on taking deep breaths and being calm and relaxed for my nursing daughter.

By the time I had to leave the mansion to meet Darcy and Charlotte—if she chose to show up; she might not have been born with as much curiosity as the Martin women—I still hadn't heard anything from Rafe. And I hadn't called to bother him, either, since I figured he had his hands full, and the last thing I wanted to do was distract him from it.

The phone rang when I was halfway to Columbia, though, and it was him. "Sorry, darlin'." My normally unflappable husband sounded frazzled and out of sorts. "I'm gonna be late getting home."

"That's OK," I said. "I'm not there anyway."

There was a beat. "Where are you?"

I told him where I was, and that Darcy had wanted to see the damage for herself. "There's no objection to that, right? I mean, it's her house."

"No objection," Rafe said. "The crime scene crew finished thirty minutes ago. I'm on my way back there myself, to board up the back door. Prob'ly best if we don't leave it hanging open."

Probably so. Not that there was much left inside anyone would want—not with a lot of the furniture slashed to ribbons—but you never know who or what might crawl through an open door and make itself at home.

"We'll see you there," I told him, and hung up.

He got there before me, and so did Darcy. By the time I pulled up in front of the house, both their cars were parked outside, and I heard hammering from the rear of the house.

I stepped through the grass to the back, and saw my husband busily nailing boards in place while Darcy was standing by with the box of nails and conversation.

They're cousins of sorts. Twice-removed, or something like that. Their grandmothers were sisters, their parents—Audrey and Tyrell—first cousins, and they look enough alike to be brother and sister.

Or maybe not. Darcy has Audrey's cheekbones and Dad's mouth and jaw, while Rafe looks a lot like the picture I had seen of Tyrell at eighteen, with a little of LaDonna in the forehead and eyes. Not the color, but the shape and setting. They're both tall, though, with the same basic coloring, and Darcy certainly looks a lot more like Rafe's sister than mine.

When I came around the corner unannounced, they both turned, and in that moment their expressions couldn't have been more different. Darcy looked startled and a little nervous, while Rafe bypassed both and went directly to action. He stepped in front of Darcy before he'd even looked at me, and I could see him weigh the hammer in his hand for its potential as a weapon. I have no doubt that if it hadn't been me standing there, but someone more dangerous, that hammer would have been entered into evidence as the murder weapon ten minutes later.

As it was, his face cleared and his grip on the hammer relaxed. "Darlin'." His lips curved as he stepped away from Darcy again.

My sister managed a smile. "Savannah. You scared me."

"Sorry," I said. "You made good time getting here. I expected to be here before you."

"I left the office ten minutes early. Figured I'd beat the traffic." She smiled, more relaxed now. I smiled back, since the traffic between Sweetwater and Columbia, even at the height of rush hour, is pretty much non-existent, and especially in the direction she was traveling.

While we talked, Rafe lifted another board from the small stack on the ground, and held it against the door frame. He nodded to Darcy, who extended the box of nails so he could grab one, and put her other hand on the board to hold it in place while Rafe hammered.

He took a step back. "That oughta do it."

It ought to. This was board six or seven that covered the back door. Anyone who wanted in, would either have to pry each board out with their bare hands—or a crowbar, if they brought one—or would have to be skinny enough to fit between the boards. Neither one of us could have, and from what I remembered about Rodney—who wasn't a big guy—he couldn't, either.

No, if someone wanted in at this point, it would be easier to kick in the front door or break one of the windows.

"Have you been inside yet?" I asked Darcy. She shook her head. "I'll take you through the front."

"Go ahead," Rafe told us. "I'm gonna grab the rest of this and put it in the car."

He bent to gather the couple of boards he'd brought but hadn't used. I gave myself a moment to admire the way his jeans stretched tight across his posterior when he leaned down, and then I turned and led the way around the side of the house to the front door with Darcy following behind. She was grinning.

"Hey," I told her with an unrepentant shrug when we were standing on the stoop and I was opening the lockbox to get the key, "that's my husband. And he's hot. I'm allowed to look."

"I never said you weren't." She turned to the street at the sound of a car coming closer. "Here's Charlotte. I wasn't sure she was going to join us."

I had assumed she wouldn't, since she wasn't here yet. But now she pulled Mrs. Albertson's tiny car to a stop behind mine, and swung her legs out. "Sorry I'm late."

"You're not," I said. "I just got here, too. Rafe's around back nailing the door shut."

Or on his way around the corner now, with a hammer in one hand and a couple of planks under the other arm. He gave Charlotte a nod in passing. "Evening, Charlotte."

"Good evening," Charlotte said, and scurried up onto the

stoop as I pushed the door open and stepped back.

"Knock yourselves out."

I'd already seen it all, so I might as well spend the next couple of minutes canoodling with my husband while they looked around inside and commiserated.

They crowded through the doorway and exclaimed in shock at the mess inside. I left them to it while I hauled Carrie over to the Chevy, where Rafe was busy dumping the extra lumber and the hammer in the trunk. "Anything going on that I should know about?"

He straightened and slammed the lid shut before shaking his head. "Nothing other than the obvious, darlin'." He leaned a hip against the back of the car and faced me. "CSI's been here and prob'ly left a mess. The place was all over fingerprints, but we won't know whose until they're processed, and we'll only know then if they're on file."

I nodded. "We had at least ten or twelve people come through yesterday, in addition to me and Charlotte, and the Allens, and Rodney, and the renovation guy and his wife."

"And all of'em's gotta be eliminated," Rafe said. "I don't think we're gonna get much from the fingerprints."

No. I didn't, either. "There wasn't anything else of interest, I guess? Anything we missed this morning?" No one had accidentally dropped a credit card with their name on it, or anything like that?

Rafe shook his head. "I had a couple of cops go up and down the street here and on the next block to see if anybody saw or heard anything last night. They're doing it again now, since so many people were at work in the middle of the day."

"There aren't any surveillance cameras or anything like that around here, I guess?"

"Traffic camera up on the main road," Rafe said with a nod in that direction. "And there's a chance somebody could have a Ring. You know, one of those doorbell cameras?"

"I've seen commercials for them on HGTV. Wish we would have had one here."

"We can put one in now," Rafe said.

"Maybe. At least we wouldn't have to worry about something like this happening again."

He straightened, eyes over my shoulder. "I don't think it's gonna happen again, darlin'."

"It's happened twice," I began, but stopped when I saw that he wasn't really paying attention to me. He had noticed a car turning down the street, and now he was watching it come closer.

I looked at it, too. "That's Rodney Clark's car."

Rafe nodded, as the dark blue Dodge Charger slowly approached, and just as slowly rolled past us. Rodney grinned insolently out the window. Just beyond the next property he turned on his signal, and rolled into the Allens' driveway on the other side of the street.

"He's sure spending a lot of time with the Allens," I commented. "He was with them at the open house yesterday, too. I mean, it isn't like his girlfriend—their daughter—is still alive." And it wasn't like Mrs. Allen even liked him particularly well. She had told me, just last month, that she thought Natalie could have done better.

We watched as Rodney turned his engine off and got out. He stood for a second, very deliberately not looking our way, before he slammed his car door and sauntered around the back end of the Dodge and up to the front door. We heard the knock, and a few seconds later he disappeared inside the yellow house.

Rafe turned back to me. "'Scuse me, darlin'."

"You going over there?"

He nodded. "They were here at your open house yesterday. And the Allens live just up the street. They mighta noticed something last night."

"And besides, you want a close and personal look at

Rodney."

"That don't hurt," Rafe agreed with a grin. "This'll gimme that, without having to pull him in for the other business."

The other business being the suspected neo-Nazi affiliation, I assumed.

"Be careful," I told him.

"Darlin', I'm always careful."

I snorted, and he added, "It's nothing to worry about. I'm just a policeman doing my job and investigating this vandalism that took place just down the street from them."

"I'll see you at home later, then," I said. "I'm going inside to Darcy and Charlotte. Thanks for fixing the back door."

"My pleasure, darlin'." He gave me a polite nod, and then turned on his heel and sauntered up the street toward the Allens' house. I watched for a second before I remembered that I wasn't supposed to be ogling him, and then I turned, too, and headed across the grass to the stoop and the front door.

Six

Darcy and Charlotte were standing in the middle of the carnage of the master suite, in the same spot where Arlene Woods had been standing this morning. Unlike then, the noose was gone from overhead, and the fan revolved by itself, with no additional threat.

Even so, the two of them didn't look happy.

"This is a mess," Charlotte said when I came through the door.

I nodded. "Maybe it'll look less bad when all the damaged staging is out of here. I mean, we'll have plenty to fix. But once all the ripped fabric and stuffing is gone, and all we're looking at are empty rooms, maybe it'll look less awful."

"Or more," Charlotte said.

Well, yes. There was a chance of that, too, of course. That the damaged staging was keeping us from focusing on all the other things that were wrong.

"Where's Rafe?" Darcy wanted to know, and I explained that he'd walked over to the Allens' to see whether they'd noticed anything, either yesterday during the open house or overnight.

"Rodney Clark just drove up. He was with them when they walked through yesterday. And he was one of the guys at Beulah's that day when we all had lunch, and—"

"I remember," Darcy said.

"If he had something to do with this, Rafe will figure it out.

In the meantime, I think we just have to carry on the best we can. I'll call Michelle tonight, and tell her she can take her staging away tomorrow. Charlotte, you and I can meet here after lunch… no, wait."

"Problem?"

"I can't tomorrow. Or at least not until later in the day. Alexandra Puckett, my friend from Nashville, is driving down to have lunch with me."

"The pregnant girl?" Darcy said.

I nodded. "That's right, you met her."

"At a barbeque restaurant in Nashville once, when we were up there." During the time we'd been trying to figure out who Darcy's birth parents were, before we'd realized that Darcy's dad was my dad.

"Well, she's coming down to visit," I said. "I contacted her the other day and suggested I could come up to see her, and she said she'd drive down instead. They're on spring break this week, apparently."

"She's still in high school, isn't she?"

"Until May. Hopefully she'll be able to keep up for long enough to graduate with her class, so at least she won't have that to worry about. If it takes her another year to start college, it won't be the end of the world."

"Where are you meeting her?" Charlotte wanted to know.

"She's coming to the mansion. She knows where it is. She was down for the wedding. I thought I might take her to the Café on the Square. Show her the law office and Audrey's place. If Audrey's there tomorrow."

"Why wouldn't she be?" Darcy wanted to know.

"I saw her outside the store earlier today. She said Mrs. Jenkins is running a fever."

"She was a little under the weather yesterday, too," Darcy nodded. "I hope it's nothing serious. Apparently some old friend of hers is coming to Columbia on Friday. I'd hate for her to miss it."

So would I, if she had a friend coming to visit. "Maybe Audrey is just taking extra care now so she won't."

Darcy nodded. "Are we waiting for Rafe to come back?"

I shook my head. "He has his own car, and I don't know how long he'll be. If you two have seen enough, we can lock up and leave. I'll call Michelle, and then, once she tells me the staging is all gone, we can meet back over here and assess the damage. Maybe around the same time tomorrow?"

Alexandra would have left to drive back to Nashville by then, and surely Michelle would have had time to remove her property, too.

They both agreed that that would work, and we parted ways on the stoop. They drove away while I locked the door and hid the key away in the lockbox. And although I took my time walking across the grass to the car and getting Carrie situated in the back seat, Rafe didn't come back out of the Allens' house in the time I stood there. Eventually I gave up and drove home, where I made dinner, and—since he still wasn't there—ate my share and left the rest warming on the stove for whenever he did get there.

It was almost eight by the time the Chevy finally came up the driveway to the house. I listened to it turn the corner and then disappear into the garage. A minute later, he unlocked the back door.

Pearl, still sharp-eared on her pillow in the corner, all the way on the other side of the house, gave out a sharp yip.

"We're in the parlor," I called out. "Bring your dinner in here and join us."

He didn't answer, but I heard him moving around in the kitchen.

"Rafe?"

"Yeah."

It was his voice, and I breathed out. For a second, I'd been worried that someone else had walked in, and what that would have meant, not just for me, but for him.

Actually, I would probably have been fine. Pearl is protective, and if anyone but Rafe had turned up in the doorway, especially someone acting threatening, I don't doubt she would have gone for his throat. Rafe, on the other hand, would have been dead in a ditch before he would have let anyone take the keys to his house.

But it was him carrying a bowl of chili and a bottle of beer through the door a minute later, his stocking-feet silent on the old wood floors. He stepped over Carrie, who was gurgling and kicking on the floor, gave Pearl a nudge with his toe and a "Good girl, Pearl," that made her wag her tail and show a happy canine grin. Rafe dropped down on the loveseat next to me, put the chili and beer on the table, and leaned back, letting out a sigh. Long, thick lashes fanned against his cheeks for a second.

"Long day," I said sympathetically.

"No shit." He opened his eyes again, and after a second, straightened. "Sorry."

"No problem. I've heard it before." Although not usually from him. He tends to censor his language around me. "Have some food. It'll make you feel better."

"I don't think so," Rafe said, but he had some food anyway. And some beer.

I left him alone until the bowl and bottle were both empty, and he leaned back with another sigh, this one more content. "Would you like me to get you some more?"

"No thanks, darlin'." He turned his head on the back of the sofa, so he could grin at me. "I gotta be careful now that I'm an old married man."

"So you don't break wind in bed?" There were beans in the chili.

The grin widened. "I was thinking, so I don't start gaining weight and disappointing my wife."

"It would take a lot to disappoint me," I said.

Not that I didn't appreciate the six-pack he kept under his shirt, and everything else that lived under his clothes, too. But I'd still love him if it went away. I'd put up with the breaking wind, too, if I had to.

He smiled. "I'm good, darlin'. But thanks for asking."

"No problem." I got to my feet and gathered up the empty bowl and the bottle. "Another beer?"

"I'm good. Gotta make sure I keep all my faculties for later." He winked.

"It would take more than one beer for you to lose your abilities there," I informed him. "And besides, we probably have an hour or two before bed. Time enough to burn off another beer."

He chuckled. "I appreciate it. But it's fine. I've had enough."

"I'll be back in a minute, then." I padded out of the room and down the hallway to the kitchen, where I tucked the bowl away in the dishwasher and the bottle in recycling, before packing away the leftovers and making sure the stove was turned off.

He was still in the same position on the sofa when I got back to the parlor, his head back and his eyes barely open. Carrie was cooing on the floor, but a little less happily than before—it would be time to change and feed her and put her to bed soon. And Pearl was napping on her pillow, her feet and eyelids twitching occasionally as she chased imaginary rabbits.

I curled up in the corner of the love seat next to Rafe and gave him a smile. "You look tired. You can go up to bed if you want. I'll take Pearl out and then change and feed Carrie before I join you."

He pushed himself halfway up. "I'm OK, darlin'. Just taking it easy."

"Rough day."

His lips curved. "I've had rougher."

No question. For him, this was business as usual. "Did anything interesting happen with the Allens?"

"Not apart from that pissant Rodney's attitude," Rafe said. "Nancy and Gary both said they hadn't heard or seen anything overnight. I didn't figure they would've, since whoever did the damage came through the back."

"Same as when Steven Morris was killed."

He nodded. "Rodney Clark didn't see nothing, because he wasn't there."

"Or so he said."

"Of course, darlin'. I asked him whether he could prove it, and he gave me this little smirk and said his buddy could vouch for him."

I rolled my eyes. "Let me guess. Kyle Scoggins."

Rafe nodded. "I took down the name and number, like I didn't know who he was talking about. But Scoggins's word ain't worth any more than Clark's."

No. The two of them would definitely alibi one another, whether they'd been there, vandalizing my house, or somewhere else.

"Nobody else heard or saw nothing, either. I hit a couple of the neighbors, and heard from the folks who talked to the others. One or two people had security systems, and I'm gonna look at the footage tomorrow, along with the video from the traffic cam on the corner of the Lewisburg Pike."

He kept sinking deeper and deeper into the loveseat as he was talking. And it isn't easy to do on a piece of furniture that's more than a hundred years old.

"Did I tell you that Alexandra Puckett's driving down tomorrow, to have lunch?" I asked him.

He shook his head.

"You're welcome to join us if you want. I'm sure she'd like

to see you." Alexandra had always had a little crush on Rafe, or at least she thought he was hot. Which he is.

"Dunno if I can get away, darlin'. I'll try."

"It's no problem if you can't," I said, talking fast, since he seemed like he was about to fall asleep right there. "I also saw Audrey. Your grandmother's under the weather."

That perked him up for a second. His eyes opened and grew alert. "What's wrong?"

"Probably just a cold or something like that. She's lethargic, has a fever, and isn't eating much. I'll check with Audrey tomorrow, and suggest taking Mrs. J to the doctor if she isn't better. I wonder if she had a flu shot this winter."

"That'd have been while she was living in Brentwood," Rafe said, about the institution where Mrs. Jenkins had spent her time before she came to live with us and then Audrey. "We can call tomorrow and ask."

"I'll take care of it," I said. "You have enough to do. But if you can spare a few minutes, she'd probably appreciate it if you stopped by and said hello."

"I'll try to get over there. And if I can make it to lunch, I'll do that, too. But don't wait for me."

I promised I wouldn't. "She's coming here around eleven, so just let me know by then. Or I can call you when she gets here and double-check."

"I'll let you know." He turned to look at Carrie when she suddenly decided she'd had enough tummy-and-back time on the floor and set up a wail. Over on the pillow, Pearl woke up with a strangled snort and a bark. "Looks like nap-time's over."

He pushed himself to his feet.

"I'll take her up and put her to bed," I offered, "if you want to let Pearl out. Or vice versa." Pearl was less work, but dealing with her involved putting on shoes and a jacket and going outside. Carrie just needed taking upstairs, but once there, there was the diaper and the pajamas.

"I'll take the baby. I haven't seen her much today." He plucked her off the floor and tucked her into the crook of his arm. "Hi there, pretty girl."

Carrie sniffled a couple of times, and then looked up at him, blinking, as he carried her toward the door. Pearl watched them until I told her, "Come on, Pearl. Time to go outside," and then she bounded to her feet, wagging her tail and the entirety of her muscular backside as she scampered for the front door.

I pulled it open for her, and then stepped onto the porch as she leaped down the couple of steps to the gravel and grass. Where she stopped dead, lifting her head. It was dark, so I couldn't see her nose vibrating as she scented the air, but I recognized the pose. I also knew what the low growl meant, when it started rumbling in her throat.

"No, Pearl—!" I yelped, but it was already too late. She gathered that compact body and threw herself into the darkness, her deep barks echoing back to me as she bulleted across the lawn and into the fields.

"Pearl!" I shrieked. "No! Come back here! Pearl!"

There was no answer, of course, just the sound of her barks getting faint as she got farther away.

"Pearl!"

I hadn't bothered to put on shoes or a coat—I was only supposed to stand on the porch for the thirty seconds it would take Pearl to do her evening business—and by the time I had grabbed my coat and was in the process of stuffing my feet into boots, Rafe was on his way down the stairs, two steps at a time, with his gun in one hand and Carrie, buck naked, wriggling under his arm.

"I got it," he told me as he brushed past, dumping Carrie into my arms.

I opened my mouth to protest, but he was already gone, out the door, down the steps, and across the lawn after Pearl. A second later he was swallowed by the darkness, even less visible in the dark than the light gray Pearl.

"Rafe!" I tried, but of course he didn't answer. And then Carrie decided to pee, right down the sleeve of my coat, and I ran back up the stairs to the nursery to get a diaper on her before she could do it again.

It took a minute to wrap her in a diaper and wrestle her tiny, constantly-moving body into a pink sleeper. Then I picked her up and ran over to the window.

She made a sort of inquiring little noise, and I patted her back, tiny and warm under the pink terrycloth, as I peered out into the darkness. "Just a minute, baby. I want your daddy home safe and sound first."

Carrie didn't say anything else, but I could hear the sound as she stuffed a tiny fist in her mouth and started gnawing on it.

I squinted into the dark beyond the driveway. Was that a movement over there? A lighter blur moving through the darkness?

Was that Pearl's low-slung body headed for home? Or someone else, coming toward the house?

I had left the front door wide open when I ran upstairs. If someone had managed to get past Rafe, he—or she—could be making his or her way toward the mansion right now.

I swung away from the window, and just as I did, there was a loud sound out there in the dark, followed by a howl, both of them practically on top of one another. I couldn't tell whether the howl was animal or human, but clearly someone—or something, like my Pearl—had been shot.

I dropped Carrie into her crib—she gave a startled yowl, but I couldn't worry about it right then—and ran as fast as I could into the hallway and down the stairs toward the gaping maw of the front door. "Rafe!"

There was no answer, of course. I hadn't expected one. From upstairs I could hear my daughter start to make fretful noises about being abandoned.

Nothing I could do about that right now. I slapped the light switches down, shutting off all the lights inside and out, and slipped through the open doorway onto the porch. And pulled it shut behind me as I stood there in the dark, feeling exposed, waiting for that metaphorical other shoe to drop.

It didn't. Nothing dropped. There was—maybe—a slight rustle of some sort far away, on the other side of the field. Like a person or animal walking or running through dry grass. Then there was a bang in the distance, followed by another. so quickly they were almost the same sound. An engine roared to life on the other side of the field.

I could hear tires grinding, followed by three or four shots in quick succession.

They didn't slow the car down, if that had been the point. I could hear it bumping and grinding across the uneven field, and the sound it made when it got to the road and sped off.

"Rafe?"

It hadn't been him in the car. Not unless they—whoever they were—had wounded him with that first shot, and then loaded him into the car. If so, those last three or four shots would have been aimed at Pearl, who wouldn't have let that happen without putting up a fight.

But it was more likely that it had been Rafe emptying a clip trying to stop the car. He was still out there somewhere. I had to believe he was, or I'd lose my mind.

I raised my voice again. "Rafe!"

There was a rustle from the darkness. I squinted in that direction.

At first, there was nothing to see but a pale blur, floating three or four feet above the ground. The little girl inside me, who had grown up on Dix's ghost stories about things that had happened around the mansion long ago, had a momentary thrill of fear.

Until they came closer, and I realized what I was looking at.

My husband—dark shirt, dark pants, dark skin receding into the darkness—cradling Pearl against his chest as he walked out of the fields and toward the house.

Seven

"Oh, my God!"

I launched myself off the porch and down the stairs.

"She's all right." Rafe's voice was tight, and I took a step back.

"Are you hurt?"

He shook his head. "She's heavy."

She was. A big, muscular dog. And he'd been carrying her a good distance, judging from the speed she'd taken off with. She must have made it well into the field before she was taken down.

"What happened?"

I fell back another step as Rafe moved toward the stairs.

"Bastard shot her." There was a cold and vicious undertone to his voice that didn't bode well for the bastard, whoever he was, once Rafe found him.

"Where? Is she… she isn't dying, is she?"

"She's fine." He headed up the couple of steps to the porch still carrying Pearl. She was awake, but her eyes were glazed with pain, and she was panting.

"Left hind," Rafe said, nodding to the door. "Open that."

I scurried in front of him and pushed the front door in. As soon as I did, we heard Carrie's wails rolling down the stairway from the second floor. Pearl whimpered, maybe because the sound hurt her ears, or maybe just because Rafe had jostled her when he carried her across the threshold.

"Get some towels and put'em on the island." He headed down the hallway toward the back of the house without waiting to see if I obeyed. I threw a—sarcastic—salute after him even as I ran for the linen closet to get him what he needed.

Carrie's screams echoed in my ears and didn't help the stress levels of everyone concerned, so after dragging half a dozen thick terrycloth towels out of the closet and spreading them on the kitchen island, I ran up the stairs to rescue the baby. By the time I made it back into the kitchen, cradling Carrie, Rafe had placed Pearl on the towels and was looking at her wound.

"Oh, my God." I turned away in instinctive rejection of the blood and torn tissue. My stomach signaled an immediate revolt, and I swallowed hard.

"Stay by her head," Rafe instructed. "Let her see you. Talk to her. Try to keep her calm and occupied."

I nodded, as I made my way around the island. I crouched to where Pearl's face was on the same level as mine and crooned at her. "You're such a brave girl, Pearl. You're going to be all right, sweetheart. Shouldn't we take her to the vet, Rafe?"

I looked up, in time to see my husband poke at the muscle surrounding the bullet wound. I swallowed hard, and Pearl whimpered. "I just want a look first," he told me, not fazed at all by the blood and the wound. "The bullet's close to the surface. I think I can get it out."

"She's going to need antibiotics, isn't she?"

He nodded. "Yeah. Prob'ly. Just let me take a look."

"Make sure she doesn't bite you."

"I carried her here," Rafe said. "If she didn't bite me then, I don't think she's gonna bite me now."

Maybe not. Although— "Her adrenaline was probably pumping then. She might be feeling the pain more now. Can't we just take her to the vet? There's an emergency vet in Columbia, I think."

He nodded. "Just let me rinse the blood off, and I'll carry her to the car."

"I'll bring it out of the garage," I said, turning to the door.

I ended up feeding my baby in the veterinarian's waiting room, while Rafe disappeared inside the clinic with Pearl and the vet. Carrie fell asleep in my arms, and I sat there in the silence—there were no other emergencies that particular night, or at least not at that particular time—and held her. The only sound was the hissing of the air conditioner, and by now it was getting late. By the time Rafe finally came back out the door, I was pretty close to being asleep myself, too.

Until the door opened and he walked out, and then my head jerked up and my eyes opened wide. "Is she all right?"

Carrie twitched in my arms, and her face scrunched up for a second. Rafe put a finger to his lips and nodded. "She's fine. They wanna keep her overnight to make sure the wound don't get infected. If she's still fine by the end of the day tomorrow, we can bring her home."

I let out a breath I hadn't been aware of holding—for the past hour and a half or so—and felt like the weight of the world had been lifted off my shoulders. "Thank God."

"She's a strong dog," Rafe said. "She's been through a lot. The X-rays showed a lot of old damage from before."

Before she was our dog, he meant. While she belonged to Robbie Skinner, who used her for dog fighting and who kept her chained in the heat and the cold under his trailer on the Devil's Backbone.

"All healed now," Rafe added. "Just like this'll be."

"Can I see her?"

"She's out cold, darlin'. The vet knocked her out for the surgery, and he's gonna keep her sedated overnight. She'll need to wear a cone when we bring her home."

Poor thing. "So we can leave?"

He nodded. "They have the number. If anything changes, they'll call." He glanced down at Carrie, nestled into my arms. "Let's go home and put the baby to bed. It's been a helluva day."

It had. And he'd been tired even before this last adventure.

"You never told me what happened," I told him when we were back in the Volvo, going in the direction of Sweetwater, with Carrie asleep in the back. "Pearl heard or smelled something, and took off into the fields. And you followed."

He nodded, eyes on the road and his hands light on the steering wheel. But there was tension in his voice. "Somebody was out there. More than one. I'm sure I saw two, maybe three."

"Doing what?"

He shook his head. "Not sure. When they saw Pearl coming—and it wasn't like they could avoid seeing her; she was running straight at'em, barking her head off—they split up. Pearl started to chase one of'em down, and one of the others shot at her. She stumbled, long enough for the bastard to get away. I was still far behind her by then."

"Was it you who tried to shoot them?" Those three or four shots I'd heard.

He slanted me a look. "Not them, darlin'. I wasn't trying to kill nobody. Just stop the car for long enough that I could get a plate number."

"And could you?"

He shook his head. "Wasn't even close enough to see what kind of a car it was. It sounded like a truck, something with a big and powerful engine. But I didn't see it."

"You stopped to take care of Pearl," I said. "That was more important."

He shrugged, but there was anger in that, too. "Bastards."

No question. It takes a special kind of jackass to shoot a dog. Especially when you're trespassing on someone else's property, and the dog is just trying to protect what's hers.

Or in this case, the neighbor's. We own the lawn, the neighbor owns the fields.

We drove a minute in silence before I broke it again. "I know you couldn't see anyone. Or anything. But would you like to make a guess as to what was going on?"

"My guess," Rafe said, "with nothing to back it up, is that this was Rodney Clark and one or two of his friends, and they followed me home earlier. Either because they did the damage to your house on Fulton last night, and I was asking questions about it, or for other reasons."

Like the fact that they were racists and he was black. Or brown. Or whatever.

"Are you going to talk to them about it?"

"I don't imagine that'll do any good," Rafe said. After a moment's thought he added, "Unless they expect me to. Then it might be best if I do what they're expecting."

"Maybe you should talk to someone about it. Get another opinion. Like Grimaldi's or Wendell's or Bob Satterfield's."

He nodded. "I'm gonna have to talk to all three of 'em, darlin'. Tammy and Wendell cause they're in charge of me, and Bob because it happened here, not in Columbia."

Of course. Although if either Tamara Grimaldi or Wendell felt like they were in charge of him, it would surprise me greatly. "Tonight?"

"Sooner'd be better. It won't take long. And then we'll put the baby to sleep and crawl into bed."

He dropped one hand from the wheel and reached for mine. I tucked it inside his. "Funny thing. That's just what I want to do, too."

"Great minds," Rafe said, and held on to my hand as we traveled through the darkness toward home.

It was a bit scary to arrive back at the mansion. As we headed up the driveway toward the big brick building, I kept expecting to hear shots from the left, from the field beyond the driveway, and feel projectiles whiz past my ears. I had heard the vehicle depart earlier—Kyle Scoggins's truck, at a guess—and Rafe had been close enough to almost see it, so there was no reason to think whoever had been out here had come back in the time we'd been gone. Why would they? But the feeling was hard to shake, and I held my breath as we passed in front of the mansion. It wasn't until we were safely around the corner and back inside the garage, that I was able to relax.

"If somebody was gonna take a potshot at us," Rafe told me, "they woulda hit me and not you. You're on the inside."

"I don't want them to hit you either," I said. "And I know it isn't likely that they're there. Why would they come back? But it'll probably be a couple of days before I can drive up to the house without feeling nervous."

He nodded and reached for his door handle. "You get the baby. I'll go open the back door."

"So if somebody's out there with a gun, they'll shoot you and not me?"

He didn't answer, just swung his legs out of the car and slammed the door. I got out on the other side, and unhooked Carrie's seat. By the time I walked out of the garage, Rafe was already on his way back toward me. "Door's open. I'll shut the garage."

It was easier to do what he said than argue, so I just hustled myself and the carrier across the grass and into the kitchen. He joined us thirty seconds later, and closed and locked the door behind us. "Safe at last."

"You're doing that on purpose," I said, and he grinned. I added, looking around, "It's strange to walk in here with no Pearl to greet us." Her stubby cropped tail slapping against the pillow and her jaws split in a doggy grin.

Rafe put a hand on my shoulder. "She'll be back tomorrow. When it gets light out, I'll go out and see if I can find anything useful. Something to tell us who these guys are, and what they wanted. Maybe call Bob and have him send a couple deputies over to help."

"Tire tracks and footprints and spent shell casings?"

He shrugged. "I don't imagine either of'em were stupid to leave anything more incriminating than that. But we have to check."

Of course they did. "I'll see you upstairs," I told him. "I'll put Carrie in her bed and meet you in ours."

"Works for me. I'll be up just as soon as I get these phone calls over with." He headed for the island as he reached for his phone. I took a better grip on the car seat and headed down the hall.

By the time he came into the bedroom, I'd had time to wash my face and brush my teeth and change into a lacy nightgown. Not because I thought he'd be up for any hanky-panky after the evening we'd had, but because, as Mother would say, once you stop making the effort, don't be surprised if you lose your husband to someone who tries harder. I could still see Felicia Robinson smiling up at Rafe, and if she had a lacy nightie and an excuse to put it on, I'm sure she wouldn't hesitate.

He stopped in the doorway and a corner of his mouth curved up as he took in the tableau. "Baby asleep?"

I nodded, and had to swallow as his eyes traveled over me from my shoulders to the top of the blanket and back. "She'll be up in three or four hours, though, I'm sure." She still woke up once or twice every night to nurse. Tonight, since she'd gotten fed late, maybe I'd only have to wake up once.

"Guess I can do what needs to be done in three or four hours." He shut the door so any noise we made wouldn't wake Carrie.

"I know you're tired," I said, watching him reach a hand back to grab a fistful of T-shirt at the back of his neck and pull it up and over his head. My mouth turned dry, and I had to clear my throat before I managed another few words. "We don't have to…"

I lost my train of thought as visions of abs and pecs and shoulders appeared, outlined in all their glory in the soft light from the bedside lamp. His head popped out the other end of the shirt, and he grinned wickedly. "What was that?"

I dragged my attention, with some difficulty, up to his face, and saw his grin widen, probably at the dazed expression on my face. "Did you say something, darlin'?"

"No," I said.

"No?"

"Nothing at all."

"Glad to hear it."

The shirt hit the floor, and he took a couple of steps forward, and his hand dropped to the button in his jeans, and I stopped paying attention to anything else. If there were people sneaking around in the fields beyond the driveway, they were welcome to do so. I had other—better—things to put my focus on.

Bob Satterfield beat Tamara Grimaldi to the front door the next morning, but not by much. Bob knocked, and as I opened the door for him, Grimaldi's SUV turned into the driveway and cruised up to the house. She parked behind Bob's official vehicle, and got out.

"Go on back to the kitchen," I told Bob, "and get yourself a cup of coffee. Rafe's back there."

He nodded and brushed past me on his way across the threshold. I stepped out and closed the door behind me while I watched Grimaldi stand for a second with her back to me and peer out across the fields.

She glanced at me over her shoulder. "Out there?"

I nodded. "I didn't go out there, so I have no idea how far

away it all happened. Rafe can tell you. I stayed inside the house with Carrie."

Grimaldi nodded and gave up the vigil. "Did I hear you mention coffee?"

"Back in the kitchen." I pushed the door open again as she came up the steps. "Late night?"

"No later than usual." She gave me a look on her way past, and her lips twitched. "None of your business."

"I didn't say anything," I protested as I shut the door behind her.

She smirked. "You thought it."

Well, yes. I had thought it. But— "There's no law against thinking."

"Guess not." She headed down the hallway to the kitchen, long legs in short heels eating up the distance. "Dog still at the vet?"

I nodded, hurrying along behind. "They wanted to keep her overnight to make sure the wound didn't get infected. We haven't called them yet this morning. But if all is well, and doesn't get worse throughout the day, we can pick her up tonight."

"I'm glad it wasn't worse," Grimaldi said, and passed from the hallway into the kitchen. "Morning."

She nodded to Rafe and Bob, who were leaning against the counter and island, respectively, enjoying mugs of steaming hot coffee.

"Anyone want me to make breakfast?" I asked.

"Your mama took care of it," Bob told me.

"I had something," Grimaldi added, reaching for the mug Rafe was handing her.

I turned to him. "Rafe?"

He grinned at me. "I'll grab an apple or something later. Don't wanna waste any daylight."

No, considering what yesterday had been like, and what

today was shaping up to be—it was so early that Carrie wasn't even up yet—I could see why he'd be worried about that.

"Let me know if you change your mind. I'm going to go upstairs and take care of the baby."

The baby monitor on the counter was starting to make little noises.

"I'll come back in before we leave," Rafe promised. "For now, we're just gonna walk around the front forty and see what we can find."

"Have fun. Don't trample the evidence."

"We'll try not to, darling," the sheriff said. "Go take care of that baby before she starts fussing."

I did. Headed back upstairs to change and feed Carrie, and get her ready for the day.

I was halfway through the feeding when I heard the front door shut downstairs, and heard their voices outside the window as they moved off the porch. By the time I'd finished nursing, and put Carrie to my shoulder to pat her back, they were off in the far distance, more than halfway across the field. Walking in a line, with about ten feet between them, heads bent and eyes fastened on the ground.

I smirked. Rafe, in his faded jeans and black leather jacket, and Grimaldi, in her business suit, both looked out of place wading through the dry grass. Bob Satterfield looked like he did this every day of his life.

And it was Bob, out on the left flank, who must have said something, because Grimaldi and Rafe both converged on him, and they stood for a minute and discussed whatever it was, before they each pulled out a cell phone and took a picture of it.

Footprint, maybe.

Once that was done, they went back into formation and kept moving across the field.

"Daddy's working," I told Carrie. "He'll be in to say goodbye before he takes off. And later this morning, you and I are going to meet Alexandra Puckett for lunch. Won't that be nice?"

She gurgled. I peered out the window at the activity—or lack thereof—in the field.

It took them the best part of two hours to walk around everything. Then Grimaldi and Bob got into their respective vehicles and took off down the driveway while Rafe came inside. "We're done, darlin'. I'm gonna head in to work now."

I nodded and presented my cheek for a kiss. "Did you find anything?"

He shrugged. "Nothing that helpful. Tire tracks on the other side of the field. Nothing distinctive about 'em, but they're spaced far enough apart that we're prob'ly looking at a truck."

"Kyle Scoggins has a truck," I said. "So, I'm sure, does the renovator who walked through the house the other day."

"And Bob and half the rest of the population of Maury County," Rafe nodded.

So no help from the tire tracks. "Anything else?"

"Footprints," Rafe said. "At least two sets, maybe three, but there's no telling whether that's just 'cause I thought I saw three people last night. There mighta been four, and the last one was careful where he stepped."

Maybe. "Anything else?"

"Shell casings from my gun," Rafe said.

"What about from the gun that shot Pearl?"

"We already know what kinda gun that was," Rafe said. "We have the bullet."

The bullet the vet had dug out of Pearl's leg yesterday. I grimaced. "What kind of gun was it?"

"Some sort of rifle. Could be a bolt-action, could be semi-automatic."

Semi-automatic? "That's an assault weapon, isn't it?" Wasn't that what we heard about on the news, the kinds of guns being used in mass-shootings around the world?

"You can use any weapon to commit assault," Rafe said, and relented. "Yes, darlin'. A lot of the recent shootings were done with AR-15s. Semi-automatic assault rifles."

"Is that what AR stands for? Assault rifle?" Or automatic rifle?

He shook his head. "Stands for ArmaLite. The folks who made it."

Shows what I know. I abandoned the minor point in favor of the bigger one. "So you're saying someone was walking around the front forty—" or the fields across from the mansion, "with an assault weapon last night? And used it to shoot Pearl?"

"Either that or a bolt-action hunting rifle," Rafe nodded.

"What's the difference?"

"For this purpose, very little." He looked at me, decided I didn't need the lecture, and added, "Let's hope it was just somebody out there popping rabbits. Somebody walking around the place with a semi-automatic is a lot more of a problem."

I guess it was. Guns that shoot one bullet at a time are bad enough. Guns that keep shooting bullets for as long as you keep your finger on the trigger are a very different matter.

"Semi-automatics don't do that," Rafe said. "That'd be a fully automatic. You gotta squeeze the trigger every time for a semi-automatic, too. But you don't have to reload every six or eight rounds. They keep shooting as long as you keep squeezing."

"They only squeezed once yesterday." Or Pearl might have been riddled with bullets. "Does that make it more likely that it was a... um..."

"Single action," Rafe said. "Maybe. But it don't rule out a semi-automatic."

No, I imagined it didn't. "Will you check on Pearl today, or should I?"

"I'll do it. After this, I don't see any way I can join you and Alexandra for lunch, though. I've still got stuff to do I didn't get around to yesterday, and now this."

I nodded. "Don't worry. We'll be fine on our own. We'll probably just go to the Café on the Square, and check in on Audrey and your grandmother—see if she's feeling better,"

"Be careful."

"It's Sweetwater," I said. "Nothing bad would happen on the square in Sweetwater."

Rafe didn't look convinced, but he didn't say anything, just bent to kiss me. "Have a good time, darlin'."

"You, too," I said, and watched him head out the kitchen door and over to the garage for the Chevy.

Eight

Michelle the stager had left word that the truck would be at the house on Fulton at ten-thirty. I got there at ten-forty-five, and watched for a few minutes as three burly guys in overalls carried furniture and knick-knacks out of the house and into the truck. Michelle was not there, or I would have tried to talk to her. She might have anticipated that, and stayed away. Or maybe she'd stopped by before ten-thirty, had looked at the damage, and then had left before I got there, cursing me.

Either way, there wasn't any point in talking to the three guys who were here. They were just moving stuff around, probably for hire. After a few minutes, I got tired of the show and put the car in gear to roll away, and that's when my phone rang.

I glanced at the display and stabbed the button. "Alexandra? Everything all right?"

"Car trouble," Alexandra's voice told me, echoing and far away. I deduced I was on speaker. "I think we ran over something a few miles back. The flat tire light came on, and I can sort of hear a noise every time the tire goes around."

"Like a nail or something? Hitting the ground?"

"Something bigger than that," Alexandra said. "This isn't a small noise."

"Are you stranded along the side of the road somewhere? Do I have to come get you?" And then arrange for a tow truck for her zippy little sports car?

"No," Alexandra said. "We're still moving. Just more slowly. We're coming into Columbia on the north side right now."

The north side? "Why…?" I shook my head. "Never mind." It didn't matter why she—or they, it sounded like she had someone with her—hadn't taken the interstate all the way to the Columbia exit, but had gotten off earlier and were, it sounded like, coming down from Franklin. "Pull into the nearest auto shop you can find. I'll come get you there."

"Looks like there's one coming up," Alexandra said. "We saw a billboard a mile back. I think I see it."

"Make sure of it before you hang up."

I waited a few seconds until she confirmed it. "Yeah. This is it."

She rattled off the address.

"I'm just a few minutes away," I told her. "I was over at the house on Fulton, the one Charlotte and I have been renovating. I should be able to get there in ten minutes."

"Take your time," Alexandra told me. "You've got that precious baby in the car, right? Drive carefully."

I said I would, and then I stomped on the accelerator, so she wouldn't have to wait any longer than she had to.

It wasn't until I was a couple of blocks from the address she'd given me, that I realized I was familiar with this particular auto shop.

I know for a fact that there are several of them in Columbia. There are probably even several on the north side of town, but this was where Rodney Clark worked. Rafe had staked it out for a week about a month ago.

There was no real reason why that should give me pause, of course, but I found my heart beating a little faster as I gunned the car up the street.

I got there just in time for the showdown, which was Alexandra sort of hiding on one side of the car, looking worried and very pregnant as she pushed herself up against the bright red metal. Her eyes were huge in her pale face, and her stomach bulged out of the short denim jacket she wore over leggings and a striped shirt.

Her significant other, Jamal, was hurling invective across the roof of the zippy little Mazda Miata. It was directed at one of the mechanics, a medium-sized, scrawny guy with a skinhead haircut and baggy blue overalls.

"What the bleep you call my girlfriend?!" Jamal bellowed, hands fisted and head lowered like a bull about to paw the ground.

He's a tall guy, almost as tall as Rafe, and he had the scrawny white kid by several inches and several pounds. He weighs considerably less than Rafe, though. Rafe weighed less, too, ten years ago. Jamal's about a decade younger, early twenties, and he hasn't filled out yet. He still looks a bit like an overgrown kid.

Not that there was anything kid-like about his anger. He was clearly about to burst with rage, and a few short seconds away from vaulting the car and beating the mechanic into a pulp. Thanks to Rafe, he knew how to do it, too. Rafe had probably even explained how to get rid of the body.

Not that there would be a body this time, or any way to get rid of it, if there was. There were too many witnesses for that. I was here. Alexandra was here. Rodney Clark was peering out of one of the bays, a smirk on his face. In the background, I could see a couple of other mechanics keeping an eye on the situation, too, as one of their number squared off against a customer.

"Imma gonna kill you, you bleeping bleep!" Jamal roared as I flung my car door open and jumped out.

"What's going on?"

"This effing effer," Jamal said, at decibels loud enough to make my ears ring, while Alexandra uttered a squeak and came running toward me, both hands under her stomach, "asked Alexandra if that's my baby she's got inside her."

I glanced at the guy, who gave me a cocky smirk.

"When Alexandra said yes," Jamal added, voice rising, "he told her she oughta be strung up for whoring for a bleepety-bleep bleep."

"Oh, my God." My mind blanked for a second, as the hideous words washed over me. My thoughts went directly to that noose revolving in the master bedroom of the house on Fulton. This was another, very unpleasant, explanation for it. I had assumed it was directed at Darcy. But I'd slept with Rafe, I'd had his baby—a baby Rodney had seen just that afternoon. A baby who looks quite a lot like her father. Was Rodney—was someone—saying that I ought to be strung up, too?

I glanced at him, back there in the background. It was obvious he found no fault with what his coworker had said. He was grinning appreciatively, watching the showdown. Maybe the whole crew was made up of racists. Maybe word around Columbia was that if you had neo-Nazi sympathies, you could find a job and friends at the auto shop on the north side.

"Get in the car," I told Alexandra, my voice tight. She slid inside the back, next to the seat holding Carrie. I turned to Jamal. "Does the Miata drive?"

"The tire's losing air."

It was. The front tire was noticeably flatter than the back tire. There was no way he'd be able to drive that car to another shop. Not without grinding along on the rim before he got there.

I turned to the young mechanic, who was still standing there smirking, looking from me to Jamal and back. "Listen, you. My brother's a lawyer. So is my sister and my brother-in-law. We have a law firm in Sweetwater. And I swear to God, if you refuse to work on this car, or if you do a shoddy job of changing the tire, or if you say anything else that's offensive...

we will have you and this entire shop and everyone in it up on charges so fast your head will spin!"

He looked at me, pale blue eyes under almost invisible brows.

"Did you get that?" I added, when he didn't say anything. "I'll do it if you push me, so you'd better not."

The young man nodded, resentment all over his face. Jamal grinned. "Pussy," he said under his breath.

The guy flushed angrily, and his hands curled into fists.

"For God's sake," I told Jamal, "that's not helping. Just get in the Volvo."

He gave me a look, but he did it. Not without a swagger, however. I waited for him to tuck himself into the passenger seat and shut the door, before I turned back to the young mechanic. "We'll be back at two o'clock. The car better be done, and done right. And you'd better not overcharge for the work, either."

He nodded sullenly.

I gave him one last, hard look, and then I folded myself back into the Volvo, and reversed out of the body shop and into traffic.

"That went well," Jamal said.

I nodded. I was still shaking a little bit, but it was adrenaline, not fear. "It would have been nice if someone had warned me that you were going to do it. I was so surprised when I recognized Clayton that I almost gave the whole thing away. Unlike the rest of you, I'm not trained to do undercover work."

Jamal grinned.

"Me, either," Alexandra said from the back seat, where she was tickling Carrie's toes through the fuzzy suit my daughter was wearing. "She's gorgeous, Savannah."

She went on without missing a beat or even drawing breath. "I mean, I know Clay. I like Clay. But the way he looked at me, and the things he said…" She shivered. "I almost believed he believed them."

"This was what Rafe drove up to Nashville for on Sunday," I said, putting the pieces together. "To get Clayton here from Chattanooga, and then set it up so you two could come down and have a confrontation with him. I guess you punctured your own tire?"

"Big ole spike," Jamal nodded. "We stopped a mile out to drive it into the tire. Even so, I thought we were gonna have a flat before we made it there."

"I wondered why you didn't come in from the interstate." Going down the Lewisburg Pike from Franklin takes so much longer. Especially if they were aiming for Sweetwater and not the north side of Columbia.

"A man's gotta do what a man's gotta do," Jamal said philosophically, and I guess that was true.

"So this whole production was to show Rodney Clark that Clayton is a kindred spirit?"

They both nodded. "Clay's worked on cars before," Jamal added. "Mostly chopping'em up, I think."

That's what I'd heard. Rafe had told me once that Clayton ended up at the TBI because he'd been arrested in connection with a ring of car thieves and a chop shop. And like with Rafe twelve years earlier, someone had grabbed him, like a twig from the fire, and shoved him into the TBI's undercover program instead of prison.

"He finished what he was doing in Gig City last week," Jamal said. "And things were a little hot down there."

I deduced he wasn't talking about the temperature.

"Wendell pulled him back up to Nashville for a few days, and he and Rafe figured out this setup. Clay's been down here since Sunday, getting settled. Yesterday was his first day on the job."

"And today you showed up."

He grinned. "If that don't make that pissant Clark think Clay's as much of a bastard as he is, I don't know what woulda. Although for a second there, I thought I was gonna have to punch him."

"He would have punched you back," Alexandra said from the back seat.

Jamal nodded. "Woulda looked good, though."

It would have. But— "Everyone else might have piled on too," I said. "You might have gotten hurt. And someone might have insisted on the police being called in. I think it worked out pretty well the way it did."

Jamal shrugged. "A little blood never hurts when it comes to making your point."

Likely not. "Maybe you'll get the chance when you go to pick up the car again."

"If the owner has any sense," Alexandra said, "he'll keep Clay far away from Jamal when we come back. No legitimate business owner would want a scene like that."

No. And if the owner of the auto shop, or the manager or whoever was in charge of it today, didn't keep Clayton away from Jamal when Jamal and Alexandra came back, I think we would be excused for drawing some conclusions about the owner or manager's opinions.

"You better make sure the car's OK before you take it on the interstate later."

"It's Clay," Jamal said. "He ain't gonna let nobody do nothing dangerous to Alexandra's ride."

Maybe not. Or at least not if he could stop it.

"And if there is something wrong with it," Jamal added, "Clay'll let me know."

Good to know. "I guess we're good to go to lunch, then?"

"As good as we'll ever be," Jamal said. "I could eat."

"Me, too," Alexandra said.

Me, three. The Café on the Square in Sweetwater was out,

though. Jamal would not appreciate the ambience, and the spindly chairs weren't designed for someone of his height. "What are you in the mood for?"

"Nothing fancy," Jamal said, which meant the Wayside Inn was also out.

We ended up at Beulah's Meat'n Three, a small cinderblock building on the road between Columbia and Sweetwater.

Beulah Odom ran it when I was a girl, and up until about six months ago. When she died, she left it to Yvonne McCoy, one of her waitresses, much to the chagrin of her remaining family: her brother Otis's wife and daughter, who had counted on it coming to them. They'd had plans of turning it from the down-home meat'n three that it was and into some sort of fancy French bistro, or maybe that was just my interpretation of the situation.

Beulah's will had kyboshed that intention, anyway. It had taken a few months, and a court case, for her to be able to keep the place, but Yvonne was in full possession now.

She was also an old flame of Rafe's, or maybe it's more accurate to say he was one of hers. She's Dix's age, a year younger than Rafe, two older than me, and one night in high school they'd decided to have sex. Yvonne once told me she'd have been happy to do it again, but Rafe hadn't wanted to, so they'd kept it to that one time. She was still very flirtatious with him, though, and maybe that should have made me dislike her—it made me dislike Felicia Robinson, after all—but somehow I didn't have it in me.

That's why, when we walked through the door of Beulah's and saw Yvonne standing there at the hostess station, I was able to greet her with a perfectly natural, perfectly friendly smile. "Hi, Yvonne."

"Princess." She grinned, and kept grinning even after she peered behind me and realized that Rafe wasn't with me. That might have been why I liked her. "How many?"

"Three of us and the baby," I said, gesturing to Alexandra and Jamal. "Somewhere a little quiet, since I'll probably have to feed her."

Jamal winced, but Yvonne nodded as if there was nothing unusual about this request. "Right this way."

She grabbed three menus and sashayed off down the aisle toward an empty booth by the window. "What can I get you to drink?" she asked when we had all slid into different sides of the booth and were in the process of removing jackets and scarves.

I ordered sweet tea, Alexandra chocolate milk, and Jamal a Pepsi, and Yvonne withdrew, leaving the menus. "Everything is good here," I said, opening mine. "All the usual small-town food, you know. Nothing fancy, but good."

"Nothing fancy suits me," Jamal said and opened his menu.

I turned to Alexandra. "How are you feeling?"

She made a face. "Like I can't wait for this to be over."

"Four more weeks?"

"Five and three days."

She looked closer to popping than that. But maybe it was because she was seventeen and didn't have any extra weight on her to balance the stomach. "It'll be here before you know it," I told her, and didn't add, *"and then you'll wish you could shove it back inside for a while longer and get some sleep."*

"Have you picked a name yet?" I asked instead. The baby was a boy, and last time we'd talked, she had threatened to name him Rafe.

Not that there's anything wrong with that, but the kid would have pretty big shoes to fill. And I'm not just talking about my husband's, but the fact that Rafe might just be the quintessential tawdry romance novel name, and the poor kid would probably grow up to be a Lothario, through no fault of his own, if they named him that.

"We're still talking," Alexandra said, with a look at Jamal.

"Maybe Ramon."

"Ramon's a good name." Neither of them were Hispanic, but maybe it was Ramone-with-an-e, and if so, that made more sense.

"Did you have a boy-name picked out, if you hadn't had a girl?"

"We talked about a few." Tyrell, after Rafe's father. Mother would have been horrified, of course, but we could have called him Ty. "William was high on the list."

"William is nice," Alexandra said.

"She turned out to be a girl, though, so she became Caroline instead." After William's mother. My great-great-a-few-more-greats-grandmother, who had taken up with one of the grooms while my great-great-grandfather had been off fighting the damn Yankees. I felt a lot of kinship with great-great-grandma Caroline. "Family names."

"Your father's name is Steven," I told Alexandra. "What about yours, Jamal?"

Jamal shrugged. "Never knew him."

Oops. "That leaves the field wide open," I said brightly, "doesn't it?"

Jamal gave me a little smirk, and I added, more naturally, "Rafe never knew who his dad was, either. Not until a year and a half ago, after his mother died. She had a newspaper clipping tucked away in her stuff, and that's the first time Rafe knew his dad's name."

Jamal nodded, with a sideways glance at Alexandra's stomach. "I'm gonna be there for this baby."

"Good for you." I left it at that. "Have you decided what you're going to eat?"

"Patty-melt and fries," Jamal said.

Always a safe choice. "Alexandra?"

"Turkey sandwich," Alexandra said. "The heartburn is killing me."

"Means the baby will have lots of hair." Or so the old wives' tales say.

I turned to Maureen the waitress as she deposited the drinks on the table. "One patty-melt with fries, one turkey sandwich, and one Cobb salad, please. How are you, Maureen?"

"Doing great," Mo said, wiping her hands on her apron. "Fries with the sandwich, too?"

I looked at Alexandra, who shrugged. "Sure."

"Better for you than onion rings," Mo said. "Or maybe you'd like some mac and cheese, or something else instead?"

Alexandra lit up. "Mac and cheese sounds great."

"Then that's what we'll do, sugar. You just sit there and drink your milk." She patted Alexandra's shoulder and winked at me before she headed for the kitchen.

"People are friendly down here," Jamal remarked, watching her go.

"Overall. There are exceptions."

And lo and behold, Maureen was dealing with one of them now. Not that he didn't seem perfectly civil to her.

After a moment, she continued toward the kitchen, and the man in question, stocky and gray-haired in a blue uniform, scooted out of the booth at the end of the row and came toward us. Or toward the front, and the cash register, with his bill in hand.

I put a polite expression on my face. "Afternoon, Sergeant."

It took him a second to place me. Then the blank expression turned to a sneer. "Mrs. Collier, isn't it?"

"It is," I said pleasantly. Or as pleasantly as I could in the face of the sneer. "Lunch break?"

"A man's gotta eat." He glanced over his shoulder, to where his companion was just scooting out of the booth.

My eyes widened, I admit it. "Officer Robinson."

She smirked, too. "Ma'am."

There was a pause. I had no idea what to say. I wanted to

ask them what they were doing here, together, but it was none of my business, and anyway, they worked together, so why wouldn't they have lunch? Rafe and Grimaldi had a bite to eat occasionally. Patrick Nolan and Lupe Vasquez eat together all the time, but of course they share a patrol car.

Then again, for all I knew, so did Sergeant Tucker and Officer Robinson when she wasn't working the front desk at the police department.

So I gave them both a polite nod and wished them a good day. Tucker sneered and Felicia smirked, and then they filed past us. Felicia made eyes at Jamal on her way past. Tucker paid the bill, and outside in the parking lot, they walked past the window and over to a Columbia PD squad car I hadn't noticed when we pulled in.

"Friends of yours?" Jamal wanted to know, as he watched Tucker wedge himself behind the wheel.

"Sergeant Tucker arrested Rafe for assault and battery thirteen years ago. His opinion of him hasn't changed. And this weekend, I saw Felicia Robinson snuggling up to Rafe down in Laurel Hill."

If they were here because of Clayton and the neo-Nazis, I figured I didn't have to explain what—or who—Laurel Hill was.

"Skank," Alexandra said succinctly.

I nodded. "I feel like someone else's husband ought to be off-limits, you know? No matter how handsome he is."

"Definitely," Alexandra nodded, with a proprietary look at Jamal.

I took them sightseeing after lunch, through Sweetwater, past the mansion, and back up to Columbia and the house on Fulton. The movers were gone, so we stopped for a few minutes to check out the inside and make sure it was empty, and also so I could get a first look at the damage without Michelle's staging in the way.

"Nice place," Jamal said, standing on the stoop behind me and looking around while I got the key out of the box and into the lock.

"Wait until you see the inside." I twisted the knob and pushed the door open. "Two days ago it looked great. Then this happened."

I walked in with him behind me, while Alexandra brought up the rear with the baby. She'd wanted to practice handling the carrier, she said, even though Jamal had grumbled about her carrying something that heavy.

"Wow." She looked around, at what was now scratched wood floors and dented walls.

I nodded. "It gets worse. The glass in the kitchen cabinets is broken. The mirrors and glass in the bathrooms have to be replaced. Most of the light fixtures have to be taken down and new ones put up. The back door is busted." We were lucky all the windows were intact.

"Any idea who broke in?" Jamal asked.

I answered as I headed for the kitchen with them trailing behind me. "At the moment we're thinking either Rodney Clark and his friends, or this middle-aged couple that came through the open house earlier in the day on Sunday. We outbid them for the house at auction, and when they were here, the wife or girlfriend," or sister or business partner, for all I knew, "complained about all our finishes. Pretty much everything she talked about ended up broken."

Jamal nodded, and winced at the state of the kitchen. I did, too. With all the pretty touches gone, the fake-fruit bowl and dainty dish towels and trio of canisters, the damage looked worse than it had yesterday.

"Whoever did it fashioned a noose of the bed sheet," I explained when we walked into the master bedroom, "and hung it from the ceiling fan."

"That's nasty," Jamal said.

I nodded. "That part of it points to Rodney and his friends. But other than that, I'm not sure we know enough right now to say who did this. It might not have been either of them."

Maybe it had been random. Just someone who saw an empty house and decided to have some fun by being destructive. It happens, more than it should. I hadn't thought I had to worry about it in this neighborhood, but perhaps I'd been wrong.

"Rafe looking into it?" Jamal asked, standing and looking around with his hands in his pockets. Alexandra was poking her head into the bathroom.

I nodded. "He spent yesterday talking to people. Today, I know he was going to look at video footage from the traffic cam on the main road, and also what the officers dragged in from video doorbells around the neighborhood. Maybe we'll get lucky."

"Long shot," Jamal said, and I nodded. "And anyway, just because you see someone drive by, or walk by, a block or two away, don't mean you can place 'em here, with a tool in their hand."

No, it didn't.

I glanced at my watch. "If you've seen enough, we should probably head out. It's almost two. And we don't want to keep Clayton waiting."

Or Rodney, either.

Jamal nodded.

"Just out of curiosity," I said, as we headed back the way we'd come, down the hallway and into the living room, "are you supposed to get into it with Clayton again when you pick up the car?"

"Rafe said to play it by ear." Jamal answered. "But it's really gonna be up to Clay. He's there with the bastards. If he thinks it's gonna take more than this morning for them to invite him into their group, he'll start something so we can give'em more. It depends on what happened after we left."

"So you don't know what to expect."

He glanced at me as he stepped past me onto the stoop. "Makes it easier when you don't. It's hard to fake surprise."

I guess maybe it was. "Are you worried?"

"No," Jamal said, with a glance at Alexandra, while I locked the door behind us and tucked the key back into the lockbox. "We're heading back to Nashville after this. Our only job was to show up and make Clay look good. We can't be seen down here again."

And the chances that Rodney and company would follow them back to Nashville were slim, I assumed. Although I was sure Rafe and Wendell, and Jamal and Alexandra, would be aware of it, if Rodney did, and would be taking appropriate precautions.

"Clay's the one in the crosshairs," Jamal added. "He's down here trying to join the KKK. We ain't in any danger. But Clay is, if they figure out what he's doing."

"Rafe'll keep an eye on him," I said. "And Grimaldi and Bob Satterfield and everyone else. Nothing's going to happen to Clayton."

"I hope you're right," Jamal said darkly and opened the back door of the Volvo so Alexandra could crawl in.

Nine

Everything was quiet when we got to the auto shop. The red Miata was parked outside, looking shiny and bright, and the flat tire was now as puffy and round as all the others.

"I'll wait until you're ready to drive away," I told Jamal, and I'll readily admit that part of the reason was so that if anything happened—like an actual fist fight with Clayton—I'd get to see it, and of course report on it to Rafe. Who'd probably get a report from Jamal and possibly Clayton, too, about everything that had gone down today.

Or maybe not from Clayton. He might have to be careful who he talked to for the next few days or weeks, so he didn't give away his purpose for being there. Rafe had done a fair bit of that sort of deep undercover work, where he'd go for weeks or even months without talking to anybody on the outside, and it couldn't be easy.

Jamal opened his door. "Stay in the car until I get back out," he told Alexandra, who nodded, but bit her lip.

"Be careful."

"It's Clay," Jamal said.

"It isn't only Clay. It's Rodney, too. And who knows who else. And if they jump you, Clay won't be able to help. Not without giving up his cover."

Jamal nodded. "I'll be careful. But nothing's gonna happen to me."

He unwound himself from the Volvo and slammed the door

before he be-bopped toward the little office attached to one end of the auto shop. One of the two garage doors was pulled down, but through the other opening I could see a car on hydraulic lifts and people in overalls walking around underneath it. Nobody seemed to pay any attention to Jamal, and they certainly didn't move as one toward the office once he'd gone inside.

"Looks like it's going to be OK," I told Alexandra.

She nodded. "It's just scary, you know."

Oh, I knew. I was intimately acquainted with that particular fear. And knew the correct answer, too, even if it didn't make anything better. "It's part of who they are. They're guys who take these kinds of risks so the rest of us can sleep better at night."

"Heroes," Alexandra said.

"Hell," I mean, heck "yes." Clayton was going undercover into a neo-Nazi hate group. A group that might possibly kill him if they figured out what he was doing. What could be more heroic than that?

Of course, there was a chance that they were all hat and no cattle, as the Texans say—full of talk but no real action—and if so, the danger was minimal. And if the danger was minimal, nobody would be happier than me (and Rafe and Wendell and Jamal and, I'm sure, Clayton himself). But at the moment we were going on the assumption that since the group had guns, which we knew they did, that they were willing to use them on other people, which we didn't know yet. And if they were willing to shoot to kill, then Clayton's actions were very much heroic.

There was a glass pane in the office door, but it was reinforced with what looked like chicken wire, and was hard to see through. I could just make out Jamal's outline through the glass. It looked like he was leaning on the counter inside. From everything I could see, nothing at all was going on that we had to worry about.

And that was borne out a minute later, when the door opened and he be-bopped back out, his skinny hips jiving as he made his way toward the Miata. He waved to Alexandra, and she opened her car door. "Thanks for the lift and lunch, Savannah."

"Thanks for coming down and seeing me," I said, even if I'd realized that the biggest part of the reason had been to establish Clayton's bona fides with Rodney. "Let me know how things go with you. With the baby and all."

She nodded.

"And be careful driving home. Chances are the car is just fine. But in case the owner here is part of this mess, and he allowed the car to go out with something wrong with it…"

"We'll stop in a minute or two and check," Alexandra assured me. "As soon as we're up the road a little bit. But if there's something wrong, Clay would have found a way to tell Jamal about it."

Hopefully so. But just in case… "Just be careful. And let me know you got home safe."

"Will do," Alexandra said, and shut the car door before skipping across the blacktop over to the Miata. She curled herself into the front seat—Miatas are very small, and not built for pregnant women—and Jamal revved the engine. The Mazda responded with a roar, and over in the open garage bay, a slight figure in blue overalls ambled toward the opening. The sunlight hit on cropped, fair hair as he reached the end of the enclosure and stopped. I watched as he lifted one hand, two fingers pointed, and mimed shooting at the Miata.

The Miata's moon roof opened and Jamal shot up a middle finger. And kept it there as the Miata squealed out of the lot and onto the road going north. Clayton gave me a scowl—but no gun hand—and turned back into the bay. I put the Volvo into gear and left the auto shop, a lot more quietly and more sedately than Jamal and Alexandra, and headed south.

The emergency clinic where we'd taken Pearl the night before was between me and home, so I pulled into the parking lot and dragged Carrie and her seat inside. Where I was told that Pearl was doing all right, and although it was a little early in the day, they'd be willing to let me take her if I promised I wouldn't leave her alone for the rest of the night, but keep a close eye on her and bring her back immediately if I thought anything was wrong. I said myself willing, handed over my credit card (and considered myself lucky they didn't ask for Carrie, too), and waited for the credit card machine to emit sneering noises. When it didn't, I scribbled my signature on the bottom of the receipt, pocketed my copy, and took Carrie over to a chair to wait for a vet tech to bring Pearl to me.

A few minutes later I heard the scrabbling of nails on the floor inside. The door opened, and Pearl stuck her head out. It was encased in a plastic cone of shame. She let out a deep joyous bark, and launched herself across the floor toward me, cone bobbing. She was towing a girl in blue scrubs who couldn't have weighed more than a hundred pounds soaking wet, barely more than Pearl herself. The girl was hanging onto the leash for dear life and was sliding across the floor behind Pearl.

She slammed into my knees—the dog, not the girl—and then tried her best to crawl into my lap. Being anything but a lapdog, she had to settle for putting both huge paws on my thighs and dancing on her hind legs instead. The vet tech peered worriedly at her, probably concerned that Pearl's wound would open up again and start bleeding.

"Good girl," I told her. "Good girl, Pearl. Calm down, sweetheart. We're going home, and if you open up your stitches again, you won't get to. You have to calm down, baby."

She wasn't listening. Of course not. She kept throwing

herself at my legs, and then she tried to stuff her head, cone and all, into the baby carrier to greet Carrie. The cone got stuck, but Pearl managed to slurp her long tongue across Carrie's face. The baby let out a protesting chirp, and then giggled. Pearl wagged her hind-quarters and panted.

"I've got her," I told the tech.

She looked worried. "You sure?"

I was, but if she wasn't, that was OK. "You can walk her out to the car with me, if you're concerned. Why don't you take the baby, and I'll take the dog."

She didn't look strong enough to handle Pearl. And Carrie was protected by the hard plastic and soft cushion of the seat, so even if the girl dropped her, she'd be OK.

Outside in the parking lot Pearl darted back and forth, tugging on the leash, obviously happy to be in the fresh air again. She scented the weather, threw her head back and sniffed at the sky, and gave a couple of joyous barks as she pranced toward the car.

"It's the blue Volvo," I told the vet tech, who followed behind with Carrie.

She nodded. "Your dog's very happy."

"She's going home," I said. "Why wouldn't she be happy?"

"How did she get hurt?"

"Somebody shot her. Somebody in the fields across from the house. We don't know who, or what they were doing there." Might have been hunting rabbits. Might not. And our chances of ever figuring it out, aside from a lucky break, were probably slim.

Hopefully it was just someone taking potshots at rabbits, someone who freaked out when they saw and heard Pearl coming, and not something worse.

I opened the front door for Pearl. She eyed the seat for a moment, and I could see her haunches bunch as she thought about jumping. "I'll give you a hand," I told her, since I could see the hesitancy. Normally, she would have bounded right into the seat. Instead, she waited while I wrapped my arms around her middle and hauled her, not too easily, into the seat. She's solid muscle, and not small, so she weighs a good bit.

I shut the door on her and then took the car seat with my daughter out of the vet tech's hand. "Thanks for the help."

She nodded, her eye on my hand for a second. The one with the wedding ring on it. "The guy who brought her in last night… was that your husband?"

"Yes," I said. *Mine. All mine.*

She nodded. "Have a good day."

I wished her the same, and then I buckled Carrie into the backseat while I tried not to smirk too widely.

"I picked up Pearl," I told my husband two minutes later. We were back on the road, still going in the direction of Sweetwater, and I figured an update was in order. "I dropped Jamal and Alexandra off at the auto shop—you didn't tell me Clayton was working there—and since the emergency clinic was on my way home, I stopped to check on her. They said I could take her home if I promised to make sure she didn't exert herself."

"She doing all right?"

I glanced over at Pearl, riding with her head out the window and her tongue lolling. My hair was going to be a snarled mess by the time we got home, but it was worth it. "She's fine. Enjoying the ride. I had to help her up onto the seat, but otherwise she seems fine." The wound was ugly, and I kept my eyes from dwelling on it, but it didn't look infected or anything like that. "She's wearing a cone so she won't lick at herself. Right now the air's getting stuck in it and flapping her ears around. She's having the time of her life."

"Good," Rafe said, sounding pleased.

"The vet tech asked if you were my husband. And Yvonne says hi." And then there was Felicia Robinson, who hadn't said anything, but who'd been there, and so had focused my attention on her again. "You're just breaking hearts left and right, aren't you?"

He chuckled. "A man's gotta do what a man's gotta do, darlin'."

"Well, Alexandra and Jamal got off OK. Clayton pretended to shoot them as they drove off, and Jamal gave him a middle finger through the moon roof. I don't know whether that means that the car is safe, or the opposite." Or whether it meant anything at all.

"The car's fine," Rafe said.

Good. I waited a second to see if he was going to elaborate, and when he didn't, I added, "It all looked very nice. I'm sure Rodney has no doubt that Clayton is a kindred spirit."

"Good," Rafe said.

"You sound busy." Or like he didn't want to talk to me. Although it was probably nothing personal.

"Just finished talking to Eddie Tremayne. He swears he had nothing to do with vandalizing your house and apologized for his wife's comments. He was hanging out with friends Sunday night, and gave me a list of four names I'm gonna have to check out."

"And his wife?"

"Home watching TV," Rafe said. "But I don't see her having the strength—or the footwear—for kicking in the door and busting up your house. Do you?"

I didn't, to be honest. "I don't think she'd be tall enough to reach the fan, either. Even if she stood on the tallest thing in the house. I guess we're back to Rodney and Kyle."

"I'm gonna talk to Eddie's friends," Rafe said. "But if they alibi him, then yeah. It's gonna look more like Rodney and Kyle."

"I'll let you get to it. Dinner at six?"

"I'm gonna be late," Rafe said. "SWAT's meeting tonight."

And he was part of the SWAT team when they needed him. Not that they had needed him in the past two months. Nothing had happened that required a SWAT team. But they were all staying on their toes in case this thing with the neo-Nazi group blew up into something bigger. And that included weekly practice sessions that usually went late.

"I'll keep something warm for you," I told him. "Be careful."

"You too, darlin'. Don't do anything I wouldn't."

Since that didn't include a lot, I assured him there was very little chance of that. And then we hung up and I focused on keeping the car on the road and the air whistling through Pearl's cone as we headed for home.

While the baby was taking her last nap of the day, I let Charlotte and Darcy know that Michelle had removed her damaged staging and that the house on Fulton was once again empty. Darcy would be working, of course, but Charlotte and I arranged to meet the next morning, to clean up the damage and to start assessing what we needed to buy and order, so we could get started on fixing the mess. I made dinner while I waited for Carrie to wake up, and left Rafe's portion in the stove while I gave Carrie tummy-time and Pearl special love and scratches on the floor in the parlor.

She was still not feeling great. I could tell now that the first exuberance of getting out of the vet clinic and home had worn off. She moved more slowly, and was less alert. Normally, she'd hear me coming from the other side of the house, and now she'd still be asleep when I came through the door. I had a supply of pain killers I was supposed to feed her every day until she got well, and the vet had warned me that they didn't just numb the pain but also had a mild sedative so an active dog wouldn't be as energetic as usual and do anything to hurt herself.

So it was a quiet evening. Carrie gurgled on the floor, Pearl snoozed on her pillow, and I had HGTV on, and was watching reruns of Hometown, wondering whether HGTV would be interested in a show about me and Charlotte, or about Darcy, Charlotte, and I, renovating houses in Maury County. Considering my usual experiences with renovations and houses for sale—I'd caught killers in them, had had them set on fire and vandalized, and even found dead bodies—it would be the most exciting show on HGTV, no question.

By eight, Rafe still wasn't home, and I was starting to get… not worried. And not exactly annoyed. But a little irritated, maybe. If he was going to be this late, couldn't he have let me know? The chicken parmesan probably looked like charcoal briquettes by now, and wouldn't be good for anything by the time he got here.

When the phone dinged with a text, I pulled it closer. And arched my brows at the message.

Unknown Caller: *Something is going on at your house on Fulton Street.*

Oh, really?

I tried to call Rafe, of course. I'm not stupid. But his phone went to voicemail—he was probably busy flexing his muscles in the black SWAT gear, and making Felicia Robinson, and any other female cops who were there, weak in the knees—and I didn't bother leaving a message, because half the time he didn't listen anyway, he just called me back to ask what I'd said. Instead, I tapped out a quick text of my own—*Went to Fulton. Got text from unknown caller saying something going on*—and called my sister. "Are you home?"

"Where else would I be?" Darcy wanted to know.

"I thought you might be at your mother's house. Or out with Nolan."

"Patrick's at SWAT practice," Darcy said, which I should have known. And would have, if I'd thought about it. "What's wrong?"

"Not sure." I told her about the message. "Rafe's going to kill me if I go there by myself. And I don't want you to go there by yourself, either. But I thought I could pick you up on the way—you're between me and Fulton—and we could go together."

The house on Fulton belonged to Darcy. If something was going on with or inside it, she had the right to know.

"Sure," she agreed readily.

"I have to load up Carrie. It might be as long as thirty minutes."

"Take your time," Darcy said. "I'm sure, if the place is burning to the ground, someone has already called the fire department. And if someone's inside, destroying things, I'd just as soon not come face to face with them."

Me, either. So while I didn't dilly-dally, I didn't scramble to get out the door as quickly as I could. I checked Carrie's diaper before getting her into her suit, and when Pearl lifted her head and gave a hopeful wag, I stopped to scratch between her furled, little ears. "Sorry, sweetheart, but it's better if you stay here and guard the house. I don't want you to have to get in and out of the car again for a day or two."

She gave a sigh, but settled back down on the pillow. I grabbed Carrie and headed out.

As a result of all that, it wasn't quite thirty minutes, but more than twenty, before I pulled up in front of Darcy's cute little rental house on the south side of Columbia. She was keeping watch, and came out to meet me as soon as I pulled into the driveway.

"Any more messages?" She slid into the passenger seat and pulled the seatbelt across her chest.

I shook my head. "Someone either doesn't care whether I get there or not, or it's someone very patient."

"Could just be one of the neighbors," Darcy said, as I

reversed back out of the driveway and continued up the road toward Columbia proper. "Your number's on the sign in the yard."

"That's what I assumed."

That someone on the street or in the neighborhood had looked out the window or walked by the house, and seen something going on inside. And had sent a text message to the phone number on my For Sale sign, hoping it would get to me.

"A little strange that they didn't introduce themselves, maybe."

Yes, that was a little strange. A quick, *"Hey, I'm Stella from 105 Fulton and something is going on in your house,"* might have been nice. That way I would have known what to expect.

Of course, the other explanation was that someone wanted me there—wanted us there—for another reason. And I was prepared for that, too. "Just stay in the car," I told Darcy when we came around the corner and approached the house at a slow crawl. "Let's see if we can see what's going on from here."

She nodded, looking left and right. "I'm not seeing anything. Are you?"

I wasn't. Fulton Street looked just as peaceful and friendly as it usually does in the evenings. Cheerful lights on the porches up and down the street, cars parked in driveways, and people watching TV and hanging out behind warmly lighted windows. It's a nice neighborhood. Our porch light was on, but the rest of the windows were all dark, just the way it was supposed to be. Nobody was moving around inside the house, or for that matter in the yard, and the front door was shut, also as it should be.

"There's a package on the stoop," Darcy said.

I squinted. So there was. A small box, maybe the size of a shoe-box, sat on the welcome mat. "Guess I should go see what it is."

I reached for my door.

"Hold on." Darcy grabbed my arm, but without taking her eyes off the box. "I have a bad feeling about this."

"What, you think someone left us a bomb?"

I tried to make it sound like a joke, but it actually wasn't funny. Darcy wasn't smiling when she looked at me, either. "I don't think you ought to touch it."

"Maybe just go over and try to get a look at it?"

She shook her head. "I don't like it being there at all. Or us being here. Did you call Rafe?"

I had called Rafe, but he hadn't answered.

"Try again," Darcy said, fishing for her phone. "I'm going to call Patrick."

If there was a bomb on the doorstep, I didn't want either my husband or Darcy's boyfriend to go near it, either. But I agreed we could use some backup here.

Rafe's phone went straight to voicemail again, though. I listened to his voice tell me to leave a message with one ear, while the other followed Darcy's conversation with Patrick Nolan, who had answered the phone. Did that mean that the SWAT practice was over, and Rafe just wasn't picking up my calls? Or was Nolan crazy enough about Darcy that he'd actually take her calls in the middle of a maneuver? And what did that say about Rafe's and my relationship, if so?

"We're sitting here outside the house on Fulton," Darcy explained. "Savannah got a message saying that something was going on, so she picked me up and we drove over. And we can't see anyone or anything. But there's a box sitting in front of the door."

Nolan must have asked what kind of box, because Darcy went on to describe it. "Looks like just your basic cardboard box. Big enough for a loaf of bread or a pair of shoes. Nothing outsized."

Nolan's voice quacked faintly, and Darcy glanced at me, at the same time as she shook her head. "No, nobody ordered anything. We weren't expecting any kind of delivery."

I shook my head, too. No, we certainly hadn't.

And then my own phone rang, and I glanced down at it. And saw Rafe's number.

"Rafe! I'm glad you called. Listen—"

"Get outta there," Rafe said, his voice tight.

My jaw dropped. "Excuse me?" He didn't even know where we were. Did he?

"Drive," he told me. "Now!"

Or maybe he did. "There's a box—"

"I know about the effing box. Just drive, Savannah!"

I had already taken my foot off the brake and moved it onto the gas, so it wasn't like I wasn't driving. We'd already moved away from the front of the house and had made it to the next property.

"I'm…" I began, and that's the last thing I heard clearly. My voice starting to tell him I was driving. But before I could get the rest of the sentence out, there was a loud noise, sort of like the gunshot from last night, and then a much louder noise, one that sort of rolled over us like a wave, and after that, everything went dark for a little while.

Ten

The car moved quite a few feet. It didn't roll over or anything like that, but it was like a giant hand had picked it up, skewed it halfway around, and dropped it again, ten or fifteen feet away. When I opened my eyes after the shock wore off, we were sitting in the middle of Fulton Street, facing the opposite direction we had been, toward our house.

Darcy, beside me, was breathing fast. I could see her chest rise and fall rapidly, even if I couldn't hear her respirations. My ears were ringing too much for that.

I could hear Carrie, screaming her head off in the backseat. Her shrill cries were loud enough to cut through whatever else was clogging up my ears.

"It's OK," I told her, and my voice sounded funny, sort of big and echoing inside my head. I cleared my throat and tried again. "We're all fine."

"You OK?" Darcy asked. Her voice sounded funny, too, so I deduced that the problem wasn't our voices, but my ears.

I nodded, carefully. "You?"

"My ears are ringing. I think I have some whiplash. Other than that I'm fine."

Good. I twisted in my seat—I might have a touch of whiplash, too—and peered at Carrie. She, too, was fine. I hadn't expected anything different, though. She wouldn't have been able to scream the way she was if anything had been wrong with her.

"What the hell happened?" Darcy asked.

Honestly? I had no idea. Not about the specifics. "I guess the bomb went off. Or whatever was in the box exploded. And took half our house with it."

That was a slight exaggeration, although not much of one. We could see the house clearly, and it wasn't a pretty sight. The front door was gone, along with half the exterior wall, including the window. The coat closet and half the bedroom on the other side of the center wall was also gone. So was the porch roof and posts, and a good bit of the roof above the living room. It was as if a giant hand—the same one that had moved the car—had reached down and scratched the middle twenty feet from the house.

"It's a good thing you didn't leave the car," Darcy said.

I nodded. Yes, if I'd left the car when I'd talked about going to check out the package on the porch, I didn't think there'd be anything left of me.

That's when I started shaking. Up until that point, I guess it hadn't really sunk in. But I'd been a few seconds and a few feet from dying. If Rafe hadn't called and told me to get the car moving…

"Does the car drive?" Darcy asked, her voice a lot calmer than mine would have been. "We should try to get out of the street. There are people coming."

There were people coming. We could see flashing lights, blue and red, flickering in and out among the trees around the corner, and as the ringing in my ears subsided—and Carrie quieted from screams to sniffles—I could also hear the sirens approach. And all around us, the neighbors were creeping out of their houses, peering around like survivors of some natural catastrophe after the winds and rain have passed.

I reached out—my joints felt creaky—and turned the key in the ignition. The engine came back to life. The steering column was locked, and it took a few seconds to figure it out, but by the time the first official vehicle came roaring around the corner, the Volvo was rolling slowly toward the curb on the other side of the street, hazard lights flashing.

First on the scene was a fire department ladder truck, with an ambulance screaming behind it. They both squealed to a stop at the curb in front of the house, cutting off our view of the smoking wreck.

Or perhaps I shouldn't say it was smoking. There was no smoke, and no fire. The stuff floating in the air was dust, I thought. Pulverized particles of wood and drywall, blown to smithereens by the bomb.

A black and white Columbia PD squad car followed the fire department vehicles around the corner. It hesitated for a second after it navigated the turn, before zipping across the street and stopping with a squeal of rubber in front of the Volvo.

The driver's side door opened, and Patrick Nolan stepped out, looking shell shocked. Darcy gave a little sob as she fumbled for her seatbelt.

Rafe didn't stop to take in his surroundings. He had his door open before the squad car had come to a stop, and by the time Nolan had both feet on the ground, Rafe was already at my door, reaching for the handle.

I pushed the button to unlock it, and had it yanked open. In the time it took me to unhook my seatbelt, he had stuck his entire upper body through the opening, ascertained that Carrie was all right, and squawking in the back seat, and withdrawn, taking me with him.

"Dammit, Savannah." He pulled me into his arms, roughly enough that I could tell he'd been worried.

"I'm fine," I said, into his shoulder. "The baby's fine." Probably better off than Darcy and me. She'd been better protected, strapped into her padded infant seat. "We're all fine."

He didn't say anything, just kept his arms around me and

breathed, slowly and deeply, into my hair.

"The house is not fine," I added. "Somebody blew up our house."

"No shit."

"If you hadn't called and told me to drive, I would have been blown up, too."

He didn't say anything to that, just held on.

"This is crazy," I told his shoulder. "Vandalizing the place is bad enough. But blowing it up? And almost blowing us up with it? That's nuts."

Rafe didn't answer, but now that I was getting a little calmer myself, from being safe and in his arms, I could feel the tension in his body. It permeated every muscle, every part of him almost pulsing with what was probably suppressed anger and need for action. The need to rip someone's head off, if he could just figure out who.

I extricated myself from the embrace. "I'm going to grab Carrie. She's going to need some comforting, too."

He let me go, and nodded.

"Why don't you go across the street, meanwhile, and see what you can find out."

The firefighters, in full firefighting gear in spite of there being no flames to contend with, were swarming around the front of the house, peering at the ground and probably looking for clues. And they weren't alone. Rafe and Patrick Nolan must have brought half the SWAT team with them, because a lot of burly cops in SWAT gear were also milling around. If anyone had wanted to take out a bunch of first responders, this would have been a golden opportunity to start shooting.

"Not like we can stay away, though," Rafe pointed out when I said so.

No. It wasn't. When something went wrong, these were the guys—and women—who ran toward the danger instead of away from it.

"Go," I told him, giving him a nudge in the direction of the house. "See what you can find out. I've got Carrie."

He dropped a kiss on my mouth. "Don't go anywhere."

I promised I wouldn't, and then he walked across the street, the deceptively leisurely saunter covering ground fast, while I headed around the car to the back door and rescued my now hiccupping daughter and cradled her close.

A few feet away, Nolan still had his arms around Darcy. I recognized Tamara Grimaldi, also in SWAT black, talking to a big firefighter with a grizzled mustache, who I assumed, mostly from his age, was the fire chief or at least the captain.

Farther down the street, some of the neighbors had gathered. I recognized Nancy and Gary Allen among them, and decided to go see what, if anything, they had seen or heard. When Rafe had told me not to go anywhere, I didn't think he'd been talking about a few yards down the street. Besides, I was sure he'd want to know what they had to say.

"Evening."

They both nodded as I came closer. So did the people they were standing with, a younger couple with a tow-headed toddler sitting on her mother's hip, while a slightly older boy, maybe four years old, was clinging to her leg. Everyone, including the kids, looked like they'd had a shock. Gary Allen's complexion was almost green, unless that was just a feature of the streetlight. Maybe I looked faintly green, too. I wouldn't be surprised, since I still felt a bit shaky, if I were honest.

"Any idea what happened?"

"A box in front of the door exploded. I have no idea what's going on. Last night someone broke in and vandalized the place, and now this happened."

Nancy nodded. "Your husband talked to us last night. We were afraid maybe there'd been another death."

I shook my head. "No death this time. Although if I'd gotten out of the car and gone up to the porch to look at the box that was there, I doubt I would be standing here right now."

Nancy's eyes widened. Gary looked over at the house, and the porch that was no longer there, with an expression like he was going to be sick. The young couple looked interested, although the husband took a step closer to his wife and kids.

"That's terrible," Gary said.

"Yes, it is. I don't suppose you've seen anyone around the house this afternoon? I was here just before two, and the box wasn't here then."

But they all shook their heads.

"And I suppose neither of you texted me that something was going on, either?"

"We didn't know that anyone was going on until a few minutes ago," Gary Allen said. "Someone texted you?"

"I figured it was one of the neighbors. Although it might have been the person who put the box there."

"What would be the point of that?"

To kill me, if I'd gone up on the porch to look at the box? Or—since that hadn't happened, and they couldn't be sure I would—just to have me here when the box blew?

"What's going to happen now?" Nancy asked, with a glance at the house.

I honestly had no idea. It could be fixed, probably. Most of it was standing. But it would take money and patience—neither of which I had a lot of at the moment—and part of me just wanted to wash my hands of it and move on. "I guess it'll depend on the insurance company. Someone will have to come out and assess, I assume. And then we'll see if they give us enough money to fix what's broken, or whether we'll just have to level the whole thing and start over."

In some ways, it might be a benefit. We hadn't bought a stigmatized property, but we'd ended up with one. One that could prove hard to sell, at least according to Arlene Woods's clients. Maybe knocking it to the ground, scraping up the pieces, and selling the land to someone who'd build a new house on the lot would be a better option than trying to repair the damage.

Over by the house, Grimaldi and Rafe had finished their conversation with the guy I'd assumed was the fire chief, and were going their separate ways. "I should go see what's going on," I said.

The Allens and the other neighbors nodded.

"Somebody will probably be by to talk to you. About anything you might have heard or seen."

"Nothing," Nancy said. "We heard what sounded like a pop, and then the explosion. I didn't see anything at all. We were on the other side of the house. Watching TV in bed."

"I was reading to Jerry here," the young mother said, patting the pajama-clad boy clinging to her leg. "Sadie was already in bed." She jiggled the toddler, who had her head on her mom's shoulder, and her thumb in her mouth. Her eyelids were heavy. "Rick was in the garage."

"Workshop," Rick said. "I do a little woodworking on the side."

"So neither of you saw or heard anything, either."

They both shook their heads. "Like Nancy said," the wife told me, "first there was a pop. Sounded like a backfire, or maybe even a shot. And immediately, the big boom. Sadie woke up and started crying. Rick came running in. And we all went outside to see what was going on."

I nodded. It all sounded straightforward. And no reason to think any of them knew anything more than they were telling me. "I appreciate it."

"Let us know how it goes," Nancy said politely.

I said I would, and then I carried Carrie toward the place where Rafe and Grimaldi were standing in the middle of the street, talking.

"—when this shit's available to any shithead with access to

a computer," Rafe was saying when I got close enough to hear. Grimaldi didn't seem shocked by the vocabulary, and they weren't words I hadn't heard before, either, but he reined them in when he saw me coming. "Darlin'. Everything all right?"

"Fine," I said. "She's fallen asleep again." And my arms were screaming. Although she didn't weight above fifteen pounds, that's plenty when you have to keep holding it up.

"I'll take her for a minute." He plucked her out of my arms before I could protest. And while I thought the jostling might wake her up and she'd go into another screaming fit, she just grunted a couple of times, and then went back to sleep, nestled in the crook of her daddy's arm. The sight of him, that big, strong warrior in SWAT black, cuddling his tiny, defenseless daughter, turned my stomach to goo, and probably gave every other woman of childbearing age who saw him a jab straight to the ovaries.

"I spoke to the neighbors," I added, shaking my arms out. "Nobody saw or heard anything I didn't."

"And what did you hear?" Grimaldi wanted to know.

I eyed her. "Other than the explosion? Not much. We pulled up. We saw the package. I thought about getting out to look at it. Darcy told me not to. And then Rafe called and told me to drive."

"Anything like a shot? A loud pop? A backfire?"

That was Rafe asking, and I nodded. "We all heard that. There was a loud sound just a second or so before the second, much louder sound when the box blew up."

They both nodded like that made sense.

"What do you know that I don't?" I wanted to know.

Rafe smirked, of course. "A whole lotta things, darlin'. But in this case, we know what was in the box."

"What was in the box?"

"A substance called ammonal," Grimaldi said. "A mixture of aluminum powder with titanium and ammonium nitrate and perchlorate."

"I'll take your word for it." Chemistry was never my thing. I know enough not to mix ammonia and bleach when I clean, but that's it. "How does something like that blow up? I mean, it was just sitting there on the porch…"

"The brand name for it is Tannerite," Rafe told me. "You can buy it all over the internet, and in fishing and hunting places. There are prob'ly half a dozen places within thirty minutes of here that carry it."

Fine. "But what is it?"

"It's a binary explosive," Grimaldi said. Unlike me, she must have excelled in chemistry at school, because she threw these terms around that meant nothing to me.

Rafe, who hadn't excelled in anything in school, dumbed it down for me. "It's a powder. People buy it for target shooting and to do baby gender reveals and that sorta thing. When you shoot at it, you get an explosion."

I blinked. "You shoot at it?"

They both nodded. "Making it go boom makes it more fun than just hitting paper targets," Rafe said.

Yes, I could imagine. Booms make everything better. "And this stuff is just available for people to get? Anyone can go into a store and buy it?"

They both nodded again. "The sheriff sees it all the time," Grimaldi said. "The first time I came across it, it was more of a shock. I couldn't imagine why anyone would drive around with a couple pounds of binary explosive in the trunk of their car. But Sheriff Satterfield told me it's common around here, and that a couple pounds of the stuff isn't something he'd look twice at."

"The Skinners used to use it for target shooting up there on the ridge," Rafe added. "There were containers of Tannerite in all their trailers."

"That's crazy!"

They both shrugged, so obviously they'd seen crazier.

"Who put it on our porch?"

"We have no idea," Rafe said. "But whoever it was, they stayed close enough to be able to shoot it and hit it."

"That was the sound I heard? Somebody shot the box?"

They nodded.

"Why didn't they just shoot me, if they wanted to blow me up?"

There was a moment's pause. Rafe's expression darkened, but it was Grimaldi who answered. "We assume they didn't want to blow you up. Or didn't want you dead. They wanted you to see the explosion. So they texted you, and waited for you to show up, but they set off the ammonal before you got out of the car."

"So I wasn't in any danger? *We* weren't in any danger?" Carrie, Darcy, and me?

Rafe growled, and his arm tightened reflexively around his daughter for a second. She made a protesting little sound, like she was going to wake up, and he relaxed again. At least enough that Carrie settled back down.

Grimaldi glanced at him, responding both to me and to the comment Rafe didn't make, but that he'd surely made before. "When we figure out who they are, we're charging them with attempted murder. If you'd still been parked at the curb when the box blew, you could have been hurt."

She hesitated for just a second, and gave Rafe another quick look before she added, "My personal opinion is that murder wasn't the goal of this, but that doesn't mean we won't charge them with it when we find them."

I nodded. "Darcy and Carrie were both on the side of the car that faced the house. They'd have been worse off than me. If nothing else, the windows could have broken and cut them." And while Darcy might have been all right—or relatively all right—had that happened, my tiny baby might not have fared so well.

Rafe growled again, and I put a hand on his back, and snuck my fingers under the edge of the Kevlar vest he was still wearing. He glanced down at me, and then made a visible effort to calm down. He rolled his head a couple of times, and then rolled his shoulders. I could feel the tense muscles from where I was standing.

"I should get her home," I said. "And Darcy, too."

"Nolan's got Darcy," Rafe said, and so it seemed. They were still standing together, but Darcy wasn't as pale anymore. Nolan had his arm around her, though, but it was probably more to reassure himself that she was OK, than it was because she needed the support.

"What about you? Do you need a ride?"

He'd come in Nolan's squad car, so the Chevy had to be parked somewhere else. Still at the police station, I guessed, or wherever the SWAT team had had their meeting.

"Don't mind if I do," Rafe said.

"You don't have to stay here and take care of anything?"

He shook his head. "The fire department'll post warning signs and cordon the property off. And it's not like we gotta worry about what's inside. Everything's broken."

The new refrigerator and stove had been intact the last time I'd been inside, and it didn't look like the bomb—or binary explosive—had touched the kitchen. But since telling him that might make him decide he had to camp out here overnight, so nobody looted the house of our appliances, I didn't mention anything about it.

"Let's go, then. I'm a little shook up. I want to get home where I feel safe."

Grimaldi nodded. "You two go ahead. I've got this. I'll talk to you tomorrow."

"Thank you," I said.

She put her hand on my shoulder for a second. "No

problem. You just go on home and don't worry about it."

I nodded. I didn't think I was going to be able to stop worrying about it—or that Rafe would, either—but we could go home and give it our best shot.

Eleven

"Gotta make a stop," Rafe said, and swung the car into the parking lot outside Beulah's Meat'n Three.

It was ten or twelve minutes later, and we'd left the lights and activity of Columbia behind, and were traveling down the dark highway toward Sweetwater. Until the little cinderblock building that housed Beulah's came into view on the left, and Rafe discovered a sudden desire for meatloaf, or maybe something else.

The Volvo bumped over the rutted gravel and dirt, and came to a stop in an open spot. There were plenty of them this late. The dinner crowd had mostly vanished, and there were only a few cars in the lot. It was almost ten at night.

"Sudden hankering for a burger?" I wanted to know.

"Yvonne called me," Rafe answered, and put the car in park. "It won't take long. You can stay here."

"I'd rather come in."

"I'd rather you didn't," Rafe said, fishing in the back for his nylon jacket. And added, "It'll only take a minute or two. And you'd be safer here."

Safer? To the best of my understanding, there was nothing unsafe about Beulah's. Not even at ten o'clock at night. But if he was concerned about my safety—and he was very rarely concerned about my safety when he was around to protect me—then of course I'd stay in the car. "Fine."

"Thanks, darlin'." He swung his legs out and closed the car

door without telling me to lock it. It was either implied, or he just wasn't worried about that particular safety issue.

So then what was he worried about?

I watched him walk toward the door to the restaurant, yanking the jacket on over the vest, and zipping it. The word SWAT in big letters on the back caught the lights in the parking lot and reflected them back at me.

He reached the door and pulled it open, and I stopped watching as he disappeared inside the low-slung building. Instead, I scanned the parking lot, to see whether anything there could give me a clue to what was going on.

And lo and behold, there it was. A dark pickup truck with a couple of familiar stickers on the back. An 88 and a Confederate flag.

I'd seen that truck before. As far as I knew, it belonged to Kyle Scoggins, Rodney Clark's BFF and his alibi for Sunday night.

The last time they'd been here—or at least the last time I'd seen them here—they'd caused a scene with Cletus Johnson and his little girl, and Yvonne had told them to leave and not come back. If they were here now, maybe that was the reason she'd called Rafe for help.

And yes, when I squinted at the windows, there they were, sitting in a booth. There were more than just the two of them; I thought I could make out four distinct bodies.

It was hard to see, though. The windows in Beulah's aren't oversized to begin with, and the blinds were pulled halfway down. All that was visible, were slices of four people sitting, from the elbows to the neck, roughly. A plaid shirt, a green thermal, something that might be a black hoodie, and something gray. And—barely visible from here—a black torso standing in front of the table at the other end.

Yep, that was my husband. I saw the light catch for a second on the badge he slapped down on the table.

None of their heads were visible, so I couldn't see any facial expressions, and it's difficult to gauge reactions just from body language from elbows to neck, especially from the side. Nobody recoiled visibly. I think maybe one or two of them tensed, and the guy in the green thermal squared his—not too impressive—shoulders.

Rafe snatched the badge up again. Words must have been spoken, I assume. Of course I didn't hear them. If anybody protested being evicted, it didn't take them long to reconsider. About a minute later, they all scooted out of the booth and started walking.

I moved my attention to the front door, in time to see it fly open. Kyle Scoggins stomped out, his face dark. He was followed by a guy I'd never seen before. A few years older; maybe thirty, maybe not. He subscribed to the same style of military haircut as Rafe: a barely-there layer of fuzz covering his scalp. He was followed by Rodney, who had his head turned and was arguing, even as he jumped off the stoop and down on the ground.

Rafe brought up the rear, with his hand fisted in the scruff of the neck of the guy in gray, whom he was wrestling along in front of him, while the guy bucked and cursed. When they reached the door, Rafe gave him a shove, and he stumbled off the stoop and into the group of three that was standing there. Two of them caught him and kept him from falling, while the third—Rodney—kept yelling at Rafe. I powered my window down an inch so I'd be able to hear more clearly.

"—as much effing right to be here as anyone!"

"You were told you were unwelcome the last time you were told to leave," Rafe said calmly, but with an edge to his voice. "You show up here again, I'm taking you to jail."

Clayton—for it was him in the gray sweatshirt—snorted. "You and what army?"

Rafe stepped right up to him and looked down from his

four or so inches of height advantage. "You sure you wanna push your luck, son?"

I smothered a snort. It was a masterful bit of condescension. Especially if you knew that Rafe would never, under normal circumstances, call Clayton 'son.'

Clay, of course, stood his ground. He knew he didn't have anything to fear. The others didn't, so they looked impressed. Or at least Rodney and Kyle did. The other man was a bit harder to read. I didn't get the impression he was as young or as hot-headed—or as easy to manipulate—as they were. He stood a step back from the others, arms crossed over the chest of the green thermal, looking watchful, his eyes flickering from Clayton to Rafe and back.

Rafe probably knew it was coming—or maybe not—but when Clayton elbowed him in the stomach, he bent over for a second. I gasped, as Clayton followed up with an uppercut to the jaw. Rafe's head snapped back, and I saw Clayton reach for the gun at Rafe's hip.

Rafe must have felt it, too, or maybe this was a move they'd rehearsed before, because he grabbed Clayton's wrist before he could get there. And when he twisted, Clay let out a squeal that sounded remarkably real. His knees buckled, too, for a second, so I imagine the pain was probably not faked. Or not entirely faked, at any rate.

"You're about two seconds away from spending the night in jail," Rafe growled at him. He was still a little out of breath, and it only made him sound angrier. He propelled Clayton forward. The other three scrambled out of the way, until Rafe could slam Clayton, chest first, onto the hood of the nearest car, and hold him there, with one arm still twisted against his back. If I hadn't known better, I would have totally believed the animosity that pumped off both of them.

Clayton bucked and kicked while Rafe held him in place, and let out a string of invective. Rafe frisked him very efficiently, though, and confiscated a knife out of Clayton's right pocket. When he flicked open the blade, it shone wickedly in the light from the restaurant. The knife disappeared into Rafe's pocket, to Clayton's very vocal, very vehement protest.

"It ain't even illegal!" he argued. "You can't take my effing knife just because you want to. I didn't do nothing!"

"You hit me, kid. That's assault on a police officer. I can take you to jail for that."

"Well, then, do it!" Clayton howled.

Rafe unhooked his cuffs from the back of his belt, and Rodney and Kyle immediately began gabbling. Clayton did, too, twisting his head practically backward to see what was going on.

When he caught sight of the handcuffs, his eyes widened, and he began squirming like an eel. "The fuck, man? I ain't going back to prison!"

"Tell you what." Rafe hauled him upright, spun him around, and pushed him back toward the others. "I don't really wanna spend the rest of the night filling out paperwork. So why don't you gimme a good reason why I shouldn't haul you off to jail."

He folded his arms across his chest and waited.

"How the hell do I do that?" Clayton wanted to know, as he tugged his sweatshirt back into place from the rough handling.

A corner of Rafe's mouth turned up. "You could start by saying you're sorry."

"Sorry?" Clayton's voice rose. "Sorry?! You want me to apologize to you? You throw me out of the restaurant and take my fucking knife and now you want me to apologize to you?!"

"If you wanna stay outta jail." Rafe's smirk widened, and I could see Clayton's eyes narrow. He spat out a string of invective, some of it quite nasty.

"That don't sound like you're sorry," Rafe told him.

"That's because I'm not, you bleepety-bleep-bleep!"

I winced at the choice of words, and watched Rafe's mouth tighten and his eyes turn flat and dangerous. "You sure you wanna go down that road, kid? You gotta chance to walk away here. Otherwise, you're spending the night in jail. And one of your friends here's gonna have to come up with bail money to get you out tomorrow."

He glanced at Rodney, Kyle, and their friend. The friend still didn't say anything. He was just watching the proceedings with his arms crossed over his chest. They weren't Rafe's arms, but none too bad for that. Kyle and Rodney—and Clayton—were all stringy and boy-like. This guy was a grownup, with grownup muscles, and Rafe wouldn't have been able to throw him around the way he did Clayton.

Of course, the only reason he was able to dominate Clayton was because they'd worked it out in advance, so maybe that wasn't a fair comparison.

"Go on, Clay," Rodney said finally. "Just say you're sorry, man. I ain't got the money to bail you out."

Kyle shook his head, too. The third guy still didn't move a muscle, and I wondered whether he was just stingy, or whether he suspected that something more was going on than what was on the surface. It was hard to imagine how, because I knew them both and couldn't tell that they were acting, but I suppose anything's possible.

Clayton gave Rodney a look. "You go around apologizing to his sort down here?"

Rodney gave a nervous giggle. "When the war starts," he said, and then seemed to think better of it. "Just do it, bro. Let's get outta here. Places to go, people to see."

Something seemed to pass between them, and for a second, I didn't see Clayton as Rafe's protégée and an employee of the TBI, but as Rodney's confederate. He was playing his part very, very well.

When he turned to Rafe, he grinned. "Sure thing, man. I'm

sorry. Please don't take me to prison. I didn't mean to hit you. I was scared, you know? You're a big dude, and I was afraid you were gonna hurt me. Skinny little white boy…"

Rafe's eyes flashed in the dark, but he put on a creditable sneer. "Get outta here. Before I change my mind."

"Yessir." Clayton threw a sloppy salute, and then the three of them scurried toward the big, dark pickup with the Confederate flag on the tailgate. Kyle got behind the wheel, and Rodney shoved Clayton in ahead of him before they both slammed the doors. The truck reversed out of the parking space, and took off out of the parking lot with a spray of gravel.

Rafe turned toward the last guy, who hadn't taken the opportunity to tuck tail and run. "Something I can do for you?"

The guy looked at him. A second passed, then another. Finally he shook his head.

"Then get going," Rafe told him. "Those three ain't welcome here. And if you're with'em, it might be best if you stayed away, too."

There was another second while nothing happened. Long enough for me to worry that something would. I hadn't been concerned about Clay hurting Rafe—obviously not—and Rodney and Kyle both came off as too cowardly to engage in an actual confrontation, especially with someone like my husband. Sure, they were probably hell on paper targets, and if they'd been behind the vandalism and box of ammonal on Fulton Street, they were capable of doing damage as long as it didn't involve risking their own skin, too. But I didn't see them actually taking on Rafe one on one, or even two on one.

This guy was different. He didn't strike me as the type who'd back down from a challenge. There was something very calculated about him, about the way he'd been standing there watching instead of getting involved.

And so I found myself holding my breath, waiting to see what would happen.

In the end, nothing did. After the silence had stretched out long enough to be threatening—or at least threatening to me; if Rafe was threatened, he didn't show it—the guy gave a short nod. "Of course, officer."

Rafe turned to watch him go. I did, too, from the safety of the car.

He disappeared into the shadows in the far end of the parking lot. After a few seconds, we heard the sound of a car door slam, and then an engine came to life. A small compact reversed out of a slot up there, and came toward us.

The car was nothing special. A ten-year-old import, white or cream or maybe silvery gray. It had no identifying marks—no 88 sticker or Confederate flag on this one—and nothing else to draw the attention, either. Nor did the driver tear out of the lot in a temper, kicking up a lot of loose stone. No, he drove carefully, making sure he gave Rafe a safe berth—safe for Rafe, I mean; there was no attempt to run him down or even make him step back—and when the car headed up the road toward Columbia, it was at an unremarkable speed that would do nothing to draw attention.

Rafe waited until the car was out of sight before heading back toward the door into Beulah's, probably to let Yvonne know that everything was OK. Two minutes later, he was back behind the wheel of the Volvo.

The first thing he did was rest his head against the back of his seat and let out a breath I deduced he'd been holding since first dragging Clayton out of Beulah's.

Not physically, of course. It isn't possible for normal people to hold their breath that long. But I thought he'd probably been tense throughout the encounter, and hadn't been able to relax until it was all over and everyone was gone, and he was back inside the car.

"Rough night," I told him sympathetically.

He nodded, without opening his eyes.

"He didn't really hurt you, did he?"

His lips curved. "Not enough to matter."

"It looked good. I didn't get the impression that Rodney and Kyle questioned the scenario at all."

He slanted a look my way, amusement still in the curve of his mouth. "Rodney and Kyle maybe ain't too smart."

Maybe not. But— "You still did it well. For a second or two, I looked at Clayton and saw him as Rodney and Kyle's friend, not yours."

"Good," Rafe said, and straightened in the seat, "because Rodney and Kyle ain't the problem. Rodney bought Clay's cover this afternoon. And if Rodney believes Clay, Kyle does, too."

"So what's the problem? The other guy?"

Rafe nodded. "I think they set up this meeting so they could put Clay up for membership in the group. I'm guessing this other guy is the one making the decisions."

"So this was another exercise in establishing Clayton's bona fides."

He shrugged. "That, and Yvonne wanted them outta Beulah's. She told'em last time they were there not to come back."

I nodded. I remembered. "So who's the third guy?"

"Dunno," Rafe said. "But now that I got his plate number, I'm gonna find out."

He turned the key in the ignition, and the car came to life.

"He looked scarier than Rodney and Kyle," I said, as we rolled over the gravel and dirt toward the exit. "Older, and more serious. Rodney and Kyle just come across as two stupid kids."

Venal and nasty kids, for sure, but the type who would break down into tears if they actually had to deal with something like being hauled off to prison. Sure, they liked to look and sound tough. But the only fight I'd seen them pick so far, was with Cletus Johnson's five-year-old daughter.

Rafe nodded. He looked both ways on the highway before turning the Volvo south toward Sweetwater. "Stupid kids can do plenty of damage if there are enough of'em. And Rodney and Kyle are the type who'll feel brave in a crowd, but get'em alone and they start sniveling."

Yes. That was my impression, too. Being part of the neo-Nazi group—if they were part of the neo-Nazi group, and we didn't actually have any proof of that yet… but if they were, it probably made them feel big and bad. When what they were, were two bullies who were too afraid to bully anyone unless they were sure of winning.

"But I agree about the other guy," Rafe added. "He looked like he knew how to handle himself."

"You could take him," I said loyally.

He glanced at me, and a corner of his mouth turned up. "You never know. I got the feeling he was military, and those spec ops guys can kill you with a paperclip."

"You can kill somebody without a paperclip."

He chuckled. "True. But he still didn't look like somebody I'd wanna mess with if I didn't have to."

Perhaps not. "So the next step is figuring out who he is, and if he's in charge of this group of homegrown terrorists."

Rafe nodded. "The car had Davidson County plates. If he's registered with an address in Nashville, but he's in Maury County now, that could be easier said than done."

"Obviously Kyle and Rodney know where to find him. Or at least how to get in touch with him."

"Yeah. But no judge is gonna give me a warrant for their cell phone records. You can't just go get a search warrant because you think somebody might be involved in something. I need proof of something before I can go get more proof."

"Isn't that why Clayton's here?"

Rafe nodded. "That's exactly why Clayton's here. And it

looks like they're moving pretty fast on getting him introduced to the rest of the group. Faster than I thought they would."

"That's good, right?"

"That's very good. Not sure there's a whole lotta time to waste. If it was Rodney and Kyle who shot Pearl yesterday, we know they've got weapons. Semi-automatic weapons."

He flipped on the turn signal and slowed down, preparatory to pulling the Volvo into the driveway. When we were headed up the drive toward the mansion, he added, "And if it was Rodney and Kyle who left the ammonal on the doorstep on Fulton earlier, they've got the means to blow stuff up. Enough of it, maybe, that they can afford to use some just to mess with you. Or with us."

"Unless that's all they have, and they decided to blow it on us."

He shook his head. "There are no restrictions on Tannerite. You can order it online. If they had enough to blow up Fulton, they can get their hands on enough to blow up something else."

"What do you think they're going to blow up?"

"No idea," Rafe said, pulling the Volvo to a stop at the bottom of the stairs, "but now that we know they got it, we're gonna have to figure that out."

He turned to me. "Any objection to keeping the car here overnight? It's late. And you're gonna have to drive me in to Columbia in the morning, so I can get the Chevy. Less'n you want me to call someone else for a ride."

Like Felicia Robinson?

"I'd be happy to drive you," I said.

He grinned, like he knew what I was thinking. "Thanks, darlin'." And then he glanced into the backseat, where Carrie was sleeping in her carrier, and added, "I'll get the baby."

"I'll get the door," I said, and held out a hand for the keys. He dropped them in my hand, and opened his door. I used the few seconds the dome light was on to sift through the keys on the ring so I had the right key for the door. I'd left through the back earlier, and in such a hurry that I'd forgotten to turn on the porch light. If I had the right key, at least I didn't have to worry about anything except getting it into the lock when I reached the top of the stairs.

Rafe, meanwhile, swung his legs out of the car and stood up. And shut the door behind him.

And almost in the same breath as that sound, came another one. Rafe's body hit the side of the car and slid down, leaving a smear of blood on the window.

I screamed, and behind me, Carrie startled awake and began crying. From inside the house, I could hear Pearl go crazy.

I would like to make you believe that my subsequent actions were calm and rational. I'd like to, but the truth is, they weren't. I was a gibbering mess, and it's a minor miracle that I was able to function at all, let alone do anything useful.

Nonetheless, the tiny part of my brain that was operating on a level more advanced than, "Ohmigod, my husband's been shot!" did manage to string some elemental cautions together.

If you get out of the car, you might get shot too.

If you get shot too, the baby will be alone, and no one might show up here until tomorrow.

Call for help before you do anything else. That way, if something happens to you, at least someone will come and find Carrie.

My nose was running and my eyes were leaking, but I knew the voice was right. And although every other cell in my body was screaming to go see how badly Rafe was hurt, somehow I managed to stay where I was and get the phone out of my purse. My fingers were shaking too much to hit the buttons for 911, so I had to ask Siri to dial the number for me.

It rang once, twice, and then— "911," the voice on the other end of the line said calmly, "what's your emergency?"

"I need an ambulance." My breath was hitching enough that

it was hard to get the words out. "Someone shot my husband."

I rattled off the address to the mansion. "He works for the Columbia PD. Notify Chief Grimaldi. And Sheriff Satterfield. And hurry."

I dropped the phone in the console, in the middle of the operator's exhortation that I stay on the line with her. I wished I could, I wished I didn't have to leave the safety of the car, but Rafe was hurt, and not getting up, and if he died out there, alone, while I sat inside the car waiting for the ambulance to show up, I'd never forgive myself.

So I slid my door open—and I had the sense to reach up and turn off the dome light before I did it, so I wouldn't be outlined like a silhouette in a shooting gallery. And then I slipped out on the gravel and dropped to my knees, and, ignoring the pain as the small stones dug into my skin, started crawling around the car to see what—if anything—I could do for Rafe.

Twelve

It took an eternity, or seemed to, before I'd cleared the corner of the car. No one shot at me, though, so I kept going, across the front of the car and around the next corner. I could see Rafe now, half-sitting, half-lying on the ground with his back against the side of the car, with one leg bent at the knee and the other straight out. His head was bent, and fear shot through me. Every foot I gained across the gravel hurt my knees, and fear had lodged like a cold lump of ice in my stomach.

But still, no one shot at me. I kept expecting it, waiting for the sound of the shot a second before a bullet plunged into my skull, but it didn't come.

Pearl was still going crazy inside. It sounded like she was throwing herself at the front door so she could get out, and I hoped she wasn't opening the wound back up. Nothing I could do about it right now, though.

"Rafe!" I hissed his name a couple feet away. "Rafe!"

He didn't lift his head. I crept a little closer and reached out. And déjà vu flashed through my head, of coming out of a closet in the Colliers' trailer in the Bog—don't ask—after shots had been fired, and seeing him slumped over on the bedroll in his room with blood soaking his T-shirt from a bullet in his shoulder.

It had worked out OK that time, in spite of my spending eight interminable hours thinking he'd died. I probably wouldn't be that lucky again.

My hand landed on his arm. The fabric of the windbreaker was wet and warm, and I drew in a breath that sounded more like a sob. "Rafe?"

Somewhere in the back of my brain, I noted that there were sirens in the distance, coming closer. I could still hear Carrie squalling from inside the car, her cries more like hiccups now. Pearl continued to bark, but I didn't hear her throwing herself at the door anymore. Hopefully she'd realized the futility of it, and it wasn't because she was too hurt to stand.

"Rafe?" I put a hand against his cheek and tried to lift his head. "Can you hear me?"

His skin was warm, so that was one thing to be grateful for, anyway. Whatever was wrong—wherever the bullet had hit him—he was still alive. If I could keep him that way until the ambulance arrived, maybe he'd be OK.

He opened his eyes. They were blank for a second before he seemed to recognize me. When he did, he gave me a sort of quizzical look. The tip of his tongue came out to moisten his lips. "Savannah?"

"Yeah. It's me." Tears were running down my cheeks now, and I dashed them away, probably leaving streaks of blood across my cheeks. "Just hold on. The ambulance is coming."

He shifted against the door of the car, and winced. "Hurts."

"I'm sure it does." And that isn't something he admits to often, so it had to be bad. "Can you tell where you were hit?"

He twitched again, and made another face. "Chest? Ribs?"

That didn't sound good. Although it also didn't sound like something I'd want to mess with, even if I'd had some idea how.

"Just sit still," I told him, my heart knocking hard against my own ribs. "The ambulance will be here in a minute. Maybe less."

He closed his eyes again, and I added, only half-joking, "You aren't going to die on me, are you?"

His lips curved ever so slightly, even though his eyes didn't open again. "Nah."

"Just hold on." I grabbed his hand and did just that, while I listened to the sirens coming closer. After another few seconds, I could see the lights flashing between the trees down the road, and shortly after that, the ambulance screeched into the driveway. Two paramedics jumped out. One of them ran toward me, while the other scurried to the back of the ambulance to wrestle a gurney out of the back.

"What happened?"

The male paramedic—I recognized him from last month, when he'd come to my rescue in the Allens' house—squatted next to Rafe.

"He was shot," I said, my voice shaking. "From over there somewhere." I waved in the direction of the field. "Probably a semi-automatic. Someone shot our dog with one last night."

The paramedic nodded.

"He thinks he got hit in the chest or ribs."

"We'll take a look," he told me. "Sir? You awake?"

He reached for the zipper to Rafe's windbreaker.

"Careful," my husband muttered, without lifting his head.

"Yes, sir."

The second paramedic came rattling across the driveway, pushing the gurney ahead of her, as the first pulled the zipper down and spread the edges of Rafe's jacket apart.

I gasped.

He nodded. "There we go."

Yes, indeed. The butt end of a bullet was sticking out of the mesh of the Kevlar right below—unless I missed my guess—Rafe's left nipple.

"There's no blood," I pointed out.

The paramedic shook his head. "No, ma'am. The bullet didn't penetrate the vest. He might have a cracked rib or two, but the vest stopped the bullet from penetrating."

"Then where did the blood come from?"

I gestured up at it, in a messy streak down the side of the car, where Rafe had fallen against the door and had smeared blood across it, going down.

The paramedic stared for a second, before his mouth formed a four-letter word that didn't make it past his lips.

"Arm," Rafe said, as another car took the turn into the driveway on two wheels and powered up the incline toward the mansion. It came from the south, the direction of Sweetwater, so I wasn't surprised to see Bob Satterfield swing his long legs out of the driver's seat.

I was, I admit, more surprised to see the passenger door open and my mother hop down on the gravel. "Savannah!"

She looked around.

"Over here." I waved at her. "Better brace yourself," I added to Rafe. "This is the first time Mother's seen you hurt since last summer."

He winced. It might have been the reminder of last summer, when he'd been in—it seemed—worse shape than this. Or maybe it was the knowledge that Mother was bearing down on him.

There wasn't anything he could do about it, though. Just sit where he was while the paramedic used a pair of scissors to cut the sleeve of the jacket straight up from the wrist.

"Dear me," Mother said, and swayed. Bob ignored her, to squat next to me, and Mother had to pull out of her vapors without assistance.

"He's OK," I told her. "It looks bad, but it isn't actually that big a deal."

"There's blood," Mother pointed out. "Rafael...!"

He managed an almost passable smile, although the wink suffered a little. "Just a scratch."

I snorted, although he was right. It wasn't much more than a scratch. The bullet that had hit him in the chest could have killed him if it hadn't been for the vest. The one that had hit his arm had just taken some skin and flesh with it, leaving a bloody furrow before imbedding itself in the side of my car.

"Any other damage?" the paramedic asked, while Bob and Mother hovered over us. Down at the street, another car took the turn into the driveway with a squeal of brakes. I glanced that way and saw Grimaldi's SUV come up the drive.

"Would you get Carrie out of the car?" I asked Mother. "Take her inside and see if you can calm Pearl down?"

"Of course, dear." She gave Rafe one last look before heading around the car to open the back door and pull Carrie out. "Hush, baby. Grandma's got you."

"Thank you," I called after her, and she gave me a wave as she headed up the stairs to the front door. Pearl's barks took on a frantic, whiny quality. She adores Mother.

Grimaldi, meanwhile, parked her SUV behind Bob's vehicle, and came jogging toward us while the paramedic finished patting Rafe down. Grimaldi got there in time to hear his verdict. "Looks like the two bullets are it. It could have been a lot worse."

It sure could.

"Thank God for SWAT practice," I said, since if it hadn't been for that, and the crazy explosion that meant that Rafe hadn't taken the time to change his clothes, that bullet might have—would certainly have—caught him in the heart.

Everyone nodded. Grimaldi, who was sort of Catholic, looked like she was thinking about doing the sign of the cross.

"Let's get him on the gurney," one paramedic told the other, and Rafe shook his head.

"Ain't nothing the matter with me."

"There's plenty the matter with you," I told him.

He gave me a look. "Nothing that going to the hospital is gonna fix, darlin'. I can just slap a Band-Aid over the arm, and there's nothing nobody can do for broken ribs. Just tape 'em and wait for'em to heal."

"Then they can bandage your arm and tape your ribs," I said. "I want somebody to look at you. You might need stitches."

He glanced down at the arm, where blood was still seeping out, but more sluggishly now. "I don't need stitches."

"You might. And it's something a doctor should decide."

"I don't wanna leave you and Carrie alone."

And OK, it was a compelling excuse. "We can go with you," I said.

"Your mama's just putting the baby to bed. I don't wanna wake her up again."

I didn't particularly want to wake her up, either, so I conceded the point. "Maybe Mother and Bob can stay with her while I go with you."

Bob shook his head. "This happened in my jurisdiction. I can't babysit."

I turned to Grimaldi. She shook her head. "He works for me. I need to hear the report, too."

"Just put a bandage over it," Rafe told the EMT. "I'll wrap my own ribs. I've had worse."

While that was certainly true, I gave the paramedic a look. He shrugged, looking apologetic. "There's nothing we can do, ma'am. If the patient refuses medical care, we can't force him. He's lucid and in his right mind—"

I snorted, and Rafe's lips curved. The paramedic continued, doggedly, as if he hadn't noticed the byplay. "And he has the right to refuse treatment."

"Fine." I sighed. "Just patch him up, then, and we'll take him inside. Y'all—" I looked at Grimaldi and Bob, "can get your report there."

They both nodded.

So the paramedics cleaned the wound and bandaged Rafe's arm and told him to have it checked by his regular doctor tomorrow, and to keep an eye out for infection. Then they told him to take it easy for a few days, and it would take the ribs six weeks to heal. No wrapping or taping necessary, as it would make it harder for him to breathe. "Take over-the-counter pain meds if you need them," the male paramedic said, wrapping up his gauze and scissors. "No working out, no straining, no fights."

No SWAT. And I'm sure crime-fighting was part of the things he wasn't supposed to do, too.

"C'mon." Grimaldi put a hand out. "Time to get up."

Rafe scowled at her, but took it. And promptly turned pale when she tried to haul him to his feet. Bob and the male paramedic moved in, and between them, they managed to get him upright. Not without some effort, though—he's a big guy, and muscle weighs a lot. And also not without hurting him considerably in the process. When he was at long last standing, he was breathing through gritted teeth, and his skin color was practically gray.

"You sure about that trip to the hospital?" I asked, and got a scowl for my trouble.

"It ain't gonna make me feel any better, darlin'. There's nothing anybody can do for broken ribs. They just gotta heal."

Fine. "If you wouldn't mind helping him inside," I said, "we'll just leave the Volvo here for the night. I assume one of you is going to want to dig out that bullet?"

Grimaldi and Bob both nodded, and exchanged a glance.

"You can fight over it," I told them. "Let's just get Rafe inside for now. At least no one's shooting at us anymore."

Like earlier, outside the house on Fulton, it would have been a golden opportunity for anyone who wanted a chance to take out important personnel. The Columbia chief of police, the Maury County sheriff, Rafe, the two paramedics...

"Whoever it was is long gone," Bob said, with a glance over his shoulder into the fields. "I guess we're starting the day with another search tomorrow."

"And likely to find no more than we did today," Grimaldi nodded, as she followed Bob and the male paramedic around the front of the car, as they supported Rafe toward the stairs. I tagged along behind, while the female paramedic wheeled her unused gurney toward the back of the ambulance.

Rafe must be starting to feel more himself, or maybe it was just getting up that was difficult. He navigated the steps just fine for a man who'd just been shot. Inside the doors, Bob and the paramedic steered him toward the parlor and Aunt Ida's loveseat, and deposited him, carefully, on it.

"If there's nothing more I can do for you," the EMT said, taking a step back, "I'm gonna push off. We have to be ready for the next call."

Rafe nodded. "We got this."

I rolled my eyes, but refrained from saying anything. "Thanks for coming," I told the paramedic instead. "When I called 911, I didn't know it was 'just a scratch.'"

I put quotes around the words with my fingers. Grimaldi smirked. Rafe chuckled, and promptly thought better of it. He put a hand to his ribs with a wince.

"Serves you right," I told him.

A corner of his mouth turned up, and he held out the other hand. "C'mere, darlin',"

I gave him a look, but I went. And perched on the peach velvet next to him. "Are you really all right?"

"Right as rain, darlin'. We'll have to take it easy for a couple days, is all." He winked, so there'd be no question about what we'd have to take it easy about.

The paramedic closed the front door behind him, so it was just the family and law enforcement left, and the atmosphere changed. "Somebody wanna fill me in on what the hell happened tonight?" Bob wanted to know. "I heard there was some kind of to-do up in Columbia. And now this? Is it related?"

"Someone vandalized the house Charlotte and I have been working on, on Sunday night," I told him. "This evening I got a text message saying that something was going on there. I picked up Darcy on the way—it's her house, and Rafe was at work, and I didn't want to go alone—and when we got there, there was a cardboard box on the porch. Before I could get out of the car and over to it, it blew up."

Mother gasped. I hadn't heard her come down the stairs from the second floor—she was probably stepping softly so she wouldn't wake Carrie—but she was standing in the doorway listening. "Savannah!"

Pearl raised her head from the pillow by the wall, and slapped her stubby tail. Mother walked that way and—would wonders never cease?—sat down on the floor next to Pearl so the dog wouldn't try to get up to greet her. I tried to recall whether I'd ever seen my mother on the floor before, unless she was in a dead faint. She must have played with us when we were kids, I assumed. Most parents do. But I couldn't remember it.

"We're all fine," I told her. "You've seen Carrie and me. And Darcy wasn't hurt. We were both a little shook up, though. Patrick Nolan took her home."

Grimaldi nodded. "I was still there when dispatch called me to come down here. The fire department pulled out, finally. I had a couple of uniforms string incident tape all around the property. Hopefully that'll keep people out."

Hopefully. "Half the front wall is gone," I told Mother and Bob. "The porch roof. Some of the roof in the living room. Some of the wall between the living room and the bedroom next door. The coat closet is just splinters."

They'd both been to the house during the couple of months Charlotte and I had been working on it, so they could picture what I was talking about.

"Dear Lord." Mother shook her head, one hand pulling Pearl's ear through her fingers. "What will you do, Savannah?"

"Never mind that," Bob said. "Somebody left a bomb on the doorstep?"

"Not a bomb," Rafe said. "Ammonal."

Bob's brows arched. "Plenty of that around here."

"What?" Mother said, wrinkling her brows and then immediately smoothing them out again.

"Not a bomb," Bob explained. "An explosive. One that needs a spark to light it."

"So someone set it on fire?"

"Someone shot at it," Rafe said.

Mother's eyes opened wide, and her jaw dropped.

"Lotta shooting going on the past couple days," Bob said laconically.

A lot of shooting. Culminating in tonight.

"Any idea who it might have been?" Grimaldi wanted to know.

"I'll tell you who it wasn't."

They all turned to me, and I added, "It wasn't the guy Rodney and Kyle and Clayton was with at Beulah's. He took a right out of the parking lot and went north, and he wouldn't have had time to get down here before us."

Rafe nodded.

"What guy?" Grimaldi and Bob asked together. "What happened?" Grimaldi added.

Rafe explained which guy and what had happened. "I have the plate number. Just haven't had a chance to look it up."

"Geez," I said, "whyever not?"

He gave me a look. "I'll do it tomorrow."

Grimaldi reached out a hand. "Give it to me. You're on medical leave for the next week."

"I'm what?"

"Medical leave," Grimaldi repeated, enunciating clearly.

"One week. And light duty after that." She wiggled her fingers.

Rafe stared at her. "It's in my head."

"Then tell me what it is, and I'll write it down."

She looked around for something to write on and with.

"I didn't go on leave when I got shot before," Rafe said.

"You weren't working for me when you got shot before." Grimaldi accepted a pen and the back of a receipt I dug out of my purse. "If you had been, you would have been on medical leave. It's SOP. I looked it up."

"I got shot," Rafe said, "and you took the time to look up standard operating procedure before you drove out here?"

"I looked it up in January, when you agreed to work for me. I figured I'd need it sooner or later."

I probably shouldn't have giggled, but it was funny. Rafe gave me a dark look, before turning back to Grimaldi. "I can't go on medical leave. I'm in the middle of an op. I've got a guy undercover I gotta keep up with."

"Someone else will keep up with him," Grimaldi said. "It wasn't like you were going to do it yourself, anyway. You made arrangements."

Of course he had. I didn't know what they were—it was less than twelve hours since I'd first discovered that Clayton was in Columbia; I hadn't had time to ask—but Clayton clearly couldn't be seen with Rafe. There had to be a middleman of some kind he'd report to.

"What the hell do you expect me to do for a week?"

"Take it easy," Grimaldi said. "Give those ribs a chance to heal."

"A week ain't enough for that!"

She didn't say anything, just looked at him. Rafe turned his fulminating glare on Bob, who shrugged. "Sorry, son. But SOP is SOP."

Rafe growled.

"We could go to Nashville," I suggested. "You could hang

out with Wendell and Jamal. And supervise."

Jamal, not Wendell. Wendell supervised Rafe. But he could probably be trusted to keep Rafe in line and make sure he didn't over-exert himself.

"That's not a bad idea," Grimaldi said, eyeing me with approval. "Make it look like you're in worse shape than you are. Maybe even dead."

"Here we go again."

"At least you know he's alive this time," Grimaldi pointed out, and since she'd taken the brunt of my grief and anger the last time I'd thought Rafe had gone down in the line of duty, I kept myself from sniping back. Until she added, "You wouldn't be able to go, though."

I opened my mouth to protest, and she said, before I could, "That'd defeat the purpose. For anyone to believe he was dead or in bad shape, you'd have to stay here and be visible."

"Can't we put out word that he was life-flighted to Vanderbilt? They have a good trauma unit." And if Rafe was supposed to be there, then I could go with him.

There was silence around the room.

"That's not a bad idea," Grimaldi said, somewhat reluctantly.

Bob nodded.

"You said the car had Nashville plates," I told Rafe. "You could go up there and track it down. And do some surveillance on the guy." It would keep him out of trouble and mostly sitting still for the next day or two, at least.

"I guess maybe that'd be OK." He didn't sound thrilled, but he sounded like it might be a solution he could accept, at least for the interim.

"I can't do anything about the house on Fulton anyway," I told him. "We'll have to have a structural engineer come out and look at it. We may have to tear it down. But Charlotte and Darcy can handle it for a couple of days while I go to Nashville with you. You said Mrs. Jenkins's house is livable again, right?"

He shrugged.

"Or if you prefer, you can go by yourself and bunk with Wendell. I'll stay here, and we can put out word that you're dead." Although how we'd get anyone to believe it, I didn't know. We'd already played that trick on the people of Sweetwater. This time, I wasn't sure they'd believe it unless we paraded the body through town on a bier.

"No," Rafe said, "Not doing that again. Let's go with the 'life-flight to Vanderbilt.' At least that way I'm just almost dead."

"Any chance they were out there, watching, and know you're not almost dead?"

All the law enforcement in the room shook their heads. "They were gone as soon as they saw me fall," Rafe said. "Or at least as soon as they heard the sirens. Wouldn't wanna risk getting caught out there."

Everybody nodded.

"So nobody actually knows that you're alive and well. Other than the people in this room."

"And the EMTs," Bob said. "But I'll put them wise."

"And I'll move back in for a couple of days and take care of Pearl," Mother said, from down on the floor. "Or we can move her to Bob's house."

Bob didn't looked thrilled about the idea, but he nodded.

"You can take my car," Mother added, "since I assume you can't drive either of yours."

No, that probably wouldn't be a good idea. The Volvo was going to need some bodywork, not to mention the blood cleaned off the side. We couldn't take Carrie on the bike. And plenty of people had seen Rafe drive the Chevy, so it was better to leave that behind, too.

"Let's talk about how we're going to handle this," Grimaldi said.

Thirteen

We were on the road an hour later, and in Nashville an hour and a half after that. I was driving, and Rafe was sitting as straight as the passenger seat allowed, barely breathing, and wincing every time one of the tires hit a pothole. Carrie had complained for a few seconds about being woken up again, but as soon as we hit the road, she fell back asleep.

"You OK?" I kept asking Rafe every five or ten minutes, and every five or ten minutes he'd tell me, "Just drive," through gritted teeth.

"Are you sure there isn't anything that can be done to make you feel better?"

He nodded. "I'm sure."

We pulled into the circular driveway outside Mrs. Jenkins's house just before one, and of course it was as spooky as something out of an old horror movie. None of the lights were on, and the mostly bare tree-branches—of which there are many in the front yard—rubbed together, making creaky noises. The house itself—three stories, red brick, with a tower on one corner—rose up like Count Dracula's castle.

I suppressed a shiver, but not well enough to hide it. Rafe's mouth quirked. "Nervous?"

"I spent a long time living here," I told him, "so no, not really. But it looks haunted. And unlived-in."

"That's 'cause it is unlived in. Once we're back inside, it'll help."

I cut the engine and turned to him. "Just stay there. I'll come around and help you out."

He arched a brow and opened his door. And was still sitting there, breathing hard, with his feet on the ground, when I got to the other side of the car.

"Don't try to be a hero, Rafe. All right?" I reached for him. "You have nothing to prove as far as that goes. And it's OK to accept help when your ribs were broken a couple hours ago. Brace yourself on me and see if you can stand."

It turned out he could stand, but it wasn't easy, and he kept up a low-voiced and vicious string of curses as he grabbed for the top of the car.

"Good!" I said encouragingly. "Now let me help you up the stairs."

"Take the baby first."

I honestly didn't think anyone was going to run up to the car and take off with the baby while I helped Rafe up the handful of steps to the front porch, but maybe he just needed a chance to catch his breath.

"Sure." I hauled the car seat out of the back and carried it up onto the porch, where I put it next to the door. "Ready? Or do you want me to grab the bags, as well?"

I hadn't packed much. We hadn't packed much when we left here in a hurry, either, and all of our warm-weather clothes were still here. It was getting warmer, so I'd felt safe in leaving most of the colder-weather clothes in Sweetwater. We just had a small bag with some necessities—underwear, socks, makeup, toothbrushes—while Carrie had the bulk of the luggage. Babies need a lot, and while she had a crib and changing table and all that here, her entire wardrobe and a lot of her stuff had had to come with us.

"Ready."

He was already—or still—gritting his teeth, but when I stepped up next to him, he put an arm across my shoulders and let me take some of his weight. The trick was staying as straight as possible, not bending, and also not jarring those ribs unnecessarily. It took us several minutes to navigate the steps he'd usually take in a bound or two, but we got there. I propped him against the wall and fished the key out of my purse. The door was different—an ugly metal security door, as far as it could get from the lovely, carved Victorian door that used to be here—but the key worked. I pushed the door open and flipped on the light.

And quailed. "Oh, my God."

"It ain't pretty," Rafe agreed.

It wasn't. The lovely foyer that used to be there, all dark, carved wood and gleaming, polished floors, was gone. I was looking at new wood, unstained, and in place of the old plaster walls, new unpainted drywall. It smelled different, too. There was still a whiff of smoke in the air, even two months after the fire, but otherwise it was all sawdust and drywall mud and something that might have been someone's lunch burrito. A half-empty bottle of Gatorade stood inside the door, and I resisted the temptation to kick it, since if it fell and spilled, that would only make things worse.

My eyes filled with tears, though, and Rafe reached for me. "C'mere, darlin'. It's OK."

"It's not OK," I sniffed, moving carefully into his arms. "It's ugly. And it doesn't look or smell like home."

"It will. Once they get finished and it's all shined up."

I wasn't too sure about that, but there was honestly no point in crying about it, since part of the crying wasn't about the house at all, but about everything else that had happened tonight. So I sniffed one last time and withdrew. "Let me help you in."

"I got it." He grabbed the jamb with one hand and propelled himself up and through the door, and into the foyer. "Get the baby."

I got the baby. "I'll just grab the rest of the stuff from the car."

We were driving Mother's Cadillac, since we couldn't take either the Volvo, the Chevy, or the Harley.

"Be sure you lock it up tight," Rafe called after me. "This neighborhood, a Caddy be gone by morning."

"I'll lock it. And please lose the jive. You don't talk like that the rest of the time."

"I be multi-lingual," he told me, with a grin. I rolled my eyes, but made sure I locked the car up nice and tight after I'd hauled all the luggage out of the trunk and up the stairs into the house. Rafe watched, looking frustrated, like he wanted to help but knew he couldn't.

"By the time we're ready to go back, I'm sure you'll be feeling better," I told him. "In the meantime, you're just going to have to let me deal with it. The last thing you want, is to do something that keeps those ribs from healing. It's much better just to take the time you need, and heal as fast as you can, than fight it and have it take longer."

Which he knew, anyway. It wasn't his first injury.

"I know, darlin'. It's just hard, watching my wife haul everything while I stand here, looking useless."

"You're not useless," I said, moving some of Carrie's paraphernalia past him. "You're decorative. And anyway, if someone came at us with a knife, you could totally take him out before he cleared the trees."

"Nothing wrong with my aim. I just can't bend over."

"That's all right. Just pull the door shut—everything's inside—and lock it. And let me help you up the stairs."

"I think I can manage." He grabbed the banister—half of which was still unstained wood, spliced into the 1880s wood on the top half of the staircase—and began hauling himself from step to step. I watched for a few seconds—he was doing all right—before I gathered up Carrie and her diaper bag and prepared to follow.

"Wait till I'm up," he told me, without turning his head. "If I fall, I don't wanna take you with me."

"If you fall, I'd rather be there to catch you."

"Just stay there. It's just a couple more steps." He reached the top and turned. "There."

"I'm going to put Carrie in her bed," I told him as I moved briskly up the staircase, "and go back for the rest of the stuff. If you need help, let me know."

"I'll be fine." He turned into the bedroom while I carried Carrie past and into the nursery down the hall.

It still smelled smoky up here, and I probably should have expected that. The place had been aired out, of course, but we'd packed up and left the day after the fire, so nobody had changed the bed linens or taken down the curtains, and the smoke hung on in the fabrics. I wrinkled my nose against it, but decided that since it was now after midnight, we could suffer through for one night. I'd just plan to do laundry tomorrow.

Since it was close to the time when Carrie was likely to wake up anyway, I changed her diaper and then sat down in the rocking chair to nurse her. She went right back to sleep, and I lowered her gingerly into the crib and tiptoed out of the room and across the hall to my own bedroom.

Where I found my husband still vertical, standing at the window staring out. His hands were curled into fists and were resting on the sill.

"Something wrong?" I asked, crossing to him to peer out. I'd just been kidding about the guy with the knife, although it wouldn't be the first time something like that had happened, so maybe someone was down there.

"What do you think?"

I looked at him, and felt my lips twitch. He had managed to shrug out of the leather jacket we'd put on him before we left Sweetwater. It was lying in the middle of the floor, where it had dropped. To make things easy for both of us earlier, I had buttoned him into a regular shirt rather than the usual T-shirt, so he wouldn't have to lift his arms above his head over and over again. And he had managed to unbutton it. It was wadded up on the bottom of the bed.

Then he had unfastened his jeans and pushed them down, and that's where the process had failed. They'd gotten caught on his boots, and were pooled around his ankles. And of course he hadn't been able to bend to undo the laces, so that's as far as he'd gotten. And now he was standing here, frustration simmering in his eyes, in a pair of boxer briefs and nothing else.

"Need help?" I asked innocently.

He gave me a scowl. "If you don't mind."

I smiled sweetly. "I don't mind at all."

A corner of his mouth turned up, and I leaned in to kiss it before I dropped to my knees and began undoing the laces of the black boots.

I'll leave the next thirty minutes to your imagination. The boots came off, and the jeans and socks, too. And eventually the briefs. And all of my clothes. By then, I'd maneuvered him onto the bed, and made sure he didn't hurt himself going down.

"What was that thing you said earlier?" I wanted to know, as I nibbled my way down the side of his neck and across his chest.

He tilted his head to the side to give me better access. "Not sure I know what you're talking about, darlin'."

"Careful. That's it. You said we had to be careful. Do you think this is careful enough?"

"I think this is just fine," Rafe said, bringing his hands up to stroke my back. "You doing all right?"

"I'm doing just fine. I just want to make sure I'm not hurting you."

"No, darlin'."

I moved down his stomach and lower, and his hands slid

from my shoulders up into my hair. "You just keep doing that. It don't hurt at all."

Yeah, I didn't think so. But I kept doing it, and one thing led to another, and a bit later we were curled up together, wrung out and relaxed. Or perhaps I should say that I was curled up, with my head on Rafe's (good) shoulder and a hand on his stomach. He was flat on his back, taking care not to move so he wouldn't jar his ribs or the bandage on his other arm.

"Hell of a day," I told him, too drowsy to moderate the four-letter word. Mother wasn't here to hear me, so what did it matter?

"M-hm." He murmured agreement into my hair.

"Do you have any idea what's going on?

"I have an idea." He yawned. "How 'bout we talk about it in the morning?"

Worked for me. "We're safe here, right?"

He nodded. "Don't worry, darlin'. I've got you."

And I had him. And for now, that was good enough.

Due to the late night, Carrie made it all the way past six before she woke up hungry and squalling. I left Rafe asleep—deducing as I did it that he must be in pain, because he normally needs less sleep than I do—and shrugged on a robe before I padded down the hallway and into Carrie's nursery. After changing her diaper, I sat down in the rocking chair and started feeding her.

I was still sitting there fifteen minutes later, when there was a key in the lock downstairs and then footsteps on the floor of the foyer. "Hello?"

The voice wasn't familiar. "Hi," I called back, feeling a little… let's call it exposed. "What's going on?"

"That was gonna be my question." I heard steps coming toward the stairs.

"Stay down there," I told him, and my voice might have been a little shrill. At any rate, it was enough to wake Rafe, because I heard rustling from the bedroom down the hall, and then a curse when he obviously came up against his own inability to get out of bed.

"Victor?" his voice called out. "That you?"

"Yeah, man," the guy downstairs answered. "Rafe?"

"Yeah. Hang on a minute. I broke a couple ribs yesterday. It's gonna take me a minute to get down there."

"No problem," the man called Victor said. "I'll just get the coffee going."

OK, then. He was clearly familiar with the place, and Rafe was familiar with him, so I didn't have to worry about being attacked. And since he was staying downstairs, I didn't have to worry about him walking in on me nursing my baby, either.

None of this had distracted Carrie, of course, so I stayed where I was and finished what I was doing while I listened to the sounds from downstairs and from down the hall.

On the first floor, Victor's footsteps faded as he headed down the hallway toward the kitchen. Closer to hand, there was more rustling from the bedsheets and squeaking from the mattress, and some grunts and muttered curses as Rafe figured out how to get upright and dressed, not necessarily in that order. After a minute or two, I heard his footsteps come down the hall toward me.

He stopped in the doorway, still barefoot and with jeans hanging low on his hips. "You OK?"

"Fine," I said. "I just didn't expect anyone to show up at six-thirty in the morning."

"That's Victor. He's in charge of the renovations."

Good to know. My eyes zeroed in on his side. "That's a nasty bruise you've got there."

It was the size of a salad plate and the color of eggplant, blooming across his ribcage on the left side. He put a hand to it and winced. "Yeah."

"Are you sure some bandages wouldn't help?"

"It'll be fine, darlin'." He sauntered into the room, bent just far enough to be able to drop a kiss on my lips—he tasted minty fresh, unlike me, who hadn't taken the time to brush my teeth before taking care of the baby; I kept my lips closed—and pushed himself upright again with a grunt. "I'll go downstairs and see what Victor wants."

"I'll finish up here and get cleaned up and dressed," I told him. "Then we can discuss what we're planning to do today."

Not laundry, obviously. Not if there was going to be a crew of workers downstairs.

"See you down there."

"Are you OK by yourself on the stairs?" I called after him.

He raised a hand, but without turning around. "I'll be fine."

Sure thing. If you call 'fine' muttering a curse on every step of the staircase because stepping down jarred his rib case each and every time.

There wouldn't have been anything I could have done about it, though, so I just listened until he was on level ground again, and then I went back to focusing on Carrie while he padded down the hallway to the kitchen and the coffee I could smell brewing.

By the time I made it downstairs, Victor was gone again, and Rafe was leaning against the counter with a mug in his hand. "He was just coming in to check how much his guys got done yesterday," he told me. "They'll be here in another thirty minutes, so unless you wanna spend the day listening to sawing and hammering, we should prob'ly get outta here."

That sounded like a good idea. I had no idea where we'd go and what we'd do until late afternoon, when presumably they'd finish. But hammering and sawing wasn't likely to make Carrie happy, so we might as well find somewhere else to be.

"How about I bring down your boots and clothes, so you don't have to navigate the stairs again?"

He nodded. "Thanks, darlin'."

"No problem," I said. "Are you OK with the pair of pants you're wearing, or do you want something else?"

He glanced down. "These are good."

They were. My eyes snagged for a second on the faded spots, like the zipper, where the fabric was faded to almost white and practically worn through, and then I met his eyes again. They'd turned darker, and I grinned. "No time for that, if Victor's crew will be here in thirty minutes."

"I could make something happen in thirty minutes." He eyed the kitchen table behind me.

"Maybe not in your condition," I suggested gently, and he made a face.

"Maybe we'll just wait a couple days for anything gymnastic."

"I think that's probably a good idea." But I took the time to give him a kiss before I headed upstairs to gather up clothes and boots for him, and the diaper bag for Carrie, so we could get out of here and let the renovation crew get to work.

Fourteen

The TBI headquarters building squats at the top of Gass Boulevard like a brown brick toad, bristling with antennae. When we pulled into the parking lot, I realized that the last time I'd been there had been the morning after the fire and the day we'd packed up and moved operations to Sweetwater. A lot had happened in just a few months.

"Do you miss it?" I asked Rafe as we headed for the entrance.

He looked at me. "I was here on Sunday."

"But you don't really work here anymore. Not the way you used to."

"I spent ten years working for the TBI and never seeing this place, darlin'."

Well, yes. Now that he mentioned it. "Never mind," I said.

He shot me a grin. "I'm good at undercover work. That's still what I'm doing. Sort of."

Sort of. "Are you making any progress on sniffing out bad cops in the Columbia PD?"

"We got rid of Enoch," Rafe said. "And cleared Jarvis. That's something."

"Any reason to think Tucker is dirty?" I probably shouldn't admit it, but I was secretly hoping he would be. And that Rafe would get a chance to take him down.

He smirked. "None I've found so far. I'm still looking."

"At Tucker specifically?"

He shook his head. "At everybody."

That probably involved Felicia Robinson, too. Someone else I'd love to think guilty of something, but she was probably just a stupid young woman who didn't have the sense to stay away from another woman's husband. "Any reason to think anyone at the PD is involved in the current mess?"

"No," Rafe said as he punched his access code into the keypad next to the door, and then reached for the handle. "Nothing I've seen so far."

"These types of organizations are happy to have military and former military, you said."

He nodded. "Folks who know how to handle weapons and explosives. For that race war they think is coming."

"They'd probably be happy to have cops, too, then."

He let the door shut behind us. "Sure they are. I just haven't seen anything to indicate that any of Tammy's cops are involved. Bob would know if it was going on in his department. Tammy might not, being new. But I'm looking."

"And I guess the other sheriffs are responsible for their own people."

He nodded. "They gotta be. I don't know'em or the folks they work with. And I have enough to do with Tammy's crew and with Clay."

And with getting shot.

I stopped in the middle of the foyer and looked around. "What are we doing here?"

"I gotta update Wendell and Jamal on what happened last night," Rafe said, nodding a greeting to the security guard as he scribbled his name and mine—and maybe Carrie's—on the visitor sheet. "Morning, Vince."

The guard nodded back. "Morning, Rafe. Good to see you. This the wife and kid?"

We spent a minute with Vince—grizzled and in his sixties— admiring Carrie as she cooed in her car seat, and then we headed for the elevators and Wendell's office.

It was barely after seven-thirty, but when we got to the door, it was open and Wendell was there, sitting behind the desk.

He's grizzled, too, and black where Vince was white. He's also the closest thing Rafe's ever had to a father. Tyrell Jenkins died before Rafe was born, and all old Jim Collier ever did for him, was teach him to survive. But Wendell's been taking care of Rafe—to the degree that Rafe lets anyone take care of him— since Rafe was twenty. They've been through a lot together. And while neither would come right out and say it, they're as close as if they were family.

He looked up when we stopped in the doorway, and while he gave me and Carrie a look, his attention was pretty much all for Rafe. "You all right?"

Rafe shrugged the good shoulder. "Likely be sore for a couple days."

More than a couple of days, I figured, but I didn't argue. He was trying to reassure Wendell that he wasn't badly hurt, and how he chose to do it, was up to him.

"The bullet missed?"

"Mostly."

Wendell nodded. That seemed to be all he needed. "What brings you here?"

"Gotta stay low for a couple days," Rafe said, and pulled one of the chairs in front of the desk an inch in my direction. I sat on it. He took the other one and started to lean back, before he was reminded that his ribs hurt. He sat up straight, scowling, instead. "Got somebody I need to track down."

He explained about the car with the Nashville plates and the altercation outside Beulah's Meat'n Three.

"Clay all right?" Wendell wanted to know.

"If not, it ain't because of me."

"It all looked beautiful," I added. "I don't think anybody

would have guessed that it was all for show."

Wendell studied me for a second before he turned his attention back to Rafe, who told him, "Clark and Scoggins bought it. I'd stake my life on that." And probably had. "I dunno about the third guy. He's older. Looks like he's been out there longer and knows more. That's why I wanna track him down."

That and the fact that he was who Rodney and Kyle had brought in to meet Clayton, I assumed. Which made it seem like he was higher up the food chain than they were. Maybe the guy in charge of their little group of white supremacists, or at least someone who might know the guy in charge.

"Give it to me," Wendell said, opening his computer. Rafe recited the license plate from memory, and then silence reigned while Wendell tapped keys and waited for results. "Looks like the car is registered to a woman named Jennifer Vonderaa." He rattled off an address. The zip code put it on the western edge of Davidson County. Bellevue, specifically. A sort of sleeper community west of downtown by ten or fifteen miles. I thought, at some point, I might have shown some property not too far away.

"It wasn't Jennifer driving it last night," Rafe said.

I shook my head. The guy had been male, and looked like he'd been born that way. And he'd been alone. No Jennifer in the car with him.

"Guess you'll have to ask her who was driving her car yesterday," Wendell said.

Rafe nodded. "We'll go check it out. Look for the car. See if she's living alone. He might be the husband or boyfriend."

Wendell scribbled the address on a piece of paper and handed it over. "Need backup?"

"Not for this. If that changes, I'll let you know."

Wendell nodded. "I'll keep Jamal on standby."

"How is he doing?" I asked. "I saw him and Alexandra in

Columbia yesterday. They did a great job of making Clayton look like a bastard."

Wendell's lips quirked, and so did Rafe's. "Clark and Scoggins wasted no time taking him to their leader," he said. "You can let Jamal know whatever he did worked."

"Oh, it was beautiful." I described the scene, both coming and going, all while I marveled at the fact that it had all happened less then twenty-four hours ago. "They both did a great job looking like they hated each other on sight. And Rafe did a great job pushing Clayton around last night, and Clayton did a great job being pushed around. Rodney and Kyle swallowed it all, whole."

"Good to know," Wendell said. "Anything else you need before you go?"

I looked at Rafe. He shook his head. "We'll just track down Jennifer Vonderaa. If we need anything after that, we'll let you know."

"I'll give you a hand up," I told him, and he shook his head.

"Thanks, darlin', but I'm fine." He put a hand on each arm of the chair and levered himself upright.

I watched as his nostrils flared, and shook my head. "That stubbornness is going to kill you one day."

"Just get the baby," Rafe said, breathing a little faster than usual.

"Did you take a painkiller this morning?"

He gave me a look.

"Why not, for God's sake?"

Wendell was watching the two of us batting the conversational ball back and forth, an amused look on his face. It went away with the next thing Rafe said.

"Don't want my reflexes slowed down. Somebody tried to kill me yesterday. If they try again, I don't wanna die 'cause I'm a second too slow."

Good point. "In that case, you should definitely take any

help you can get."

I picked up the car seat with the baby and headed for the door. "I want to stop in the ladies room. I'll meet you in the hallway."

I assumed Wendell probably had questions he didn't want to ask in front of me, and this way, they'd have a couple of minutes to themselves without actually having to ask me to leave.

The business must have been quickly concluded, though, because by the time I came out of the bathroom with Carrie in a dry diaper, Wendell was nowhere to be seen, and Rafe was leaning against the wall next to the open office door. "Ready?"

I nodded. "You know, normal people have normal jobs. She's probably at work at this time of the morning."

"Not everyone works nine to five," Rafe said, falling into step next to me as we headed for the elevator. "But that's all right. I'll be happy to take a look around her place without her there."

I glanced at him. "Isn't that illegal without a search warrant?"

He gave me a look back. "When did that ever stop either of us?"

Well, never. But… "You're a police detective now. Doesn't that make a difference?"

"Only in court." He pushed the button to summon the elevator. "Besides, I don't plan to get caught."

"I didn't think you were planning to get caught." I mean, he probably wouldn't. He can melt through locked doors when he wants to, and not leave any sign that he was there. "If you find anything, won't it be useless if you didn't have a search warrant for it?"

"We'll deal with that if it becomes a problem," Rafe said. "And anyway, she's not a suspect. I just need a line on her husband or boyfriend."

"Or brother." The elevator doors opened, and I stepped in. "Or son."

Rafe followed me. "Or the neighbor who decided to borrow her car when she was away at a bachelorette party in Miami this weekend."

He pushed the button for the ground floor and shook his head. "We're just looking for a thread to tug, darlin'. She might be related to this guy, or it could be totally random. She might not know anything about him. Or he could be asleep on her couch or in her bed right now. It's a place to start."

The doors closed and we rode down in silence. It was just a few seconds before we were back on the ground, and on our way across the stone floor of the lobby.

"What's happening in Maury County today?" I asked, as Rafe headed into the parking lot toward a creamy Cadillac. It took me a second to remember that the Volvo was still in Sweetwater and that we were driving Mother's car. "Is anyone doing anything about catching whoever shot you?"

He unlocked the doors remotely and opened the back door so I could put Carrie and her seat inside. "There's no real question about who shot me."

I clicked the car seat into the base and straightened. "There isn't?"

He shook his head as he shut the door. "You know who didn't go north from Beulah's? Kyle Scoggins's truck."

That was true. "Kyle and Rodney shot you?"

"Clay shot me," Rafe said, opening my door next.

I stopped in front of it, my mouth open. "Clayton? Clayton shot you?"

He nodded. "Get in, darlin'. I don't wanna stand here any longer than I have to."

No, I could imagine that. Not that anyone was likely to take a potshot at him in broad daylight in the TBI parking lot. But safer not to take any chances. I slid into the car. "What do you mean, Clayton shot you? How do you know?"

He shut my door and then walked around the Cadillac and got behind the wheel before he answered. It took a little time and a little swearing, and he was in pain by the time he was situated. I could hear it in his voice when he told me, "All part of the master plan, darlin'."

"Maybe you should share this master plan with me," I said, as he turned the key in the ignition and the Caddy purred to life. My voice was tight, even in my own ears. "Because if you knew that you were about to be shot, and you didn't tell me, I'm going to be upset. I was really scared last night. I thought you were dead."

He shook his head. "I wouldn't do that to you, darlin'. If I'd known it was gonna happen, I woulda let you know."

"So how do you know it was Clayton?"

He put the car in gear and we rolled out of the parking space. "It's what makes sense. They were together. They went south. They didn't have time to drop Clay off. And I'm pretty sure, when he's able to report in, he'll say that they told him they were there the night before and shot Pearl."

So Rodney and Kyle, without Clayton, had tried to shoot him the night before, too. And had gotten Pearl instead. "I want to kill them," I said.

"You're gonna have to settle for life in prison, darlin'." He took a left on Gass Boulevard and sent the car rolling down the hill in the direction of the parkway. "We're gonna put them away, though, and for a long time. Not only does attempted murder of a police officer come with a long sentence, but when you add the hate crime to it..."

Right. "And then there's everyone else we think they're planning to kill."

"If we're right," Rafe said, slowing down for the light at the bottom of the road. He put his turn signal on. "After last night, Clay should be established with the group, even if he's only met

Clark and Scoggins and the new guy so far. They may wanna introduce him around, so we could see some movement down there soon."

And we were up here, missing it.

"We'll be back later," he told me. "It ain't likely to happen today. I'm sure some of these people are gainfully employed upstanding citizens, who can't just drop everything and run down to Columbia because they've found a new recruit. But at least now we've got people keeping an eye on the auto shop and on Scoggins again."

Good to know. Although I wasn't sure how helpful that was going to be, since we also had Clayton on the inside now, and nothing was likely to happen that he didn't know about.

Then again, he hadn't been able to let Rafe know that he was about to be gunned down last night, so Clayton might not be the help Rafe hoped he would be.

The Cadillac hit the parkway going north, and a few minutes later, we were headed west toward Bellevue. "I'll find this place on a map," I said, pulling out my phone, "so we know where we're going."

"You do that. And when you're done, maybe take a quick look on social media for Jennifer Vonderaa."

Good idea.

As we zoomed down the highway, I found the address and got it placed in my head so I'd know where Rafe had to go once we got out to that part of town. That done, I switched over to Facebook and looked for Jennifer. Her last name was unusual enough that she wasn't hard to find, and I held up the phone for Rafe's perusal. "This her?"

He glanced at the profile picture and nodded.

I took the phone back. "It says in her profile that she's in a relationship, but there's no name for the boyfriend. I'll check for pictures."

He didn't look right or left as we zoomed through the area

where, six months ago, a woman named Carmen Arroyo had died and her newborn baby had gone missing. A newborn baby we had thought, at the time, might be Rafe's. Either he didn't realize where we were, or it didn't bother him. I'm sure he hadn't forgotten.

"No pictures of her with anyone in the past couple of months," I reported as we left the wooded area with the old cabin behind, and rolled down the road toward the garbage dump, on one side of the highway, and the Tennessee Women's Prison on the other. "A couple of girlfriends, but no guys."

I didn't take my eyes off the phone when I added, sort of off-handedly, "Do you ever hear anything from Carmen's sister? Or her mother?"

"No," Rafe said, eyes on the road as we drove along next to the chain link fence that encircled Southern Belle Hell. It was tall and curved in at the top, so anyone who tried to make it over would have to fight gravity not just vertically, but horizontally as well. I didn't imagine many people made it out of there.

"It's got nothing to do with me," Rafe added. "I didn't kill her. I didn't knock her up. It ain't my baby."

"Did you ever figure out whose baby it was?"

"No," Rafe said, "and it's none of my business. Talk about something else."

Fine. "I'm back to October, and there's still no picture of a boyfriend. Have you ever tried to climb a fence like that?"

"Like what?"

I pointed, and he looked at it. "No, can't say as I have, darlin'."

"You never thought about breaking out of Riverbend?"

He grinned. "I guess I can't say the thought never crossed my mind. But the security there's better than that."

Riverbend Penitentiary is a maximum security prison full of very bad men, and while I'd met a few cold-blooded women in my time—including the one responsible for Carmen's death—they weren't the kinds of killers Riverbend housed.

"Could you do it?"

He looked at the fence again. "Prob'ly. Although it don't look like it'd be easy."

"I imagine it isn't meant to be."

"I imagine not." He gave the fence one last look over his shoulder before we got too far away. "Any particular reason you wanna know?"

"No," I said. "Just making conversation. Riverbend's around here too, isn't it?"

He nodded. "Over that way." He pointed past the factories that were coming up on our right as we crossed the river and powered up the hill toward Centennial Boulevard. "I ain't taking you there so you can look at it."

"That's all right. I have no need to see it." I dropped the phone to my lap, since looking at it was making me faintly nauseated. Or maybe it was the smell of the dump. "So if you were a woman with a boyfriend, why wouldn't you have his name or picture on your Facebook feed?"

"You don't have mine there," Rafe said, and continued before I could answer, "We don't know that he's her boyfriend. He could be her brother or her neighbor or something else. The relationship could be with one of the women you saw a picture of. But when we get there, you can ask her."

"Really?"

He grinned at me. "No, darlin'. We wanna try to keep this low key as long as possible. Telling her you've been looking her up on social media wouldn't do that."

"Are you at least going to let me get out of the car when you talk to her?"

"Yes, darlin'," Rafe said, "I'm gonna let you go knock on the door all by yourself. And do all the talking."

Oh, really? "Why?"

"So as I can go around back and take a look around."

Ah. "You want me to keep her occupied while you snoop."

He nodded.

"How come I don't get to snoop?" I mean, I wanted to see, too.

"One of us has to keep her busy, darlin', or the other one can't look around. I'm better at looking around, and you're better at talking."

"She's female," I said. "She might like talking to you more."

He shook his head. "If she's hooked up with a guy who's in a hate group, I'm not gonna be her type."

Well, no. Hard to imagine any red-blooded American woman not being attracted to Rafe, but he had a point. If she wanted him—and everyone who looked like him—dead, then she wasn't likely to be charmed by a hot grin and an overabundance of sex appeal.

"I'll talk to her," I said.

He nodded. "Much better that way. I'm faster at going through locked doors, and she's more likely to keep talking to you."

I nodded, but a little of my disappointment must have shown, because he added, "You're gonna have to get her to tell you who was driving her car last night, darlin'. It isn't just about keeping her occupied, although you're gonna have to do that. We don't want her walking in on me tossing the place. And we need information. That's the real reason we're here. You gotta find out about this guy."

Right. I squared my shoulders. "I can do that."

"I know you can, darlin'." He flipped on the turn signal for the exit on Old Hickory Boulevard and glanced at me. "Where to from here?"

"Right at the bottom of the ramp and left at the light. Then three-quarters of a mile straight until you take a left on Sawyer Brown."

He nodded. "D'you know what you're gonna say to her?"

I had no idea, and told him so.

"Give it some thought. You gotta have a reason for knocking on the door."

I guess I did. "Any suggestions?"

"You hit her car and ran away, and you're feeling guilty? You thought the guy was hot and you wanna meet him again? He hit on you and you wanna make sure his wife or girlfriend knows what he's doing when she ain't around?"

"He *was* kind of hot," I said pensively, and grinned when he arched a brow in my direction. "You know what I mean. He looked like there was a six-pack underneath his shirt. And he had that military look. Some women like that."

"I never figured you did."

"I don't," I said, since the guy hadn't looked appealing to me at all, and not just because of the skinhead thing. "For me to pull off saying he's hot, he's going to actually have to be hot. Or she has to think he's hot, anyway…"

"If they're brother and sister, she prob'ly don't wanna hear that some woman drove here from Columbia because she thinks her brother's hot."

And even less so if they were married or involved, I imagined.

"So maybe we just won't use that excuse," I said, as Rafe turned the car onto Sawyer Brown Road. "In about half a mile, you're taking a right on Willow Springs."

He nodded. "Maybe you'd best not say anything about yesterday. Come up with some other sort of excuse for why you're knocking on the door."

"I'm a real estate agent," I said. "I don't need an excuse beyond that."

"Then you'll have to tell her who you are."

Unless I told her I was someone else instead. I dug into my purse and came up with a business card. "Problem solved."

He glanced at it. "What's that?"

"This is Arlene Woods's card."

He looked blank, and I added, "She's the agent who showed the property on Fulton on Monday morning, and who called me about the damage after the vandalism. You met her."

He slowed down for the turn onto Willow Springs. "You don't look nothing like Arlene Woods."

Thank you. "I don't have to. She doesn't have her picture on her card. I'll just introduce myself as Arlene Woods and hand over the card. Chances are she'll believe that's who I am. And then I can talk to her about her house and how many people live there and things like that."

"Sounds good," Rafe said. "That's it coming up on the left. With the green mailbox."

I peered through the windshield at the house with the green mailbox.

We were on a solid middle-class street of smallish houses that had been built during the building boom in the nineties. The nineteen-nineties. There was a boom in the eighteen-nineties, too—the Victorians. These were not Victorians. Victorian houses, like Mrs. Jenkins's Queen Anne, can last centuries if they're well maintained. These had been shoddy when they were put up, and by now, twenty years later, were showing the ravages of time.

Jennifer Vonderaa lived in a small cottage with a short driveway ending in a front-loading single car garage. The brick exterior only extended to the front of the house. Once you got around the corner in either direction, it was all vinyl, and not nice vinyl, either. It was a yellowy off-white, and looked dingy. Here and there, the vinyl showed the patchy florescent green of environmental staining; it would have been easy to get off with a power washer, but Jennifer either didn't have the money or didn't care enough.

"No sign of the car," I said, as Rafe pulled up on the

opposite side of the street.

He shook his head. "Prob'ly in the garage."

"It didn't look like the kind of car that needed garaging." Unlike Mother's Caddy, which had never spent a single night outside until last night.

Rafe glanced beyond me into the backseat. "Baby's asleep."

"We can leave her here. I can't go inside the house anyway, if you're planning to be snooping around in there, so I'll be able to see the car the whole time I'm standing on the front step. Or I can take her with me and if she wakes up, she wakes up."

"Just take her. I feel better about that." He pushed his door open. "I'm gonna go around to the back. You knock on the door."

I nodded, and watched him cross the street before I opened my own door and then Carrie's. With the car seat looped over my arm, I headed up the empty driveway and then along the concrete path to the front door.

Fifteen

There was a doorbell on the jamb next to the door handle. I pressed it and waited. It ding-donged deep inside the house, but didn't bring forth anyone to answer the door, so I added a couple of knocks for good measure. And then another ring and another knock.

When I heard the lock tumble on the inside, I took a step back and pasted a friendly smile on my face. Only to have it drop off when the door opened and I looked up at my husband.

"The garage door was open," he said blandly.

Sure it was. "Is the car in the garage?"

He shook his head. "House is empty, too."

"Maybe she went to work."

"Might have." He stepped back, into a small foyer with ugly, twelve-by-twelve tan tiles on the floor. "C'mon in."

"Are you sure I should?"

"I just want another quick look around. And I don't want you standing outside the door, drawing attention, while I do it."

I nodded, stepping across the threshold. "What are you looking for?"

"Not sure," Rafe said, shutting the door behind me, "but something about this house don't feel right."

I sent out my own spider senses in every direction, but if something felt wrong, it was too subtle for me to pick up on. My instincts aren't as finely tuned as his. Everything looked and felt normal to me. There were the usual small sounds in the background: the white noise of modern life. A clock was ticking faintly. The refrigerator was humming. So was the air conditioning. It was a little colder in here than it ought to be, and the place smelled strongly of pine cleaner. There was no sense that anyone was standing just out of sight, holding their breath.

"I'll take another look around," Rafe told me. "You can look around, but don't touch nothing."

He disappeared through a cased opening into the living room. I stayed where I was and looked around.

The place was small and nothing fancy. Tan builder-grade carpets covered the floor in the living room. They probably hadn't been replaced since the house was built. There was a border with magnolia leaves and flowers running along the ceiling in lieu of actual crown molding. The furniture had seen better days, too, and consisted of a brown corduroy recliner sofa and a dark brown coffee table with a couple of remotes on it. The TV was neither new nor particularly impressive: a smallish flat-screen sitting on a pressed wood console in front of the window that overlooked the street. The blinds were pulled down.

Beyond the living room, Rafe's footsteps moved from carpet to something hard, probably sheet vinyl or fake hardwoods, or maybe more of the ugly tile. I heard him move around behind the wall. And since he'd told me I could, I made my way into the living room and from there, into the eat-in kitchen on the back of the house.

As I had surmised, the flooring back there was more of the ugly tile, and the cabinets were cheap oak with picture-frame doors. Not all that different from the shaker fronts that were popular now, but different enough that they looked outdated and kind of tired.

"This isn't very pleasant," I said, looking around.

Rafe gave it a blank look, like he hadn't really noticed. He probably hadn't. He looks at these things from a very different perspective than I do.

Instead, he waved me over to where he was standing, next to the refrigerator. "Take a look at this."

Jennifer, like a lot of other people, used her fridge to hang pictures, recipes, reminders for doctor's appointments, and the like. Rafe was pointing to a photograph of a man in camouflage, with streaks of black and green on his face, cradling a rifle.

"That's the guy from yesterday," I said. "A hunter?"

He shook his head. "Military. Iraq or somewhere like that. Look at all the sand."

There was a lot of sand in the picture. "Maybe there's a name on the back."

I reached out and, when Rafe didn't tell me not to, grabbed the picture by the edges, very carefully, and flipped it. "No."

I scanned the fridge. "Any other pictures of him?"

Rafe shook his head. "This is her." He pointed to a photograph of a woman in a chunky, knit sweater who peered myopically out of a pair of square glasses.

"You recognize her from the DMV photo?"

He nodded. "No pictures of her with the guy."

No. That could mean something, or nothing at all. There are very few pictures of me and Rafe cuddled up together, and none of them are on the fridge, either in Nashville or in Sweetwater. Rafe is camera-shy, from all those years of being undercover. It was hard to get him to stand still for the wedding photos.

"The spec ops guys aren't supposed to have their photos taken, either," he told me when I commented on it. "Safer for them if nobody knows who they are."

"So you think he's in special operations, not just a regular soldier."

"I know an operator when I see one," Rafe said. "Could be a SEAL or a Ranger or Delta Force or something else, but he ain't a grunt."

"If you sent the picture to someone in the military, could they tell you who he is?"

"It'd be easier if we knew which branch of the military he was from, but I imagine I could find out. Put it back up there."

He pulled out his phone while I nudged the photograph back under the magnet that had held it in place.

"Fort Campbell's only about thirty minutes away," he added while he focused on the picture and snapped a shot of it. "Home of the 101st Airborne. The Screaming Eagles."

And more like forty-five minutes away, if someone who wasn't Rafe was driving.

"Also the 160th Special Aviation Regiment. The Night Stalkers."

"You seem to know a bit about it."

He dropped the phone back into his pocket and looked around the kitchen. "I spent a couple months in Clarksville once."

"That's right." It was all coming back to me now. "It was in that PI report Todd paid for. Back when he was trying to convince me you were big and bad and I should stay away from you."

He nodded. "Military grade weapons walking off the base and showing up with gangs in Nashville and Memphis."

"And Todd thought you were part of it."

"I was part of it," Rafe said. "Just not the way Satterfield thought."

"But this guy wasn't." I glanced at the photograph on the fridge.

He shook his head. "I got a good look at him last night. He ain't somebody I've ever seen before. And anyway, we got everybody who was involved in that mess back then. It's six or seven years ago now. I don't imagine he was old enough at the time."

Maybe not. Although he couldn't be a whole lot younger than Rafe was, now and then.

"I'll take a look around the living room," I said. "Check the name on any mail sitting around and stuff like that."

He nodded. "I'll check the bedrooms. I still got a bad feeling about this." He walked in one direction while I walked in the other, trying to wrap my brain around what might be setting his finely honed radar tingling.

There was nothing much to look at in the living room—no piles of junk mail on the table, no convenient bills sitting around—so I ended up standing by the front door, up on my toes, peering out of the small window in the top of the door.

Willow Springs seemed to be made up of people who went to work in the morning and didn't come back until the afternoon. Nothing stirred outside, except for a mail truck that crept slowly up one side of the street, circled the cul-de-sac, and came down the other side. It rolled to a stop next to the mailbox, and the carrier spent a few seconds shoving another handful of mail into the box before the truck continued on down the street. Looked like maybe Jennifer hadn't picked up her mail in a while. Maybe she was in Columbia with her boyfriend, or significant other. Or brother or whoever he was. A bird swooped down from above the house and started pecking at the lawn. A few seconds later it was joined by another one.

A phone rang nearby, sort of muffled, and I reached into my purse to grab it before it could wake Carrie.

It wasn't my phone that was ringing, though. The ring tone was the same as mine: a standard version of the Hallelujah-chorus I use for people I don't know. But my phone was silent, and I withdrew my hand again while I looked around, trying to isolate the sound.

By the time I had traced it to the pocket of a coat hanging on a hook in the entry, the phone had fallen silent. I reached into the pocket anyway, and drew it out. And realized, as I was doing it, that I was leaving fingerprints on the plastic shell.

The screen was still lit up, proclaiming *Missed Call* in green letters. I peered at the number, but of course it didn't mean anything to me.

As I stood there, the phone dinged, and the *New Voicemail* icon came up. Nudging it was almost automatic. I might have spared a single thought to whether it was a smart thing to do or not, but by then Rafe was coming toward me from the back of the house. "Did something happen?"

"It wasn't my phone," I began, but then the voicemail began playing, so I closed my mouth again to listen.

"Hi, Jennifer. It's Gwen. It's ten, and you're still not here. Call me. Barry will have your hide if you skip work again without a good excuse, so call me and give me one."

She hung up without leaving a number, or for that matter without saying goodbye.

"Barry," I said. "Do you suppose…?"

He shook his head. "Barry must be her boss. Gwen's a coworker. And Jennifer didn't show up to work this morning."

"Maybe she's in Columbia with her boyfriend and her car."

"Without her phone?"

Well, no. Probably not. Unless… "Maybe she's afraid someone will track her down if she carries a phone. It has GPS, right? Or something?"

He nodded.

"So if she wanted to make sure she couldn't be traced, maybe she'd leave the phone at home."

"If she wanted to make sure she couldn't be traced, don't you think she'd leave the car at home, too?"

Well… yes. If she was trying to disappear, she probably wouldn't do it in the car that was registered to her.

"New theory," I said. "Maybe she's trying to get away from the boyfriend. Or brother or Führer or whatever he is. The guy on the fridge. Maybe he took off in her car for Columbia, and she took the opportunity to go in the other direction. And she isn't afraid the police will track her down, but she's trying to make sure the guy won't know where she is."

"Possible," Rafe admitted, peering out the window at the sound of an engine outside.

"Anything we need to worry about?"

He shook his head. "Lady across the street coming home. From the gym, looks like. Maybe you'd like to go over there and ask her when's the last time she saw Jennifer, and whether she knows who the guy is."

I supposed I could do that. "What are you going to do?"

"Take one more look around," Rafe said. "I didn't spend any time in the garage yet. I turned around when I heard your phone."

He peered out the window. "There she goes, into her house. Out you go."

He opened the door, and I slid sideways, Carrie's car seat still clutched in my hand. Through it all, the baby had stayed asleep.

"Let me see that phone," Rafe said, extending a hand for it. I gave it to him, and then he shut the door behind me, and Carrie and I made our way down the driveway and across the street to talk to the lady there.

The house was identical to Jennifer's across the street. The woman who opened the door looked nothing like Jennifer, or at least not the Jennifer in the picture. She was half a century older, for one thing, with bright magenta lipstick and a frizzy cap of dark hair. A pair of hot pink tights bagged around her scrawny legs, under an oversized T-shirt proclaiming her too sexy for her shirt.

"Yes'm?" She looked me up and down.

"Sorry," I said, dragging my eyes away from the disastrous fashion sense. "Um… I was across the street, and saw you drive up. I'm looking for Jennifer. She didn't come to work this morning, and Barry sent me to look for her."

She cut her eyes to the house across the street before looking back at me. "What's your name, sugar?"

"Oh," I said, wondering whether I dared to claim to be Gwen. Probably best if I didn't, since she might have met Gwen before. "I'm Arlene."

"Nice to meet you, Arlene." She looked me up and down. "Don't meet a lot of girls with that name these days. Family name?"

"Grandmother," I said brightly. "You?"

"Dorothy Mangrum. You can call me Dot." She grinned, showing off a set of gleaming white dentures.

"Nice to meet you, Dot," I said politely. "So about Jennifer… She's not answering the door, and when I called, I heard her phone ringing inside. Have you seen her lately?"

"Saw her yesterday morning," Dot said promptly. "I was going to Jazzercise, and she was going to work, I guess. It was half past eight or so."

"And that was the last time you saw her? She didn't come home in the evening?"

"I'm sure she did. Leastways her car did. I saw it in the driveway when I went out to dinner with my gentleman-friend."

I nodded. "Speaking of gentleman-friends…"

She rolled her eyes. "Just come right out and ask, Arlene. You wanta know about the soldier, right?"

"If you'd like to tell me," I said politely.

Dot clearly wasn't impressed, because she rolled her eyes eloquently. "You gotta ask for what you want in life, Arlene, or you're not getting squat."

Fine. "Tell me about the soldier, please. Was he Jennifer's boyfriend?"

"I guess he was," Dot said readily, "although I can't imagine what somebody like him would want with somebody like her."

"What's wrong with her?"

"She's a little mousy," Dot said, "ain't she?"

"Is she?"

She looked at me. "Didn't you say you worked with her, sugar?"

Well, yes. I had said that. "Different department."

She put her hands on her skinny hips. "They have departments at the daycare now?"

Oh. Um… "Fine," I said. "I don't actually know her. But you can call over there and check if you want. She didn't show up to work this morning, and Gwen did call and ask where she was."

She dropped her gaze to Carrie, still sleeping in the baby seat over my arm. "You one of the mothers, or something?"

"Something." And definitely one of the mothers. If not one of the mothers who took my child to Jennifer's daycare. "Tell me about the soldier. Does he have a name? When was the last time you saw him?"

"I'm sure he has a name," Dot said, leaning a shoulder against the door jamb and settling in for a chat, "but I don't know what it is. He wasn't friendly, if you know what I mean."

"And she never mentioned his name to you?"

"Between you and me, she ain't that friendly, either."

OK, then. So no name. "How long has he been coming around?"

She thought about it, pursing those magenta lips. "Couple months, maybe?"

"Were they dating? Or old friends? Brother and sister?"

"Not brother and sister," Dot said definitely. "Don't look much alike. Think they were probably romantic, but he didn't seem that into her."

"Did he seem into someone else instead?"

She shook her head. "Just seemed like a cold fish. Good-looking, though."

Yes, he had been decent-looking. What I'd seen of him through the windshield last night.

"But you don't know anything about him. Where he came from? How they met?"

"No," Dot said, glancing past me. "Who's that?"

She straightened. I figured I knew, but I looked over my shoulder anyway. "That's my husband."

The look she gave me was approving. "Good for you. What's he doing in Jennifer's house?"

"Looking for her," I said.

"He work at the daycare?"

No. The idea was ludicrous. Not that he doesn't do a perfectly fine job taking care of our daughter.

But I didn't want to tell her that he was law enforcement, not without his say-so, so I just ignored the question. "I should probably go. Thanks for your time."

"Anytime," Dot said, her eyes still on Rafe. "If he has any more questions, he can knock on my door anytime. You tell him that."

I said I would. "You said you saw Jennifer yesterday morning. When was the last time you saw the boyfriend?"

"He was headed out when I started book club last night," Dot said. "Must have been around six, maybe."

"What does he drive?"

I already knew he'd been in Columbia in Jennifer's car, of course, but he might have a vehicle of his own, too.

"He was driving her car."

"Was he alone?"

"Not sure, sugar. I only saw him, but the car was already driving away. She mighta been in there, too."

I nodded. "Thank you. I should go."

"He's looking upset."

I shot another glance over my shoulder. Yes, he did. Not with me, though. He had his phone out, and was talking fast.

"Excuse me," I told Dot, and turned away.

"You're excused, sugar."

But I didn't hear the door close. And when I reached Rafe, standing at the bottom of Jennifer's driveway, and glanced over my shoulder, Dot was still standing there in the open doorway. She gave me a little finger-wave.

Rafe was dialing again.

"Something wrong?" I asked him.

He held up a finger, and I waited while the phone rang on the other end. It was on speaker, so when it was picked up, I heard both sides of the conversation.

"Agent Collier." The voice was male, warm and friendly and a little bit familiar, but not familiar enough that I was able to place it. It wasn't Wendell, nor Bob Satterfield, nor my boss, Tim Briggs, who always sounded very friendly indeed whenever Rafe said anything to him.

"This is an anonymous phone call," my husband said.

I arched my brows, and from the sound of the voice when it came back, the guy on the other end of the line was doing the same thing. It was less warm and friendly now, more crisp and businesslike. "Go ahead."

Rafe rattled off the address to Jennifer's house. "You're gonna wanna get over here. There's a dead body in the freezer."

Sixteen

I felt myself sway, and he put out his free hand to steady me while he kept talking. "You're gonna wanna confirm the identification, but it looks like the owner, Jennifer Vonderaa. She didn't show up for work this morning."

"Go on," the voice said. I assumed its owner was taking notes.

"You're also gonna wanna coordinate with Chief Grimaldi in Columbia and Sheriff Satterfield in Maury County, and probably the TBI, too."

"Funny coincidence," the voice said dryly, "I know someone at the TBI I can call in."

"There's enough Tannerite in the garage to blow up the whole neighborhood."

The guy behind the voice was definitely arching his eyebrows now. "Any suggestions for what I should do about that? Maybe call in an explosives team?"

"It's a binary explosive, Detective," Rafe said. "You'd have to shoot at it to make it blow. As long as it's just sitting there, it's safe."

"Good to know," Mendoza answered. I had recognized his voice by now—and yes, it was partly because Rafe had identified him by title. Although I had heard his voice before, more than once, so the name would have come to me eventually. "Anything else I need to know?"

"Not right now. Call in your TBI contact so it's on the

record. We can talk when you get here."

Mendoza didn't answer, just hung up. Two seconds later, the phone rang again, and Rafe picked it up. "How long's it gonna take you to get out here?"

They exchanged a few more words, and then Rafe dropped the phone in his pocket and turned to me. "Sorry. I just had to get that called in as soon as possible."

"No problem." I was still feeling a little light-headed, and I appreciated his hand under my elbow. "Jennifer's dead?"

He nodded. "There's a big freezer in the garage. When I opened it, there she was."

I got a little wobbly again, and his hand tightened on my arm. "What happened to her?"

"Hard to say," Rafe said. "I didn't try to lift her. There was no blood that I could see. Not on the front of the body, anyway. And she wasn't strangled."

I didn't ask him how he knew. "What do you think happened?"

"I think he probably broke her neck," Rafe said. "It's quick and easy to do if you know how, and anybody who's been through special forces training would be used to unarmed combat."

I nodded. He was used to unarmed combat, too, and had trained Clayton, Jamal, and José, so he—and they—probably knew how, as well. Although I could live very comfortably without having that hypothesis confirmed. "That's cold, no pun intended. Most people would just kill her and leave her there. He put her in the freezer?"

"Might be coming back," Rafe said.

And wouldn't want to walk into a house with a stinky, bloated corpse lying on the floor. I nodded, even as I asked, "Why would he come back?"

"For the explosive." He glanced at the garage door. "I wasn't kidding. There's enough ammonal in there to blow up a building. One that's a lot bigger than your house. You saw the box that sat on your doorstep. There's enough ammonal in that garage to take down something five times bigger. If they went to the trouble of buying all that, they must be planning to use it for something."

"So he might also have been thinking that he wouldn't want anyone to notice the smell before he could come back and get his ammonal."

Rafe nodded. "We'll have to stake the place out and wait for him. That'll be a fun job for somebody."

"It won't be you, right?"

He shook his head. "No, darlin'. This is grunt work. Mendoza'll put a couple patrolmen on it. Or maybe I can talk Jamal into moving in."

"Just as long as you don't have to," I said. And added. "The… um… body will be gone, right?"

He nodded. "The body'll be going to the morgue in an hour or two. Just as soon as Mendoza gets here and calls it in."

"Is there a reason you can't call it in?"

"Mainly it's 'cause I don't wanna have to investigate," Rafe said. "It happened in Mendoza's jurisdiction; let him deal with it. I got my hands full with Maury County."

Made sense. "So he's on his way?"

Rafe nodded again. "You wanna stick around, or take the baby and go before he gets here?"

"Is there a reason you don't want me to be here when he shows up?"

A corner of his mouth turned up. "No, darlin'."

I sniffed. "I married you, you know. And Mother loves you. I'm sure she regrets asking Mendoza if he'd marry me when you weren't there on our wedding day."

"Not a problem," Rafe said. "This is gonna take some time, and prob'ly be boring. If you wanted to do something else, you could. I can get a ride back to town."

It sounded like he wanted to get rid of me, so I decided I'd let him. "Fine. I'll go somewhere and do something else. The lady in the house over there is named Dot Mangrum. She says she saw Jennifer yesterday morning and the guy last night, leaving. She thought Jennifer might have been with him, but if she's in the freezer, he probably left alone."

"I imagine he did," Rafe said, glancing over my shoulder at Mrs.—or Miz—Mangrum. "You think I oughta go talk to her?"

"I don't know if she knows anything she didn't tell me, but she seems to appreciate good-looking men, so it couldn't hurt. Or you could send Mendoza over when he shows up,"

Rafe looked at me. "You're doing that on purpose."

I grinned. "I'm not blind. I can tell that he's good-looking. Although not as good-looking as you."

Or good-looking in a very different, more civilized, Armani-clad way. Quite nice if you like the type, but it couldn't compare to the rock'em, sock'em sex appeal of the man I married.

He seemed like he was actually a little perturbed by my mentioning Mendoza's good looks, though, so I took a step closer and went up on my toes. "I love you."

It was supposed to be a sweet kiss, just a quick brush of lips before I put Carrie in the Cadillac and left. It turned into something else when he looped an arm around my waist and yanked me up against him.

And promptly grunted when I slammed against his probably-still-painful ribs.

I eased back a fraction of an inch. "Serves you right for trying to be macho."

"I don't have to *try* to be macho," Rafe said, which was certainly true.

"Why don't we give this another shot?" I went back up on my toes. This time he didn't yank, just leaned down to kiss me. And the quick brush of lips turned into something slower and deeper, something that didn't hurt him, even though I did have to grab hold of his jacket with my free hand so I wouldn't dribble into a puddle at his feet.

When I opened my eyes again, he grinned. "That's better."

I nodded. "I hope you're not actually worried about Mendoza. Because I wouldn't be interested in him even if I hadn't already met you by the time I met him. He isn't my type. He might be Mother's type, but he isn't mine."

"Judging from Bob," Rafe said, "he ain't so much your mama's type, either."

Maybe not. I hadn't thought about it, but Mother had picked a different kind of guy the second time around, just like me. Daddy had been the perfect Southern gentleman, a suit-clad lawyer with a degree from Vanderbilt and an antebellum mansion. Bob, while certainly no slouch in the gentlemanly arena, was a cop, and a lot less polished.

"Huh," I said.

Rafe nodded. "Go on home, darlin'. I'll talk to Miz Mangrum and wait for Mendoza and the medical examiner. I'll let you know what happens."

He opened the door to the Caddy and waited until I had put the car seat into the back. Carrie was still asleep, but would probably wake up screaming for sustenance any minute now.

"I'll see you later," I told him, and got in the car while he headed across the street and up to where Dot Mangrum was still standing in the doorway watching us.

I drove by Mrs. Jenkins's house on Potsdam, but Victor's crew was still there, working. There were a couple of white vans parked in the driveway, the kind with ladders lashed to the top, and the front door to the house was hanging open. Through it, I could see a couple of workers doing things to the floor and banister. I could also hear the steady thump of Mariachi music emanating through the open door.

It would be awkward, not to mention loud, to sit upstairs while they worked, so I didn't pull into the driveway, just kept going down Potsdam Street. On Dresden I took a left, and headed into the more affluent part of East Nashville. Ten minutes later, I pulled into the parking lot behind the LB&A office on Woodland Street.

LB&A—short for Lamont, Briggs, and Associates—is the real estate firm I work for. I'd joined them back when the place was called Walker Lamont Realty, and then I stayed on after Walker left—or was hauled off to prison—and the name changed. When I'd moved down to Sweetwater in January, I'd thought about switching to a brokerage down there, but the future was uncertain, what with Rafe still attached to the TBI in Nashville just as much as he was to the Columbia PD, so I hadn't done anything about it. With modern technology, it wasn't a problem to scan and email documents back and forth over much longer distances than the few miles between Columbia and Nashville, so it hadn't seemed worth the trouble until I knew for sure that it was going to be necessary. And besides, it wasn't like I had so much paperwork that it was a problem. The only listing I had was the house on Fulton, and God knew what was going to happen to that after yesterday.

Carrie was still asleep, so I spent a couple of minutes in the car making phone calls to Darcy and Alexandra Puckett. Darcy had already been updated about last night's events by Patrick Nolan as well as Dix, and she told me that she had an appointment with a structural engineer at four, and she'd call me after that with whatever his recommendations were. Alexandra agreed to meet me for lunch so I could update her on what had happened since the last time I saw her, which was less than twenty-four hours ago. So much had happened in the last day that lunch with Jamal and Alexandra at Beulah's felt like it was last week, and not just yesterday.

That done, I hauled the car seat out of the back of the

Cadillac and headed for the back door to the office.

The reception area is in the front. The biggest, fanciest offices are in the back, farthest from the general population and closest to the kitchen and bathroom, and to the rear door into the parking lot. Back when Walker was here, the big office in the far back was his office, and across the hall from it was Brenda Puckett's domain. Tim had occupied the slightly smaller and less fancy office opposite that. He's been working his way into Walker's desk chair ever since.

He was sitting in it now, his skinny butt solidly planted on the leather, and his golden curls gleaming in the overhead light. "Well, look who's here. Top of the morning to you, Savannah."

His smile was, as always, just a little bit malicious.

"Same to you," I said, and put Carrie's seat on the floor before I plopped into one of the chairs across from him.

While I did all that, Tim looked past me to the door. "Is Rafael with you?"

Tim and my mother are the only two people in the world, or at least the only two I know, who call Rafe by his full name. Mother does it because she's particular that way. She calls my brother Dix by his full name, too, and has never called Catherine anything but her full, complete name. Tim, meanwhile, pronounces Rafe's name like a caress, like he enjoys wrapping his tongue around the syllables, and imagines wrapping it around something else instead. Between you and me, it sounds indecent enough to make me squirm.

I shook it off. "He's in Nashville," I told him, "but not here."

Tim made a moue. "Pity."

"He just found a dead body in a house in Bellevue. He'll be busy for a while."

"Goodness gracious," Tim said, "it's like dead bodies just follow the two of you around."

And don't you forget it.

Since threatening Tim makes no difference to his feelings for

Rafe, I changed the subject. "Remember that house I was renovating in Columbia? It went on the market a couple of days ago?"

Tim nodded.

"Well, we have to take it back down. Somebody vandalized it Sunday night. It needs repair. And yesterday, somebody blew the front wall and half the roof off."

Tim stared at me, speechless.

"My sister is meeting with a contractor this afternoon. He'll tell her whether it can be saved or whether we just have to tear it down and start over."

Tim shook his head. "Why do these things always happen to you, Savannah?"

"I guess I'm just lucky that way," I said. "At any rate, I need you to withdraw the listing. The house isn't available anymore."

"Go see Lauri." He waved toward the door. "Fill out the paperwork."

"We have a Lauri?"

"New receptionist," Tim said.

When I'd first started at Walker Lamont Realty, Brittany had occupied the front desk. That had lasted until last fall, when Brittany's ineptitude had slid over into deliberate graft, and then Tim had offered the position to me. I'd turned it down flat—I might not be a successful realtor, but there was no part of me that wanted to sit behind the reception desk for eight hours a day—and Tim had put Heidi Hoppenfeldt on it.

"What happened to Heidi?"

Heidi was a fixture around LB&A. She'd been Brenda Puckett's protégée back when Brenda was alive, and then she'd become Tim's dogsbody after that.

Tim grimaced. "She left."

The reception job had been the final straw, I guess.

"I'm sorry," I said. Sincerely, since Tim was probably

feeling the loss. Heidi had taken care of all the small and unpleasant things that Tim didn't want to have to deal with. Now, I assumed, he'd have to do them himself.

Unless Lauri took care of them for him.

"She went to ReMax."

One of the biggest real estate firms in the world. Where nobody was likely to make her a general dogsbody or saddle her with the reception desk.

"Good for her," I said, and then thought better of it. "I mean…"

"I know what you mean. Go see Lauri. She'll pull your listing for you."

I nodded, and pushed myself to my feet. "Thanks, Tim. You doing OK?"

"Fine," Tim said. "Shut the door on your way out."

That was clear, anyway. I grabbed the baby and headed out. And pulled the door closed behind me with an irritated little snap before I set off down the hallway toward the reception desk and Lauri.

When Brittany worked here, the front desk had always looked like it belonged to a teenager. Brittany was young, blond, vacuous, and interested in things like fashion magazines and celebrities. There'd been bobble-heads and cutesy tchotchkies all over her desk.

Now the desk was ruthlessly organized, with not a pencil out of place, and every piece of paper was organized into stacks by size. A new nameplate—Brittany hadn't had one—sat facing the front door. *Lauretta Biegler* it said.

Lauri sat behind it, as ruthlessly organized as her desk. She looked like she was in her late thirties, with brown hair scraped straight back into a heavy knot at the back of her head, and flawless makeup. Her tiny gold hoop earrings were as different as they could be from the huge circles Brittany used to wear, the kind that were big enough for me to stick my arm through. And she was dressed in a severe, blue jacket and crisp white blouse: a far cry from Brittany's T-shirts and jeans. It was possible there was a pair of jeans under the desk—I couldn't see Lauri's lower body from where I was standing—but I'd stake my life on there being a skirt, and nylons, and high heels there instead.

"Yes?" she said when I came into view, her voice crisp.

"Hi." I tried a friendly smile. She didn't smile back. "I'm Savannah. I work here." Sort of.

"A pleasure to meet you," Lauri said, and didn't sound like she meant it.

On the other hand, she didn't sound like she actively didn't mean it, either. It was something she said because it was what she was supposed to say, nothing more and nothing less.

There were no chairs in front of Lauri's desk, so I remained standing. "I have a listing down in Columbia. A house I've been renovating. It went on the market last week, and yesterday, somebody blew a hole in it."

Lauri looked at me. "Who?"

"We're not sure." My money was on Rodney and Kyle, especially after Rafe found a supply of Tannerite in Jennifer Vonderaa's garage, but there was no proof. And as far as I knew, no way of getting any, either.

"Why?" Lauri said.

"I have no idea. Either because they could, or because they wanted to." A message to me after they'd seen me with Jamal and Alexandra that afternoon? Or a message to Rafe, after he'd implied that Rodney might have been behind the vandalism Sunday night?

"What are you going to do?" Lauri wanted to know.

This had nothing to do with withdrawing the listing, but I told her anyway. "My sister is meeting with a contractor this afternoon, to see whether we can fix it or we have to tear it down. In the meantime, I need to take it off the market. Tim said you could help me."

"Of course." She opened a drawer, thumbed through a couple of folders, and came up with a form. "Address?"

I told her the address and she looked up the other pertinent information on the computer that sat on the corner of her desk.

"Sign here." She pointed. I scribbled my name on the line, and she took the form back. "I'll take care of it. Anything else?"

"No," I said, a little flummoxed by this kind of efficiency. Brittany had been anything but organized, and whenever I'd needed something like this, she'd hand me the form and tell me to fill it out myself, and bring it back when I was finished. "Thank you."

"No problem." She went back to the computer, presumably to take care of my problem. Brittany would have opened a fashion magazine and left my form sitting on her desk for a few days, until she was good and ready to deal with it.

I recognize a dismissal when I see one, though, even if this one wasn't as blatant as the one Tim had given me. I took Carrie and headed back down the hallway toward the back of the building and the exit closest to the FinBar.

The place I was meeting Alexandra is just down the street from the office. Once upon a time, I'd eaten there with rather boring regularity. It's one of those new and fancy sports bars, with lots of polished brass and hanging ferns. When I got there, I asked for a booth out of the way—there were plenty of them available, since the lunch rush hadn't started yet—and explained that I was early for a lunch date with a friend, but that I'd take a sweet tea and an order of pretzels with beer-cheese dip while I waited. If I was going to occupy a table for close to an hour while I waited for Alexandra, I was going to have to order something to eat, before we actually ordered lunch, and beer-cheese dip sounded like it would hit the spot.

The waitress popped a bubble and left. I extracted myself from my coat, and then I extracted Carrie from the car seat and took her into the bathroom to change her diaper. By the time the waitress came back with the tea, we were back at the table, and Carrie was dry and happy and nursing.

I took a sip and settled in to wait. And since there was nothing else to do, I fished my phone out of my purse and called Rafe. "Hi."

"Darlin'." I could hear noises and voices in the background.

"I just wanted to update you," I said. "I'm at the FinBar waiting for Alexandra Puckett to meet me for lunch. Victor's people are still at the house, so I went to the office. Tim sends his love." He hadn't said that, but it was a safe bet he did. "Are you still in Bellevue? Did Mendoza show up yet?"

"The ME just got here. And a crime scene crew. It's gonna be a while before they're done. Mendoza and I are looking around for anything that can give us an idea who this guy is or how to find him."

"What about her phone? It's still there. And surely she must have called the guy?"

"There's a number," Rafe confirmed. "But it goes to a burner phone. No way to trace where it is or who it belongs to."

"Burner phone?"

"Cheap, over-the-counter phone with prepaid minutes. Anybody can buy the phone and the minutes with cash. And this guy woulda had the sense to do that."

"Have you checked?"

"No," Rafe said patiently, "but anybody who knows to use a burner phone knows to buy it in a way where it can't be traced back to him."

I guess that made sense. "If he's that smart, why do you suppose he didn't take the picture from the fridge with him when he left? He had to know it could be used to trace him."

Or could hopefully be used to trace him, anyway. Facial recognition and whatnot.

"Maybe he forgot it was there."

"Stupid of him," I said, "if he did."

Rafe didn't contradict me. "Or maybe he's planning to get it when he's coming back for the ammonal."

Maybe. It wouldn't have taken any time at all to get it before he left the last time, though, so it still seemed stupid to me. "How long will you be staying out there?"

"Till Mendoza leaves," Rafe said. "I'll hitch a ride back to town with him. We have to figure out how to put somebody in the house while we wait for this guy to come back. Hopefully he's not out there now, watching us. Hopefully we can get done what we need to do before he decides to come back."

"I'll let you go," I told him, since he sounded stressed out. "I don't suppose you have any idea what he might want to do with all this ammonal he's hoarding?"

"No, darlin'. I surely don't." And he sounded frustrated about that, too.

"Maybe something will turn up. Or maybe he'll turn up looking for it, and then you can ask."

"Maybe so," Rafe said, but he didn't sound like he believed it. "I'll talk to you later, darlin'."

"Love you," I said, and hung up so he could go back to work and worry, and I could finish feeding my daughter and waiting for Alexandra.

Seventeen

Before Alexandra got there, the phone rang again. The number was unfamiliar, but I was still a real estate agent, and still—technically—had a house to sell, so I answered in my perkiest voice. "Good morning, This is Savannah. How may I help you?"

A sniff, then— "Miz Collier?"

"Yes?" I said, drawing it out while I tried to place the voice. She knew Rafe's name, which I haven't really used for business, so chances were it wasn't about business.

Another sniff. They weren't the superior kind, but the watery ones. "This is Felicia Robinson."

I blinked. Why would Felicia Robinson be calling me, all teary?

And then it clicked. "Yes," I said smoothly, "of course. Officer Robinson. What can I do for you?" And had I ruined it by sounding perkily happy when my husband was supposed to be dying?

Or didn't that deception apply to Felicia? She was another cop, maybe it was OK to tell her the truth.

But no. Some of this information was need-to-know—Clayton's involvement certainly was, for Clayton's safety—and Felicia had had lunch with Sergeant Tucker at Beulah's the other day. If I told her the truth, she might tell Tucker, and I wasn't sure I trusted Tucker. I had no reason not to, especially as far as this situation went—Rafe had even said so, that he didn't think Tucker was involved—but I knew he didn't like Rafe, so I didn't want to take any chances.

"I heard," Felicia said, and had to take a breath to be able to continue, "that Rafe was shot last night…?

"Yes." No lie, that one.

"How is he doing…?" She sounded like she was holding her breath, prepared for the worst.

"Not well," I said. He'd just found a dead body, so that wasn't a lie, either. And in addition to that, his ribs hurt.

Between you and me, I'm not the world's greatest liar, especially not face to face, so it helps to tell the truth as much as possible. Or a version of the truth.

"The chief said he might die…?"

"Yes," I said. That one was a total lie, although he might. Not from being shot, but I'd long ago come to terms with the fact that Rafe lived a dangerous life and might die from it.

"Do you know who…?" She had an irritating habit of trailing off at the end of every sentence. I hadn't noticed it before, so maybe it was just the circumstances. Or just because this was the first conversation we'd had that had been longer than a sentence or two. Maybe she'd always done it, and I just hadn't noticed.

"We have a good idea. The same two people who have been under investigation in connection with the Laurel Hill mess. Rodney Clark and Kyle Scoggins."

There was a beat. "I went to school with Rodney and Kyle," Felicia said, shocked into finishing a sentence on a strong note for once.

"Did you? Were they always racists?"

"No," Felicia said, but she didn't sound totally sure. "Not Kyle, at least. Rodney, maybe a little. Although he got a lot worse after Natalie was killed."

And maybe that was understandable, since he believed— since everyone believed—that Natalie's killer was Steven

Morris, a black man.

But no, that was still no excuse for wholesale hatred of a whole demographic, and especially no excuse for joining a white supremacy group and advocating for a race war.

"Will you tell me if…?" Felicia trailed off again. I guess it happened when there was something she didn't want to put into words.

"Of course," I said, since there was no reason at all I would ever have to call her back and tell her that Rafe had died. He was alive and well and working hard in Bellevue.

"And I'm sorry I haven't been…"

…*nice to you?*

"No problem," I said. "It happens all the time." Some women develop unhealthy attachments to Rafe without him doing anything to cause it other than being himself.

"Thank you." She gave another watery sniff.

"Tell you what," I told her, with no ulterior motive other than to make her feel better, "if you want to do something to help, why don't you ask Grimaldi if she can give you something to do?" Rodney and Kyle were under surveillance twenty-four/seven now. Surely Grimaldi could find a shift for Felicia in all of that. Because while I hadn't liked the way she'd treated me, or the way she'd fawned over my husband, I felt bad for her now. She was barely more than a girl, and obviously distraught, and over something that was a non-issue. And Rodney and Kyle needed to be surveilled. Might as well use her feelings for something good.

"You wouldn't mind?"

"Not at all," I said. "I want whoever did this to pay. If you can help bring that about, all the better."

"Thank you." She sniffed again.

"No problem," I told her. "Thanks for calling."

She hung up, and I tucked the phone away in time to greet Alexandra as she arrived at the table and began the arduous process of trying to wedge her pregnancy into the booth across from me.

After lunch was over, Alexandra and I walked back to the LB&A parking lot together—she parks there too, since her mother used to be an employee—and I waved her off before I dialed Rafe again. "Any news in your part of the world in the past hour and a half?"

"Not much. The crime scene crew is still combing Jennifer's house, but there's not much doubt who killed her. If we get lucky, there'll be a fingerprint somewhere we can use to at least identify this guy, even if it won't get us any closer to finding him."

"I assume you've told Grimaldi and Bob to keep an eye out for Jennifer's car?"

"Yes, darlin'." His tone of voice was patient. Too patient. I deduced I was being annoying. I mean, of course he'd have thought about that.

"I'm sorry," I said. "I just want to do something useful, you know? Something that helps. But I don't know what that is. Short of driving up to Clarksville, to Fort Campbell, and flashing the picture from the fridge around…"

"No," Rafe told me, "don't do that. Just go on home, darlin'. Put the baby down for a nap. Curl up with a book. Kick Victor's crew out, if you have to, so you can get some peace and quiet. If it takes another day or two to finish the repairs, it don't matter. We're staying busy in Sweetwater for right now. And when I get home, we'll grab some food and talk about it and see what you can do to help."

I grimaced. It wasn't what I wanted to hear—like Felicia, I wanted to do something that would actually help—but if that was all I could do right now…

"Any idea when you'll be home?"

"Closer to five," Rafe said. "We got some stuff to set up

yet."

I glanced at my watch. Going on one-thirty. "I guess I'll see you then."

"Thanks, darlin'. I'll fill you in when I get there."

I told him I'd be waiting, and then I drove home, put Carrie down for her afternoon nap amid the sounds of hammering and sawing—if I was going to be upstairs anyway, I might as well give Victor's construction workers the run of the downstairs while they wanted it—and settled in with my laptop.

The crew cleared out by three-thirty, and it was quiet again. By then I had cruised through four years of Jennifer Vonderaa's Facebook feed and was working my way through the 3,462 people on her friends list to see if there was a connection to the spec ops soldier anywhere. I had also checked the property assessor's office—one of my first go-tos as a real estate agent—and ascertained that she owned the house she'd lived—and died—in by herself.

So I was striking out on trying to find him. I kept checking Jennifer's connections, and their connections, and everybody's photo feed, but without any luck, and then Carrie woke up, and I changed her, and fed her, and burped her, and put her on the floor for tummy time, and then my phone rang, and it was Darcy.

I put it to my ear. "What's going on?"

"I just finished talking to the contractor." And she wasn't happy about it, judging from the disgusted tone of her voice.

"Uh-oh." I braced myself. "What did he say?"

"That it's going to cost a lot to fix the house again."

Tell me something I didn't know. "Is it possible to fix the house again?"

"Of course," Darcy said. "It's possible to fix anything. The question is how much it costs."

"And how much would this cost?"

"A lot," Darcy said.

"Is the structure sound?"

"He said it was. The roof and walls can be replaced. The foundation wasn't affected. So the house can be fixed. The problem…"

She trailed off.

"Yes?" I said.

"I don't want to sound greedy. But I already paid to renovate the house once. I hate having to pay for it again, if we're not going to be able to charge more. Our profit dwindles each time we have to put more money into fixing it up."

Yes. That was definitely true.

"Hopefully the insurance company will pay out enough to cover this second round of renovations," I said optimistically.

"That's another thing," Darcy answered. "The house was insured for what we paid for it originally. Not what it was worth after the renovations were done. So they may decide to go with the original value. And if so, we're out of luck. And out a lot of money."

Yes, we were. "Have you spoken to anyone with the insurance company? Have they been out to look at the damage?"

"I called them on Monday," Darcy said, "after the vandalism on Sunday night. They didn't come out on Tuesday, or if they did, they didn't tell me they were there."

"And you didn't call and tell them about the explosion?"

"I didn't see any reason to," Darcy said. "If they haven't been there, they'll see it when they get there."

I guess that was true. "So we're waiting."

"Unless we want to make a decision without knowing what the insurance company says."

I changed gears. "Have you called Charlotte?"

Darcy said she hadn't.

"I'll do that, then. Not that it's really up to her. It's up to you." Since it was her money, and all Charlotte and I had put in, was a lot of sweat equity. "Do you know what you want to do?"

"No," Darcy said. "Right now I'm so discouraged that I wish we'd never bought the house. It sounded like such a good opportunity at the time. And now it's all messed up."

I nodded sympathetically, not that she could see me. "Maybe we just need to take a little time to breathe. There's a lot going on, and not just with the house. Maybe we just wait a day or two and see what the insurance company says? They'll be out by the end of the week, surely?"

"Surely," Darcy said, sounding exhausted and disgusted and sad. "Yeah, that sounds like a good idea. Let's just not make a decision right now. Let's wait and see."

"Sounds good." I changed the subject quickly. "Are you and Nolan getting together tonight?" Because she sounded like someone who could use some loving, tender care, and Nolan would provide it.

"He's working," Darcy said.

Come to think of it, a lot of them were probably working. Rodney and Kyle were back under surveillance, and there was spec ops guy on the loose somewhere, possibly in Columbia. I'm sure they were all working.

"Maybe you should go to your mom's house and hang out with her and Mrs. Jenkins."

"I don't want to risk making Aunt Tondalia worse," Darcy said. "She still wants to go out and meet this old friend of hers on Friday, and she's still not doing well."

"Surely, if she's ill, Audrey won't let her?"

"Right now, they're hoping for the best," Darcy said.

"Well, I'd suggest you come up here, but there's nothing to do here either, and not much fun. Maybe you could call Charlotte, and the two of you could go out somewhere and drown your sorrows in a pitcher of margaritas?"

"That's not a bad idea," Darcy admitted. "Maybe I'll do

that."

"Good." Then she could tell Charlotte the news instead of me. "She could probably use the cheering up, too, and not just because of the house. Her divorce should be final soon, and that's never much fun, even if the jerk did knock up someone else and then kidnap her and the kids."

Darcy agreed. "I've been through a divorce. I'll cheer her up."

"Sounds like a good plan," I told her. "You two talk, and if you come to any decisions about the house, let me know. If you don't want to discuss it, that's fine, too. Let's just let it sit a day or two, and then we'll decide."

And hopefully by then, spec ops guy would be found and arrested, and he, along with Rodney and Kyle and anyone else who was part of their small group of bubbas, would be locked away somewhere where they couldn't hurt me or mine, or for that matter anyone else, ever again. And all we'd have to deal with, was whether or not we wanted to renovate a house we'd already renovated once.

Rafe came home, as expected, a little after five. By then I was ready to get out of the house again, and let him know it.

"There's nothing to do here. I can't cook dinner. There's no TV in the living room." And for that matter no furniture or any walls. "I've been sitting up here with Carrie for three hours, doing research on my computer, and I'm going crazy."

"Let me take you two out for dinner," my husband said gallantly, without mentioning that he'd been busy combing a crime scene for clues all day, and all he wanted to do was relax his no doubt aching ribs.

I bit my lip, chagrined. "Are you OK?"

He smiled. "I'm fine, darlin'. Anything that needed lifting or bending down for, I told Mendoza to do. I've been standing around giving orders all day."

That was surely an exaggeration, but since it made me feel better—and since his smile seemed genuine—I let it pass. "I just spoke to Darcy. She and Charlotte are going to go get drunk and drown their sorrows in tequila."

"Bad news?"

"Nothing we didn't expect. Fixing the house on Fulton is going to take a lot of money. Darcy's discouraged, since it would be her money, and since she's concerned that the insurance won't pay what the house is worth now."

He nodded.

"Your grandmother is still under the weather. You may want to call and check on her."

"Just as soon as I take a shower," Rafe said, peeling his shirt up and over his head.

My tongue got stuck to the roof of my mouth. I unpeeled it—Carrie was gurgling on the floor, and besides, Rafe was injured, so it wasn't an invitation to anything—and told him, "I've spent a couple hours on Jennifer Vonderaa's Facebook page, looking for this guy. No luck so far."

"Try Tinder," Rafe said, turning back to the hallway, shirt in hand and muscles moving smoothly under his skin. "Or one of the other matchmaker sites. Maybe they met that way."

Maybe they had. It wasn't a bad idea.

While he soaped and rinsed off the crime scene, and while Carrie gurgled on the floor, I started checking out matchmaking sites.

It became obvious very quickly that I'd have to join to search. Turns out they don't just let anyone cruise the meat market without registering first. Even the free sites wanted me to register. I tried to imagine myself explaining to Rafe that I'd had to set up a profile on a dating site in order to look for Jennifer's boyfriend, and couldn't do it.

"Surely the TBI or somebody must have access to these sites?" I asked him when he came back out of the bathroom, barefoot and bare-chested, with a pair of jeans riding low on his hips, towel-drying his hair. "I can't do it without signing up, and I'm not sure I want to. What if I make a mistake and I start getting emails from guys wanting to pick me up?"

"I'd kill 'em all," Rafe said, rubbing the towel across the top of his head. The bruising on his ribs was staring to turn yellow around the edges, but was still deep black-purple in the middle. "Don't worry about it, darlin'. We'll find the guy. And yeah, I'm sure both the TBI and Mendoza have access to the sites. Nothing you need to handle yourself."

"If Mendoza has a Tinder profile, he must be inundated with women."

The thought slipped out before I could catch it, and Rafe gave me a look.

"Sorry," I added. "So would you, if you had a Tinder profile."

"I don't need a Tinder profile to find women."

No, he didn't. And Mendoza didn't, either. But this time I stopped myself before I said it. "Ready?" I asked instead, brightly.

That got me another look. "I look ready to you, darlin'?"

Well, no. He didn't. "Sorry. Guess I'm just hungry." And eager for him to cover up, since watching him shirtless did things to my libido that I couldn't do anything about while my daughter was cooing on the floor.

He grinned, in that way that made my stomach do a swoop. "Hold that thought."

I promised him I would, and watched him walk back across the hall, where he pulled a clean shirt around all those muscles and came back into the nursery buttoning it. "I could go for a burger. Gabe's OK?"

Gabe's is a tiny, hole-in-the-wall dive that Rafe favors, that—yes—does have excellent burgers. The rest of the ambience leaves a little to be desired, however. "Is it safe, with the baby?"

"'Course it is. Hand her to me, would you? I can't bend."

Of course he couldn't. I scooped the baby off the floor and handed her over, and watched as he cradled her against his shoulder, one big hand on her fuzzy butt. "Are you going to be OK going down the stairs?"

"I'll be fine, darlin'. Just grab her stuff."

I grabbed her stuff, while I told him, "Felicia Robinson called to ask how you're doing."

"I hope you told her I'm hanging on by a thread," Rafe said, and turned toward the door. "C'mon. I'm starving."

I smiled, and followed him out the door and down the stairs.

Gabe's has deliciously greasy burgers with mounds of crispy French fries and golden onion rings, and I didn't even suggest that maybe I ought to have salad. Rafe was right: they did love Carrie. The waitresses all cooed over her, and even the gray-haired bartender gave her a look and an approving grunt.

"'Scuse me, darlin'," Rafe told me after he'd devoured his burger and onion rings, and half my fries. "Wanna word with Gunner."

Gunner was the bartender, it turned out, since that's where he went. The phone came out, and I assumed the picture of the picture of Spec Ops Guy was flashed. Gunner took a long look, and they talked for a few minutes before Rafe came back to the table.

"Military?" I asked.

He nodded. "Former Marine. And he employs a couple other vets in the kitchen. They come in here sometimes, looking for work, after they muster out. Word's gotten out that Gunner might give'em a job."

"Did he recognize him?"

"He wasn't sure. Said he mighta seen someone who looked

like that a month ago, but can't say for certain."

"Did the guy fill out an employment application?" That would give us a name and phone number, anyway. Maybe even a social security number. At least we'd know who he was, if not where to find him.

His lips curved. "No, darlin'. He wasn't looking for work. And a place like this don't really use applications, anyway."

Bummer. "So if he wasn't looking for work, what did he do?"

"Sat at the bar and drank a beer," Rafe said. "Made small talk. Compared tours. Gunner served in the first Gulf War. This guy said he was in Afghanistan and Iraq."

"Did he give a name?"

"Said his name was Lance." Rafe shrugged.

"That's somewhere to start, isn't it?" There were probably thousands of people named Lance in the armed forces, maybe tens of thousands, but it was less than the number we'd started with, which was everyone with a Y chromosome.

"If it's his real name," Rafe said. "Gunner's called Gunner because he was a Gunner. His real name's John."

Ah. Yes, that did make it more difficult.

"Did anything else happen? When he was here?"

"Not that Gunner said. This place don't look like a white supremacist's hangout, so if he was trying to recruit, he musta thought better of it."

Obviously. Half the wait staff was black, and so was half the clientele. Gunner looked like he might have some Native American in him, or maybe Hispanic.

"So he left," I said.

Rafe nodded. "If it was him and not somebody else with a short haircut and white skin."

"What happens if we can't find him?"

He didn't sound concerned. "We'll find him. Sooner or later. He'll be back for the rest of the ammonal at some point. No reason why he'd pay for it and then leave it all there."

"Are you sure he isn't planning to come back and blow the house up?" With the body inside. "What would happen to the freezer if he shot at the ammonal and the garage blew up?"

"First of all," Rafe said, although I could tell he was thinking, because his eyes got a sort of faraway look, "he'd have to get a clear shot at the stuff. It wouldn't work to shoot it through the wall. The velocity of the bullet wouldn't be high enough to set off the explosive."

"Maybe he has a garage door opener."

Rafe nodded. "Second, if he did manage to set off the ammonal, the garage would turn into splinters and so would part of the house. You saw what happened last night."

I nodded.

"The freezer would either stay where it was or get blown over. But it wouldn't turn to sticks the way the walls would."

"So blowing it up wouldn't be a way to get rid of the body?"

He shook his head. "If he wanted to get rid of the body, he'd be better off taking it outta the freezer and putting it in the car along with the ammonal. And then pitching it outta the car somewhere between here and Columbia. Or here and wherever he's going."

"Is there any reason to think he's going somewhere else?"

"No," Rafe said. "Rodney and Kyle are down there. Laurel Hill is down there. Lance was down there yesterday, to meet Clay. Clay's also down there. It makes sense that whatever they're planning has something to do with down there. But hell if I know what it is."

I had no idea either. So I changed the subject. "I don't suppose the body's there anymore?"

"No, darlin'. It's at the morgue. The ME has confirmed that her neck was broken. It was most likely quick and painless. She might not have known what was happening."

Or she might, and might have had a few seconds, at least, of fear and pain before it was over.

I pushed my plate away. "I'm ready to go."

"Me, too." He signaled for the check.

Eighteen

The call came at a quarter to midnight. I was sleeping the sleep of the just, worn out by energetic lovemaking. Rafe, of course, was wide awake as soon as the phone rang. He grabbed it from the bedside table and put it to his ear while I was still blinking my eyes open.

"Yeah?"

There was a second's pause, and then he said. "I'll be there in twenty." He was already flinging the covers off. I murmured sleepily as the cold air hit my body.

The phone kept quacking, though, and his body must have reminded him that he still wasn't healed, because he ended up staying flat on his back and talking into it. "Are you sure you don't wanna hit'em now? Why give'em a chance to regroup?"

Whoever was on the other end said something else, and Rafe sighed. "Fine. I'll see you in the morning."

He shut the phone off on what was probably the other person's goodbyes, and lay back down, pulling the blankets back up.

"Problem?" I asked, still half-asleep.

"No, darlin'." After a second he added, "Sorry I woke you."

"You didn't. The phone did." I hesitated for a moment. "Grimaldi? Wendell? Mendoza?"

"Mendoza," Rafe said.

"Did something happen at the house? Jennifer's house? Did somebody show up for the body?"

"Not the body," Rafe said. "Which is a damn shame, or we coulda gotten'em on conspiracy to commit murder."

"Won't you get them on that anyway? They shot you, right?" And if they were having target practice in Laurel Hill, in skull masks and armbands with swastikas, they must be planning to shoot other people, too. "Who was it? Was it Lance?"

"Rodney and Kyle and Clay."

"Lance must have sent them instead of going himself. The coward. Although it sounds like Clayton's still safe, anyway. They don't know who he is."

"Seems that way," Rafe agreed.

"Why aren't you on your way to interrogate them? Won't Mendoza let you be there?"

"Oh, he'll let me be there." Judging from Rafe's tone, there wouldn't be anything Mendoza could do to keep him out. Not that I imagined Mendoza would try. "He just don't wanna do it tonight."

"Do you feel like that would be better?"

He was staring up at the ceiling, still wide awake. I could see the faint light from the nightlight in the hallway reflect in his eyes. "They're rattled right now. They're mostly just kids. Chances are, neither of'em's been arrested before. Other than Clay, anyway."

Of course. "And Clay has no reason to be rattled." Although I'm sure he was pretending to be.

"If we push'em now," Rafe said, "they might give us the name of the other guy and whatever plans they have for the ammonal."

"So why won't Mendoza confront them tonight?"

"He thinks they'll be even more likely to talk after a night in jail," Rafe said. "They're sitting in there, with the drunks and the dregs, getting more and more worked up. He thinks by tomorrow morning, they'll tell us whatever they have to, to get outta there."

That also made sense. "Do you think Mendoza's wrong?"

"No," Rafe said grudgingly. "It could work that way. But it could work my way, too. We'd get the answers either way."

And his way would allow him to get rid of some aggression right now. I got it. "If that's the only reason, you're probably just going to have to do it Mendoza's way." They were Mendoza's prisoners, in Mendoza's jurisdiction.

Rafe grunted. Other than that, we lay in silence a minute.

"Mendoza's keeping 'em together for the night," Rafe said. "And keeping 'em monitored, just in case they say something we'd like to know."

That was reasonable. "Do they get a phone call each?"

"Tomorrow. If they're arrested."

"They haven't been arrested?"

He shook his head. "Just detained for questioning. And that's happening tomorrow at eight."

"And it's OK to do that?"

He sounded amused that I asked. "Sure thing, darlin'. We're letting 'em get a good night's sleep before talking to 'em."

"Considerate of you," I said dryly. "If you have to be downtown early tomorrow, we should probably try to get some more sleep."

"I guess."

Another minute passed.

"You wanna help me burn off some energy?" my husband inquired.

My lips curved. "I guess I could do that. If you've got energy to burn."

He reached out, and slipped a hand around my neck. "You mind coming over here? It'd make it easier."

"I don't mind at all," I told him, and slid across the bed.

"Can I come with you?" I asked the next morning as he

prepared to head out. "The construction workers are coming back, and I don't have anything to do other than sit here while they hammer and saw downstairs. It's awkward and boring."

He opened his mouth, and then closed it again. And shrugged. "Sure. If Mendoza don't want you there, he can tell you to leave."

Fair enough.

"Don't be surprised if he does," Rafe added.

"I won't. But I've met these guys. I've watched them. They shot my dog and my husband. They blew up my house." Or at least we thought they did. "I'd like to hear what they have to say."

"Not sure we're gonna ask 'em anything about that," Rafe said. "We gotta figure out the best way to handle this. They got all that ammonal for something, and we don't know what it is. If they won't tell us, the best thing may be to let 'em go, and then see what they do."

I nodded.

"And if we wanna do that, we can't come up with too many good reasons for arresting them. If we do, they're gonna be suspicious if we don't."

Good point.

"Let's just see what happens," I said, and headed for the door. "Thanks for letting me come."

He didn't answer, just smiled. I thought about what I'd said, and blushed. He chuckled.

"You know what I mean," I said.

"I do, darlin'." He took the baby carrier with our daughter out of my hand and nudged me out the front door ahead of him. "And it was my pleasure."

"Not solely," I told him, and preceded him down the front steps to the car, just as the first white painter's van pulled into the driveway from Potsdam Street.

Police headquarters are across the Cumberland River in downtown, just on the other side of the bridge. It's a quick and easy drive. Fifteen minutes from when we walked out of Mrs. Jenkins's house, Rafe had parked Mother's Cadillac in the secure lot behind the building, and ferried Carrie and myself into the building and up to Mendoza's office on the third floor.

"She insisted on coming," he told the detective when Mendoza arched his brows at the sight of me. "If you don't want her here, you're gonna have to tell her."

Mendoza smiled, and a dimple popped up in each of his cheeks. He's so handsome it's a little spooky, like one of those perfect specimens of Latin lover you see on Telenovelas. "Mrs. Collier."

"Detective." I smiled back, sweetly. "If you don't mind, I would really like to see what they have to say for themselves. Tamara Grimaldi would have let me."

"I'm not Tamara Grimaldi," Mendoza informed me. "But you can stay if you want. As long as you don't expect to do anything but watch and listen."

Fine by me. "Are they still in a cell?"

"They're in holding," Mendoza said. "And being quiet starts now."

I made a face. Rafe's lips twitched, but he didn't say anything. Not to me. Although he did put a hand on my lower back and circled it a couple of times. "I guess we'll interview'em one at a time?"

"*I* will interview them one at a time," Mendoza corrected. "At the moment, we don't know if we want you to appear in this."

Rafe opened his mouth, and Mendoza overrode him. "They know who you are from Columbia. They probably tried to shoot you."

Rafe nodded. I did, too.

"I'm not sure we want them to know that we've made the

connection with Columbia. They walked into a crime scene in Nashville, where someone had killed a young woman and put her in a freezer. That's reason enough for me to talk to them."

That was true. And put like that, there was no reason for Rafe to get involved. I opened my mouth to tell him I agreed with Mendoza, and shut it again without speaking.

Carrie, looking around wide-eyed, made a cooing noise, and Mendoza switched his attention to her. And smiled again. "Well, hi there, gorgeous."

He bent over the carrier to tickle her and make her giggle. It was another of those moments where every woman in the vicinity would have felt their biological clock start to tick louder.

Rafe scowled, but told Mendoza, "Fine. I'll stay back and let you interview them."

"And if I decide we can get better results by bringing you in," Mendoza answered, straightening, "then we will."

Rafe nodded. "Take Clay first. I wanna know if he knows any more than he's already been able to tell us."

"Let's go down to the interview rooms, then." Mendoza gestured toward the door. I headed that way with the baby. Rafe followed, and Mendoza brought up the rear.

"Wait here," he told us a couple of minutes later. We were all standing in a small room that had a window into an empty interview-room, the sort you see on TV. I'd been in one very much like it once or twice. I might even have been in that particular one. It was better to be on this side of the wall.

Mendoza headed out, letting the door close behind him, and Rafe grabbed a chair and pulled it up to the window. "Have a seat."

I sat, and gave the toys attached to the handle of Carrie's car seat a jingle-jangle so she'd have something to look and swat at. "Been a while since I was in one of those."

"I was in one of'em back in January. It mighta been that

one." He looked through the window into the interrogation room. "Goins pulled me in for questioning about Doug Brendan's accident."

I remembered. Detective Goins had interviewed me, too, although he'd done it in his office. I hadn't been suspected of killing Rafe's superior at the TBI. I'd just been suspected of covering up for Rafe, or perhaps of being fooled by him, so Goins had treated me with more care than he did Rafe.

"Do you suppose he's here?"

"Goins?" Rafe said. "I imagine he is. That's why I called Mendoza directly yesterday. Didn't wanna risk ending up with Goins on the case, and having him accuse me of killing Jennifer Vonderaa, too."

"That was probably a good move." Since Goins was stupid enough, and racist enough, to believe it. "It's too bad he doesn't live in Maury County, or I'd suspect him of being involved with the white supremacy group."

"He don't need to live in Maury County for that," Rafe said.

True. "Any reason to think he is?"

He shook his head. "Just your garden variety bastard. If he was involved, he's be breathing down Mendoza's neck by now."

I guess maybe he would. "That's a shame. I'd like to have him be guilty of something, so he could lose his job and not be a detective anymore. People like him don't belong on the police force."

"People like him are everywhere," Rafe said, and turned to the door when it opened. "Clay."

He nodded to Clayton as the younger man stepped through. Mendoza came in after him, and shut the door.

Clayton nodded back, and spared me a glance before he focused on Rafe again. "You OK, man? I thought you were wearing a vest, but then you went down and didn't get up."

"A couple broken ribs, a couple of Band-Aids," Rafe said, as if neither was important enough to worry about. "Although you coulda given me a heads-up."

I nodded. Advance warning would have been nice.

"No time," Clayton said, rubbing a hand over his barely-there hair. He subscribes to the Rafe Collier style of haircut. On Clayton, scrawny and pale, it makes him look like a skinhead. On Rafe, it just looks dangerous. "We lit outta the parking lot outside the restaurant, and Rodney and Kyle, they were bitching about how you'd been pushing me around and how you needed to be taught a lesson. And before I knew it, there we were, in the fields opposite the house, and one of'em handed me a rifle and told me that since I was the one you'd been pushing around, I was gonna have the honor of taking the first shot. And I tried to tell'em I've already been inside—"

In prison.

"—and I don't wanna go back, especially not for shooting a cop, but I couldn't argue too much, or they were gonna question whether it had been a good idea, hooking me up with the group…"

Rafe nodded.

"And so I took the shot. And because there was no blood, I figured I might as well take another one. Because if there wasn't any blood, I figured Rodney and Kyle were just gonna take the gun, and then they'd start shooting…"

"You did good," Rafe told him, like the fact that Clayton had shot at him, and hit him, twice didn't matter at all. "If it hadn't been for the vest, you woulda killed me with the first shot. And the second was just close enough to take a slice outta my arm. It all looked real good."

Yes, it had. Good enough that I had to fight back a shiver.

I shook off the memory and smiled at Clayton. "It scared the daylights out of me."

He ducked his head and looked embarrassed. "Sorry."

"Don't be," I told him. "You did your job. And you

obviously did it well enough that Rodney and Kyle decided that they didn't need to take their own shots."

"I said," Clayton told us, with a vicious undertone, "that Rafe was down and that the place was gonna be crawling with cops in a few minutes. They couldn't wait to get outta there."

The corner of Rafe's mouth turned up. Mendoza, leaning against the wall a few feet away, shifted from one foot to the other.

"Tell me about last night," Rafe said.

Clayton made a face. "Rodney gotta text. He called Kyle and told him to be ready to roll in twenty, and that we needed the truck. Then he told me to get my coat on. I asked him what was happening, and he said that we'd been given a mission."

He made air quotes around the last word.

"What was the mission?" Mendoza wanted to know, and Clayton glanced at him.

"You gotta understand, they don't tell me everything. Not yet." He looked at me. "I didn't even know it was your house they were planning to blow up until I saw you drive up, and I recognized the car. And by then it was too late to let anybody know anything."

"Not your fault," I told him, since it wasn't, and since there wasn't anything he could have done about it anyway. Not without blowing his cover. "Just out of curiosity, do you have any idea why they did that?"

"'Cause they could?" Clayton said, irritated, and then added. "Sorry. Yeah. It was because of Jamal. You came and got him and Alexandra from the shop, and Rodney didn't like the way you talked to me. He'd seen you working on the house, and he'd been inside it that Sunday, so he knew it looked nice, and he figured, if he could damage it enough, it would take you time and more money to fix it."

I nodded. "Did he happen to mention whether he was the one who broke in and vandalized the place Sunday night, too?"

"If he did, he didn't say anything about it," Clayton said. "When he picked me up, he said he wanted to see if I could shoot. I figured we were going to a shooting range or something, or a field with a bunch of cans on a fence. Instead, he dropped down in a neighborhood full of people. When I recognized the car, I was afraid he was gonna tell me to shoot you. But then all he wanted—he said—was to see if I could hit the box."

"Congratulations," I told him. "You hit the box."

"Yeah, no kidding." He made a face. "For the record, I didn't know it was gonna blow. I just figured it was a stupid initiation thing and all I had to do was make it jump or something. I didn't expect it to blow half the roof off."

We stood in silence a second while we all remembered the roof blowing.

"Then what happened?" Rafe said, and Clayton turned back to him.

"Rodney said I'd proven myself to be worthy. He's kind of a jackass. And then we drove to the restaurant south of town and met Kyle. And the other guy showed up. And then you showed up—" He nodded to Rafe, "and the rest of it you know."

"Tell me about the guy."

"Rodney calls him Lance," Clayton said, "but I don't think it's his real name. Kyle asked about it, and Rodney told him that the guy who led The Base called himself Spear."

Both Rafe and Mendoza nodded. I had no idea what The Base was, but I nodded, too, so it would look like I did.

"Does he have a connection to The Base?" Mendoza wanted to know, with a glance at Rafe. I deduced The Base was a big deal.

But Clayton shook his head. "If he does, nobody mentioned it. He sure didn't. He didn't say much of anything. Just showed up, and sat down. He and Rodney did some kind of handshake. Rodney introduced me. Lance asked why I wanted to join them.

I gave him the cover story. Arrested just over a year ago. Got out after a year. Wanted somewhere to start over. Came here."

"And he bought it?" Mendoza asked.

Rafe's lips twitched.

"Nothing not to buy," Clayton said. "It's all true. Except that I didn't spend the last year in prison. But the arrest's on record. It was in the paper and everything. With my picture. Unless he's stupid, he already verified it."

"Did you get the impression that he was stupid?"

"No," Clayton said. "I got the impression that he's as cold-blooded as a snake, and not stupid at all. And that was before I knew he'd killed somebody."

There was a moment's silence.

"What about last night?" Rafe wanted to know.

"I told you Rodney gotta text. We drove over to Kyle's place and parked my car, and then we drove Kyle's truck to Nashville."

"Did either of them talk about what was going to happen once you got there?" Mendoza wanted to know.

"I asked," Clayton said. "Rodney said we had to pick up the rest of the explosive for Friday."

I could see Rafe's lips tighten, and knew what he was thinking. It was already Thursday morning. If Lance was blowing something up tomorrow, there wasn't much time left to figure out what it was and stop it.

"What are they setting up to blow?" he asked Clayton.

Clayton shook his head. "Dunno. Rodney said I'd find out tomorrow."

"So doesn't Rodney know," Mendoza asked, "or did he just not want to share it with you because you're new?"

"No idea. Him and Kyle could just be minions, running around doing errands for this guy, and he's keeping it all to himself until it's time. Or Rodney might know, but he likes yanking my chain." He shrugged.

"Did Rodney mention anything about Jennifer Vonderaa's body?"

Clayton shook his head. "Not a word. Just that we were there for the Tannerite. That's all. When we left the truck, he said to grab all the ammonal and load it up so we could get outta there as quick as possible, before anyone saw us."

Rafe nodded. Mendoza did, too. "If that's all, we should probably get you back to the cell."

"First," Clayton said, "tell me what's gonna happen next."

"We'll talk to Rodney and Kyle," Mendoza said. "Separately. It's up to you what you want to do. If we get this guy's whereabouts out of one of them, your job might be done. We can let them know that you were in violation of your parole and you were taken back to prison."

Clayton folded skinny arms over his skinny chest. "How was I in violation of my parole? Tannerite is legal. You can't arrest any of us for having that. The garage door was open, so we didn't break in. We didn't know about the body, and you can't prove we did."

Rafe smirked. I hid a smile, too. Mendoza gave Clayton a look. "Careful there, sport. If you don't want us to tell your new friends you went back to prison, we won't."

"I wanna see it through," Clayton said. "If they're blowing something up tomorrow, I wanna be there to help. I wanna stop it if I can. Don't take me off the job now."

"That's up to you," Rafe told him. "You wanna go back in the cell, you go back in the cell."

"And make it good," Mendoza told him, as he opened the door and gestured for Clayton to precede him.

"Rafe trained me," Clayton informed Mendoza as he walked past him and into the hallway. "I know how to do my job."

The door closed behind them, and Rafe chuckled. And then winced and put a hand to his ribs.

"Sounds like he's doing all right," I said.

Rafe nodded. "He's good. And he's right. We need him to stay in. Rodney and Kyle are more likely to hear what the target is before we figure it out. If Clay's there, maybe they'll tell him. They sure as hell ain't gonna tell us."

No, they wouldn't. At this point, Clayton was our best shot of getting a handle on this before the worst happened.

"Do you believe that Rodney doesn't know? Or is he just stringing Clayton along and making himself out to sound special?"

"Could be either," Rafe said, leaning against the wall. "If I'm reading this situation right, Lance has an agenda. He's the one driving the action. But instead of having built himself an army he can use, he's dealing with a couple of kids who are playing war games, who are doing this because it makes them feel like hot shit. They pick fights with five-year-old girls in restaurants, and get excited about their 'missions.'" His tone made air quotes around the last word. "They put a box of explosive in front of a house and shot at it to see it blow, for God's sake. They're kids. And unless Lance is an idiot, he can see that. He should be able to see it. So it's very possible he's keeping those plans close to his vest until the last minute. Because if it came to a real interrogation, I could have the information out of either of'em in two minutes flat."

I didn't doubt it. "Is that what you would do?"

He nodded. "I'd string'em along, and make'em feel like they mattered, and I'd use'em to do things I didn't wanna do myself—like go back to the house where I'd killed my girlfriend and dumped her in the freezer to pick up the explosive I was gonna use for whatever my master plan was tomorrow. But I wouldn't tell'em anything important, and I'd be prepared to do the real work myself."

"So this is a lesson in futility."

"Pretty much," Rafe said, and turned to the window as the

door into the interrogation room opened. "But it has to be done."

I nodded. And turned, too, as Kyle Scoggins walked into the room next door ahead of Mendoza, wrists cuffed in front of him.

Nineteen

"Looks about ready to piss his pants," Rafe said.

I nodded. Kyle did. Or at least he looked quite nervous, and not at all like the cocky bastard who had whispered racial slurs to Cletus Johnson's five-year-old and then swaggered out of Beulah's like he was untouchable.

He was trying, I'd give him that. He walked in with his head high, and he nudged the chair out from the table with his foot like he couldn't be bothered to use his—cuffed—hands. And when he sat, he slouched back, trying to look at ease. But I could see his Adam's apple move when Mendoza took the seat across from him and laid a manila folder on the table, aligning it precisely with the edge.

Deliberately, he placed a ballpoint pen at a perfect forty-five degree angle to the corner on top of the folder, and then placed a small recorder next to that. Finally, he folded his hands on top of the folder, and eyed Kyle. "I'm Detective Jaime Mendoza. Homicide."

Kyle didn't say anything, but his Adam's apple moved again.

"State your name and address for the record," Mendoza told him.

Kyle gave his full name—his middle name was Maynard— and an address in Columbia, in a voice that shook a little.

"First time in an interrogation room?" Mendoza asked him, in a tone like he found it a little bit amusing.

Kyle shrugged, but it came across more nervous than insolent.

There was another moment while Mendoza eyed him, and while Kyle fidgeted. Then—

"Tell me about last night," Mendoza said.

"What do you wanna know?" Kyle had to clear his throat before he got the words out.

"You were found breaking into a house in Bellevue—"

"We didn't break in!" Kyle said. "The door was open!"

"Did you have the homeowner's permission to come inside?"

Kyle hesitated.

"I'm guessing not," Mendoza said, "since at the time you got there, the homeowner was dead. Who told you the door would be open and you could go in?"

"Lance told Rodney," Kyle said, his voice almost inaudible.

"Speak up for the record, please. Someone told your friend Rodney?"

Kyle glanced at the recorder. It was the same sort of glance someone might give a snake, or a neo-Nazi. "Lance did."

"Is it Lance's house?"

"I think it's his girlfriend's house," Kyle said.

"Lance's girlfriend is the dead woman in the freezer?"

Kyle turned pale. "I don't know."

"Have you ever met Lance's girlfriend?"

Kyle shook his head.

"Out loud, please," Mendoza reminded him, "for the recorder. Have you ever met Lance's girlfriend?"

Kyle swallowed. "I don't think so."

"Did you look in the freezer last night?"

I wouldn't have thought Kyle could look much paler than he did, but somehow he managed. "No," he whispered.

Mendoza opened his folder and fished out a piece of paper. When he slid it in front of Kyle, I recognized Jennifer

Vonderaa's face, upside down. The angle was wrong for me to be able to tell whether the picture had been taken before death, or after, but judging from Kyle's expression, she was dead, and her head was resting on a bag of frozen peas. "You ever see her before?"

"No," Kyle whispered.

"You didn't go there to pick up the body?"

"No!" Kyle looked like he was about to vomit.

Rafe made a little sound, halfway between amusement and disgust, and inside the interview room, Mendoza nudged the small trash can under the table in Kyle's direction, using the tip of his Italian leather shoe. "Use that, if you feel the need."

"I'm OK," Kyle said, although he reached down and pulled the can a little closer. There was no sign left of the cockiness from last month, or even a few minutes ago.

"If you weren't there for the body, what did you go there for?"

"Favor for a friend," Kyle said.

"This friend being Lance?"

Kyle nodded. Mendoza must have eyed the recorder, because Kyle added, "Yes."

"Does Lance have a last name?"

"Doesn't everyone?"

I waited. After a second Kyle shriveled under what was undoubtedly a glare from Mendoza. "Sorry," he muttered.

"A woman's dead," Mendoza informed him. "Your friend Lance might have killed her. It's not a laughing matter."

"No, sir."

"And let's not forget that if I can't find Lance, you and your friends make pretty good suspects, too. You were found in the house with the body."

Kyle swallowed. "Yes, sir."

"Let's try this again. What's Lance's last name?"

"I don't know," Kyle said.

Mendoza waited a second, but when Kyle didn't say anything else, he continued on. "So you drove to Nashville to do a favor for Lance. Lance told Rodney the door would be open. And Lance wanted you to do... what?"

"Pick up the containers of Tannerite in the garage and bring them to him," Kyle said.

"Tannerite." Mendoza sounded like the word was foreign to him. "What is Tannerite?"

"Explosive," Kyle said.

"That's right. It's a binary explosive. Ignites with a shot from a .223 or higher caliber bullet."

Kyle nodded, his eyes lighting up.

Or at least his eyes lit up until Mendoza asked him, gently, "What were you going to blow up, Kyle?"

"Nothing," Kyle said, as all the animation left his face. He slumped back in his chair, looking sullen.

"No? What were you going to do with the Tannerite?"

"Target practice," Kyle said.

Mendoza nodded. "That's a lot of target practice. You practicing for anything in particular?"

"No," Kyle said.

"Ever shoot anything not for target practice? Hunting or anything like that?"

"No," Kyle said. "Was—?"

He stopped and clamped his lips together.

"From what we can tell," Mendoza said genially, "her neck was broken. One quick snap—" He demonstrated, "and—"

"*Gurk*," Kyle said, or something like it. He looked like he was going to lunge for the trash can, but he held it together.

Mendoza leaned back in his chair. We were looking at the back of his head, so I couldn't see his expression, but I could venture a good guess from the tone of his voice. "Know anyone who could do that, Kyle?"

Kyle shook his head, his eyes huge. "No."

"Your buddy Lance didn't mention that there'd be a dead body in the freezer?"

Kyle shook his head. And added "No," for the recorder.

"You think he might have mentioned it to one of your friends?"

"No," Kyle said, sounding horrified. "Rodney..." He trailed off.

"Rodney didn't mention it? What about your other friend? Clay?"

"Clay doesn't know Lance," Kyle said. "We only met him a couple days ago. If Lance told anyone..."

"It would be Rodney?"

Kyle nodded.

"Would Rodney know and not tell you?"

"No," Kyle said, although he didn't sound sure.

"Maybe I need to ask Rodney?"

Kyle nodded, relieved. "Yeah. Ask Rodney."

He sounded almost pathetically eager to throw his best buddy under the bus.

Mendoza nodded. "Let's go." He pushed to his feet.

Kyle stayed where he was. "Where?"

"Back to the holding cell for now. Until I've talked to Rodney."

Kyle got to his feet, reluctantly. "Are you gonna arrest us?"

"That depends on whether you tell me the truth," Mendoza said mildly.

Kyle's mouth opened, probably to protest that he *was* telling the truth, and Mendoza went on before he could get the first word out. "Turns out your new buddy Clay has a record. Why don't you ask him about it while I talk to Rodney? Have Clay tell you what it was like to spend a year in prison. And then, if you decide you have something else you'd like me to know, you tell me when I bring Rodney back."

He smiled as he opened the door so Kyle could go past him.

And for being such a good-looking guy, it was a remarkably unhandsome smile. Kyle gulped, and looked anything but happy when he walked out into the hall.

As the door shut behind them, Rafe turned to me and grinned. "That was entertaining."

"I felt almost bad for him," I said.

Rafe shook his head. "I don't. He's scum, and he deserves to rot."

No question, but— "You don't think he had anything to do with the murder, do you? He looked like he was going to hurl when Mendoza asked him if he was there to pick up the body."

"I figure Lance killed her. Spur of the moment, most likely. Maybe she got around to asking what he was planning to do with the three tons of Tannerite he was keeping in her garage, and she didn't like the answer."

Made sense. Or she already knew what he was planning to do with the three tons of Tannerite, and she was getting cold feet.

"Or maybe he told her he needed to use her car to go to Columbia on Tuesday night. She asked why. He said to meet a new recruit. She asked what he was recruiting for. He told her he's a neo-Nazi and is building the Fourth Reich. She wouldn't let him take the car. He killed her and took the car anyway. Maybe he filled the trunk with as much Tannerite as it would hold. And then he sent Rodney and company back for the rest."

Maybe so.

"He's planning to do whatever he's planning to do tomorrow," Rafe said, "and then I'm betting he's outta here. Off somewhere else. Never planning to come back. I'm surprised he's still driving Jennifer's car."

"He might not be. He might have killed her after he came back here on Tuesday night, not before he left. I don't see him killing his girlfriend and then driving her car to Columbia, do you? So maybe he borrowed her car to go down there, and whatever happened, didn't happen until he came back."

Rafe nodded. "There's a BOLO out on Jennifer's car, both here and in Maury County, but I don't think anyone's seen it yet."

"Maybe it's in Rodney's auto shop getting a new paint job and a new VIN," I said. "And maybe Lance is driving Rodney's car. Clay said they took his car to Kyle's house, right?"

Rafe nodded. "I should touch base with Tammy. And make sure that BOLO extends to Lawrence, Lewis, and Giles."

"Too late," I told him, nodding to the door in the other room. "Here they come."

Here they did. Rodney first, and unlike his buddy Kyle, he did manage a creditable swagger as he entered the room. While Mendoza detoured around the table and gave us a look through the mirror, Rodney made himself comfortable in the other chair. Kicked back, like he didn't have a care in the world.

After he had stated his name for the record—middle name Wilson—Mendoza went right for the jugular. "Both your friends tell me you're the one who'll be able to tell me how to get in touch with your buddy Lance."

Rodney smirked. "What d'you want with Lance?"

"Arrest him for murder, to begin with," Mendoza said pleasantly. "Although if I can't find him, you'll make an acceptable substitute."

"You can't prove I had anything to do with that woman in the freezer," Rodney said, and unlike Kyle, he didn't sound worried about it, either.

Mendoza leaned back. "Who told you that?"

"What? That there was a body in the freezer?"

"That we can't prove you had anything to do with it," Mendoza said calmly. "Did someone tell you that? Say, Lance?"

But Rodney shook his head. "Clay did. When he came down after you talked to him. He said there was a dead body in the freezer, but nobody could prove we had anything to do with it."

"That depends on whether you did have something to do with it," Mendoza said, still calm. "Unless you wore gloves when you snapped her neck, your fingerprints will still be on the body. They don't go away just because the body's frozen."

"Is that true?" I asked Rafe.

He shook his head. "Might be some DNA. That lasts. But it'll take a while to get those results back."

So Mendoza was bluffing. I turned back to the window.

"That's bullshit," Rodney said. "I didn't have nothing to do with the body. Kyle and Clay woulda told you that."

"They said *they* didn't know about the body." Mendoza put emphasis on 'they.' "But they also said you were the one in communication with Lance. So if anyone knew, it would be you."

"I didn't know nothing," Rodney said.

"Lance didn't tell you?"

Rodney shook his head.

"I guess you're not that close?"

"We're close—" Rodney began, and then seemed to think better of it. He subsided back into the chair, but still managed to look truculent.

Mendoza leaned back, too, casually. Or at least the back of him looked casual. We were looking at Rodney's face and the back of Mendoza's head. He had nice, healthy hair, jet black and a little wavy. Much like Rafe's when he lets it go, except a little darker. Rafe's hair looks black when it's cropped short, but it's actually more like an espresso brown when it gets a little length.

"Tell me about Lance," Mendoza said.

Rodney didn't answer, and Mendoza added, "Did he ever mention his girlfriend to you? Did they have problems? How long had they been together?"

"We didn't talk about it," Rodney said.

Mendoza nodded, understandingly. "Do you have a girlfriend?"

"No," Rodney said, flushing.

"You dated a girl named Natalie Allen in high school. Until she was murdered."

"That's got nothing to do with this!" Rodney said.

"You were questioned in connection with her death."

"I had an alibi! And anyway, the guy who killed Natalie is in prison."

"Steven Morris went on trial for Natalie's murder, and was acquitted. And ended up dead the next day. You were questioned in his murder, too."

"Same guy did it!"

Mendoza went on as if he couldn't hear Rodney, or didn't think what Rodney was saying was worth listening to. "That's three murders you've been involved in now, Rodney."

"I wasn't involved in any of them!" Rodney said, his voice shrill. "I didn't kill Natalie. I had an alibi! I had an alibi for Morris's murder, too. And I didn't even know there was a dead body in the freezer until the cop told me!"

"Lance didn't mention the fact that he'd killed his girlfriend and put her body in the freezer?"

"No!"

"Don't you think that's something he should have shared with you, instead of letting you walk into a house with a dead body in it?"

"Yes!" Rodney said.

"It's a little suspicious, after all. Almost like dead bodies follow you around."

"I told you...!" Rodney began.

Mendoza waved it aside. "So Lance told you to go to the house. And he said the door would be open. But he didn't tell you about the body. What were you there for?"

"To pick up the—" Rodney began, and then stopped.

"Body?"

"No! Why don't you listen? I didn't know nothing about the body! We were there for something else."

Mendoza nodded. "As it happens, I already know. Your friends told me. So why don't you go ahead and say it, for the record?"

Rodney shifted on the chair. The handcuffs rattled. "We went there to pick up the Tannerite."

"Who does the Tannerite belong to?"

"Lance," Rodney said. "Lance bought it and stored it in his girlfriend's garage."

"Did Lance's girlfriend know that she was storing enough explosive to blow up a building?"

"Dunno," Rodney said. "Never met her."

Mendoza let that hang for a second before he said, "It's a lot of Tannerite. What was Lance going to do with all of it?"

"Target practice," Rodney said, and a smirk hovered at the corners of his lips.

"Does he practice a lot?"

"He's a sniper," Rodney said.

I glanced at Rafe, who arched a brow. "True?" I asked him.

He shrugged. "Could be. If it is, it'd make it easier to identify him."

It would. But that wouldn't tell us where he was or what he was doing now. Even so, I nodded and turned my attention back to the window.

"So maybe he doesn't need practice," Mendoza was saying. "Is it the rest of you who practice?"

Rodney shrugged.

"What are you practicing for? Are you planning to join the military?"

Rodney lips curved. "No."

"Go hunting?"

"Yeah," Rodney said. "Hunting."

Rafe made a disgusted noise. I wanted to, as well. Mendoza didn't. I'm sure he could hear the gleeful tone in Rodney's voice, and he could guess what kind of hunting Rodney was talking about, but he didn't let it show. "I need to talk to Lance about his dead girlfriend, Rodney. Where can I find him?"

"Dunno," Rodney said.

"Where was he when you last spoke to him?"

"He texted me," Rodney said, "and gave me the address. I don't know where he was."

Mendoza fished a bag out of his jacket pocket, and shook a cell phone out onto the table in front of Rodney. "That's your phone."

Rodney reached for it.

"Call Lance and ask him where he wants you to bring the explosive."

Rodney looked at him.

"Or I can charge you with conspiracy to commit murder. You were there, in the house, with the body. You went there on Lance's orders. It's a short step from there to making the case that you were going to move the body. And that takes it into conspiracy."

"We weren't! We were only getting the Tannerite!"

"You can explain that to a jury," Mendoza said. "Or you can call Lance."

Rodney scowled at him. Mendoza waited. It took a few seconds, but eventually, Rodney began stabbing at the phone, his movements sharp and annoyed.

"Put it on speaker," Mendoza told him.

Rodney shot him a look, but did it. We could hear the ringing, and then the fake-friendly, canned voice. "I'm sorry. The number you have dialed has been disconnected or is out of service..."

"Dammit," Rafe said.

I nodded. "I guess, when they didn't come back last night,

he figured out that something was wrong."

"Must have." He said another bad word, as he leaned his hands on the sill of the double-sided window and stared longingly at Rodney. "Wish I was in there."

"You wouldn't be able to get him to admit to something he doesn't know."

He shot me a look. "I know that. But I'd still enjoy trying."

No doubt. "It's like you said. If all Lance is doing is stringing Rodney and Kyle along, and using them to do his menial stuff, then it makes sense that he wouldn't tell them anything important."

"Maybe," Rafe admitted. Although he still looked wistfully at Rodney like he was picturing grabbing him by his scrawny neck and shaking him like the rat he was, until he coughed up the information Rafe wanted.

I patted him on the back. His muscles were tight through the soft cotton of his shirt. "You probably wouldn't be able to manhandle him anyway, you know. Not with your injuries."

"Sure I would. He prob'ly doesn't weigh one-thirty soaking wet."

He probably did—because if he didn't, it meant he weighed less than me, and I couldn't quite condone that. But it wasn't by much. While Rodney was into his twenties, he looked like a teenager, as slender as a snake, with no discernible shoulders or muscles to speak of. Without his injuries, Rafe could have squashed him like a bug in five seconds flat. And even as it was, I wouldn't bet against him.

Not that he'd get the chance. At least not today.

"I'm going to have a talk with the district attorney," Mendoza was telling Rodney. "He's back there."

He gestured with his thumb to the window. The corner of Rafe's mouth turned up.

"He'll tell me whether we've got enough evidence to arrest the three of you."

"We didn't touch her," Rodney protested. "We didn't open the freezer. We didn't even know she was there!"

"Breaking and entering," Mendoza reminded him, getting to his feet. "The intent to remove property that doesn't belong to you. It adds up." He gave Rodney a not-at-all reassuring smile. "Just sit tight."

He walked out. Rodney watched him until the door closed behind him, and then he looked at us. Or at the mirror, since he couldn't possibly see us.

The door into our room opened, and Mendoza stepped through. In the interrogation room, Rodney got tired of watching the mirror—of watching himself—and looked away. And realized that Mendoza had left Rodney's phone lying in the middle of the table.

With another look at the mirror, Rodney pulled it toward him. And dropped both hands, still cuffed, and the phone below the edge of the table and into his lap.

"Did you want him to have the phone?" I asked Mendoza.

He glanced through the window at Rodney. "I figured we might see if he uses it for anything. Just in case Lance has more than one number. I'll get it back from him before he leaves."

"You can't keep it, can you?"

He shook his head. "Just long enough to see if he called or texted anyone else. Or emailed someone. If we're letting him go, we'll have to give it to him, though. Can't keep the phone if we're not keeping him."

He looked at Rafe. Rafe looked back.

"I think he's telling the truth about not knowing about the body," I said.

Mendoza nodded. "But we can still hang on to him if we want to."

"Even if the door was open and he was just picking up the Tannerite—which isn't illegal—for a friend?"

This time, they both nodded. "The situation being what it

is," Rafe said, "yeah."

"So is that what you're going to do? Keep them and the Tannerite so Lance won't have what he needs for whatever he's planning to do tomorrow?"

They eyed one another.

"No," Rafe said. "I vote we let'em go. And see what they do."

"It's a risk," Mendoza told him.

Rafe nodded. "But if they go back to Columbia, the risk ain't gonna be in your jurisdiction."

Mendoza's face darkened. "Screw you," he said, just not as politely. "Just because something happens outside my town, doesn't mean I don't want to stop it if I can."

"We'll stop it," Rafe said. It sounded more grim than confident, so I deduced he was worried about the consequences if he didn't. "Savannah and I'll stay on'em the whole way to Columbia. Even if they notice us—and I don't think they will— they ain't good enough to lose me."

Mendoza nodded.

"Once we get there, they'll be under observation every second. If any of'em scratches his—" He glanced at me, "—butt, we'll know about it."

I rolled my eyes.

"What if they don't get in touch with Lance?"

"We'll have to hope they do," Rafe said, "'cause I don't know any other way of finding him."

"If he really is a sniper, we can identify him from military records. It'll take a while—"

"And won't tell us where he's holed up," Rafe completed the thought, "but it's always good to know who people are. And if he's local, maybe he has friends or family—other than Rodney and Kyle—he might be staying with."

"Might be worth checking motels and short term rentals in your area," Mendoza suggested.

Rafe nodded. "We don't know that he's staying in Columbia, though. He could be in Franklin, or Pulaski, or Leiper's Fork, or Damascus. Anywhere within about an hour. He could still be in Nashville."

Probably not, unless he drove like Rafe. And he might. But it made more sense that if he was planning to do something in the Columbia area tomorrow, he'd be staying down there.

"Do they allow camping in Laurel Hill?" I asked. "If he's former military, he's used to roughing it." And could probably subsist on leaves and berries for a while. Not that there were many of those yet. Too early in the year. But there was tree bark. And he could always bring in enough supplies for a day or two.

Rafe nodded. "There's a campground. And even if he's not there, there are places where he could pitch a tent and maybe not be noticed. Good idea."

I tried not to preen.

"I'll get the sheriff of Lawrence County to send a couple folks out there to look around. And maybe we can get a chopper up. From the park service or something. Take a look from the air. Might help us spot something."

He reached for his phone.

"I'll go cut them loose," Mendoza said, turning toward the door. "You better go get ready to follow."

"Where's their truck?" Rafe asked.

"Out back." Mendoza inclined his head toward the back of the building. "I had a uniform drive it to the lot yesterday. It wasn't involved in a crime, so no need to treat it with care."

"What about the Tannerite?" I wanted to know.

"Still at the house in Bellevue. For all we know, it's Ms. Vonderaa's Tannerite, and we can't let anybody take off with it. Not unless they can prove ownership."

And since it was Lance who had bought it, at least according to Rodney, and since Lance wasn't likely to be able to provide receipts, the Tannerite stayed where it was.

"So they have to go back without it."

"No reason to make it easier for them," Mendoza said, which was certainly true. He reached for the door handle. "You two—or three," he glanced at Carrie, cooing quietly in her seat, "head out. They'll be out in fifteen, twenty minutes. There are procedures."

"I know," Rafe said, catching the door on the back swing. "I've been here before. After you, darlin'."

I picked up the car seat and the baby and preceded him out the door.

Twenty

"There they are," I said thirty minutes later, as Rodney, Kyle, and Clayton came out the back door of the police station and into the enclosed parking lot. By then we had moved into an empty parking spot on the street, and were waiting to fall in behind them when they drove off.

Rafe nodded, his eyes on them as they high-fived each other and sauntered across the lot looking for Kyle's truck. "Looking pretty pleased with themselves."

They were. But then they'd just avoided getting arrested for murder, so maybe they had reason to be pleased.

"Weren't you happy whenever you got to leave a police station without being arrested?"

He shot a grin my way. "Still am, darlin'. Part of me's still waiting for somebody to say, 'Sorry, man, your luck's run out.'"

I smiled back, before looking around. "Where's Mendoza?"

The detective had offered to ride along in his own car, to make the shadowing a little easier. So far I hadn't seen him leave the building, though.

And obviously Rafe hadn't, either, because he said, "No idea. We'll pick him up on the road. Or not. He may be good enough that I don't make him."

I doubted that, and told him so. Rafe smirked. "I'm good, darlin'. But so's he. Could be we have a draw."

Whatever. "Either way, neither of you will have a problem following them, right?"

"No problem at all," Rafe said, as the sound of an engine being revved cut through the air. "Sounds like they're coming."

"Probably going to make a point by tearing out of the lot a lot faster than they should and sticking their middle fingers out the window."

Rafe chuckled. "Prob'ly. Here they come."

Here they did. Taking the turn from the lot onto the street much too fast and without looking first, and yes, whoever was on the passenger side stuck a middle finger out the window and waved it at the building as they went by. Down at the corner, they stopped for a fraction of a second, just long enough to make sure they wouldn't be flattened by oncoming traffic, before they zoomed across three lanes of traffic to the sound of irate horns, and headed east.

Rafe pulled the Cadillac away from the curb and followed, sedately.

"You're not going to lose them before they get on the highway," I asked him, "right?"

He shook his head. "The truck's pretty distinctive. Can't hide those bumper stickers. And I'm a better driver than whoever's behind the wheel."

No question. And since I trusted him, I settled into the seat and watched the world go by as we crossed the bridge over the Cumberland River and saw the interstate overpass in the distance. The blue truck was already halfway down the incline, going hell for leather toward a red light.

They had to wait twenty or thirty seconds to make the turn onto Interstate Drive, and by the time they crossed Woodland Street and powered up the on-ramp, we were three cars behind. Rafe hung back, and at the next interstate entrance, a quarter of a mile down, let a few more cars squeeze between us and the truck.

The next hour was a lesson in evasive driving. Rafe stayed so far behind the truck I was worried we'd lose sight of them—

and sometimes we did. Then he'd speed up, just enough that we'd catch sight of them again, before we fell back once more. He'd switch lanes from directly behind, to one lane right and one lane left whenever there were more than two lanes. Past Franklin, where the road narrowed, we stayed even farther back.

"Nothing to worry about," he told me. "We know where they're going."

And assuming they were on their way home, I guess we did. I was hoping that they might take us to wherever Lance was—and I'm sure Rafe harbored a secret hope in that direction too, or we wouldn't be doing this—but most likely they were just going home.

"There they go," he added, when the truck zoomed up the ramp to the Spring Hill exit, north of Columbia.

I looked around. "Have you seen Mendoza?"

I'd been watching for him, but hadn't noticed any one car sticking around the truck long enough to be noticeable.

Rafe nodded. "He's in the gray compact ahead of'em."

"Ahead?"

There was a smallish, gray car going up the ramp ahead of the truck. It was too far away for me to see clearly, but if Rafe said it was Mendoza, I'm sure it was.

"Old trick," Rafe said. "Nobody worries about being followed by the guy who's ahead of'em."

And I guess that was true. I'd been looking for Mendoza in the cars around us. It hadn't occurred to me to look for him ahead of the guys we were following.

"I guarantee you they didn't think of it, either," Rafe told me when I said so.

"So what happens now?"

"Now we switch off. On these smaller roads, it's much more likely that they'll notice us. So we'll take the first couple blocks, give Mendoza time to circle around, and then he'll take'em for a couple of blocks. We got Tammy coming, too."

So there'd be three cars playing leapfrog with the truck. Mendoza's nondescript economy car, Mother's Cadillac, or whatever Tamara Grimaldi was driving today.

It was interesting, I guess, to watch the maneuvers. We'd stay behind the truck for a couple of blocks, then turn right or left at a light or into a business, and whoever was behind us—Mendoza or Grimaldi, in Rafe's official issue Chevy—would take up the shadowing. We'd turn around, fall in behind, and then the whole thing would happen again.

In the end, though, the truck drove straight to a tired-looking ranch house on the northern end of Columbia, and into the driveway.

"Kyle's parents' house," Rafe said.

"He lives with his parents?"

Rafe nodded.

"How come he doesn't live with Rodney?"

He shook his head. "No idea. If it's important, we can ask. When we arrest'em again."

"We… I mean, you will arrest them again?"

"I imagine so." He didn't take his eyes off the driveway, where the truck's doors opened. Kyle hopped down from the driver's seat, while on the other side, Rodney jumped out and then Clayton. Rodney and Kyle met at the front of the truck, executed some kind of complicated handshake, and then they separated. Clayton's Camaro was also parked in the driveway, and he and Rodney got into that. And the chase began again, for another ten minutes, until the Camaro zipped into the parking lot of an apartment complex not too far away. Here, Rodney and Clayton executed a less complex high five, and then Clay got back in the car while Rodney jogged up the stairs to his second floor apartment.

"No Dodge Charger in this lot," I said, looking around.

Rafe shook his head, his eyes on the Camaro as it left the lot and headed south.

"What happens now?" I asked, as he moved into traffic behind it.

"Now we give Clay time to debrief anything that mighta been said on the way home, that we don't know about, while I take you home. Then I go hook up with Tammy, and see what needs doing next."

"You're supposed to be on medical leave," I asked, "aren't you?"

"Yes," Rafe answered, "but now that we know that whatever Lance is planning, is gonna go down tomorrow, there's no time for me to be on medical leave. I have to do what I can. And so do you. Your job is to keep yourself and Carrie safe and well."

Actually, my job was real estate. "I have a better idea. How about I drop you off with Grimaldi, and then I take the car and have another look at the house on Fulton, now that it's been a day?"

"Sure," Rafe said. "Let me call Tammy."

He pulled out his phone. Twenty seconds later—after a lot of Uh-huhs—he hung up and turned to me. "Turns out I gotta go down to Laurel Hill. The chopper spotted a camp they want somebody to check out."

"Are you sure you can handle a hike like that?"

"I imagine we'll be taking a ranger vehicle," Rafe said, "but I'll be careful."

Good.

"Tammy's following us. I'm just gonna pull in here—" He made a quick turn into a fast food parking lot and pulled into an empty parking space. "All yours."

I walked around the car to the door he held open for me, and then raised my face for a kiss. "I'll see you later. Be careful out there."

"Always," Rafe said, and got into the Chevy next to

Grimaldi. She waved at me through the window, and then they took off around the building. I got back into the car, on the driver's side this time, and turned to look at Carrie. "Just you and me again, baby. Let's take a look at the house, and then we'll go home and get some food."

She gurgled, almost like she could understand me, and then we headed out of the lot in the opposite direction of Rafe and Grimaldi.

This was the first time since the Tannerite incident that I'd seen the house on Fulton, and I'll admit I sat in the driveway for several minutes just staring at it. It hadn't looked this bad in the dark the other night. In the bright light of day, I could certainly understand Darcy's demeanor on the phone yesterday, after she'd looked at it again with the contractor.

It looked like something out of a war zone, or maybe the victim of a tornado or other natural catastrophe.

There was yellow caution tape strung across the gaping hole in the front wall, and the lawn was littered with pieces of wood and shingle. Someone should get out here and clean that up, and it might have to be me. Not now, though. I'd have to change into gardening clothes and bring a pair of sturdy gloves, since some of those pieces of wood would give me splinters and probably had nails sticking out of them.

I opened the door and swung my legs out. And walked around the car to grab Carrie's seat before I made my way over to the front door—or where the front door would have been, had it not been in pieces all over the lawn.

The stoop was concrete, and hadn't gone anywhere. I stepped up on it and stuck my head past the yellow tape, into the interior of the house.

A good chunk of the floor was gone, and dank air wafted up from what used to be the crawlspace. When I looked down, I could see bare dirt.

The living room didn't look great, either. The front two rooms, the living room and the bedroom on the other side of the wall, would need total renovation. Studs, drywall, floor joists, sub-floor particle board, and hardwoods for the floor, not to mention windows and a new roof. Plus a new front door and a porch covering the front door. Siding, to replace what had been blown off by the blast. And paint inside and out, to make it all look pretty again once it was finished. Everything needed doing, basically.

I made a mental note of how much money and time I thought it would take—a lot, and a lot—and looked beyond it.

The opening between the dining room and kitchen looked all right, and so did everything beyond. On this side of the opening, there was still the evidence of the vandalism, of course, but the explosion didn't seem to have made anything worse. Not on the back end of the house.

I twisted as far as I could, and managed to place Carrie's car seat on the part of the floor that was still intact, five feet beyond the door. Then I wiggled my way onto it, after making sure it was sturdy enough to hold my weight. One of the sharp edges stabbed me in the hand, and I uttered the kind of word Mother would have been shocked to hear fall from my lips. A bead of blood appeared in the middle of my hand, and I reached for my purse and the tissues I keep in there.

But the purse was on the passenger seat of the car—I had left it there when I switched places with Rafe in the Hardee's parking lot. I left Carrie where she was, cooing on the ruined floor, and stalked into the kitchen, where I turned on the cold water and stuck my hand under the spray while I reached for a paper towel with my other hand.

Only to freeze when I heard a movement from the back of the house, down the hall in the direction of the master bedroom.

I turned the water off again, carefully, and wrapped the paper towel around my hand. "Hello?"

The cut was still bleeding, and the paper soaked through with water immediately, but I didn't stop to grab another. "Anyone there?"

No one answered. But the silence had a sort of listening quality. This house didn't feel empty, not the way Jennifer Vonderaa's house had felt yesterday morning.

I took a quiet step toward the dining room. And then another. And then I scrambled through the cased opening and across what was left of the floor toward the big, gaping hole in the house. Somehow—and I can't tell you how—I made it through the gap between where the floor ended and the stoop began, and I did it while snagging the car seat with the baby and taking it with me. And then I hurtled toward the car and around to the back door, where I shoved Carrie's seat onto the base and waited for the click that signaled she was secure.

By then, she was wailing, of course. She'd been swung around like a rag doll inside her carrier, and she was probably getting hungry anyway.

Instead of moving around the car to the driver's seat, I opened the front passenger door and went in head first, scrambling across the seat and the console—and my shoulder bag—until I could scoot myself under the steering wheel. And the first thing I did was lock all the doors before I dug in my pocket for the car key. It took a couple of tries, because my hands were shaking, before I got it into the ignition. But once it was there, and the engine came to life with a roar, Rafe couldn't have done a better job of reversing out of the driveway on squealing tires, and taking up off the street.

As soon as we were going straight, my hand fumbled through the debris of the purse for my phone, and like two nights ago, I had to ask for Siri's help when it came to dialing the number. Five seconds later, I heard my husband's voice.

"Savannah?"

"You gotta come back," I told him, my teeth knocking

together. "There's somebody in the house."

"On Fulton?"

"Uh-huh." I nodded while I glanced in the rearview mirror. Nobody was following us, and I had no idea how anyone could, since there hadn't been a car in the driveway for anyone to use. That didn't stop me from looking. "What if it's Lance? What if he decided that since the house is empty, he'd camp out there for a while? He'd know that, if he was part of blowing a hole in it two nights ago!"

"Calm down, Savannah," Rafe's voice said in my ear, even as the much less calm sound of squealing brakes came through the phone. "We're on our way."

"So am I. I'm not going back there."

"No, don't." He said something to Grimaldi, something I couldn't hear, before he came back on. "Go home, darlin'. Or go to Beulah's if it'll make you feel better. Somewhere with more people. We'll be at the house in ten minutes."

"He'll be gone by then," I said, calming down enough to think and not just run. "Won't he?"

"If he knows what's good for him, yeah."

After a second he added, a little less grimly, "Did you see him?"

I said I hadn't. "Just heard a noise in the back of the house. I called out, and I got that feeling, you know, like someone was standing there listening. But I didn't go any closer, so I didn't actually see anyone."

"Good," Rafe said. And added, "That you didn't go any closer. If it was him, and he killed his girlfriend, he'd have killed you too."

I already knew that, thank you very much for pointing it out.

"But if he knows you spotted him," Rafe added, "or at least that you heard him, then yeah, he'll get outta there. Prob'ly gone already."

"Then I'm going back," I said, now that the panic had subsided and I was far enough away to feel safe. "I'll wait for you outside."

"Don't you think you oughta go home instead?"

"No. I want to see if he was there."

"If he was there, he ain't gonna be there anymore, darlin'," Rafe told me, "but turn back by all means. Just don't get outta the car."

I promised him I wouldn't, and then I found somewhere to turn the car around, all the while promising Carrie that once this last errand was over, we'd go home and she could eat and take a nap.

Everything looked quiet when I made my way back down Fulton Street. Of course, it had looked quiet when I got there originally, too. I pulled to the curb and left the engine running, but I stayed in the car, watching the house and waiting for Rafe and Grimaldi to show up.

It was only three or four minutes before I saw them come around the corner on two wheels, but it felt longer. Any second, I expected the muzzle of a rifle to peek through the broken window in the front bedroom and blow me to kingdom come.

Or not really, although the thought crossed my mind that it might happen. So I was keeping an extra-close eye on the windows and broken parts of the house, so no one could stage an assault from there. Even though I was almost sure that Rafe was right and that Lance, if had been him, was long gone.

The Chevy came to a stop halfway in the driveway and halfway out. Grimaldi and Rafe burst out of the doors, both of them with guns at the ready. Rafe didn't even spare me a glance before he sprinted up to the hole in the wall and bounded from there into the living room without breaking stride. Grimaldi, meanwhile, legged it around the corner, long legs pumping.

I rolled down the window, the better to hear anything that

might happen—like gunshots, or orders to drop the gun and get down on the ground. But nothing happened. Two minutes later—another eternity—Rafe came back out the front and Grimaldi came around from the back, and both of their guns were back in the holsters.

I opened my door and got out, and met them in the middle of the lawn.

"Nobody there," Rafe told me, not even winded.

I opened my mouth to say that someone certainly had been there, but before I could, he added, "Water droplets in the sink and stains on the toilet bowl in the master bath."

My face twisted. "He can't shoot straight?"

"I guess he just didn't bother to lift the seat."

"Pig."

He shrugged. "Good for us."

"How so?"

"DNA," Grimaldi said.

Well, yes. There was that. But— "That takes weeks, doesn't it? Or months, even. That won't help us find him by tomorrow."

"No," Rafe admitted. "But when we do find him, and if we take him alive, it'll help prove he killed Jennifer Vonderaa."

I supposed that was something of a silver lining. Although I'd rather catch him today and stop whatever he was planning to do tomorrow.

"Maybe I should have confronted him. Maybe I could have done something to keep him here—"

"No," Rafe said. "You did just what you were supposed to do. You don't put yourself and Carrie in danger to catch the bad guys."

"But if I had—"

Grimaldi shook her head. "This isn't a guy you want to mess with, Savannah. He snapped Jennifer Vonderaa's neck with no problem. He could do the same to you, just as easily. Or shoot you. Or do something else to you. Your husband's right. You did what you were supposed to do. You got out of there and called us."

I made a face, but didn't argue further. They had a point. I obviously don't have what it takes to tackle the bad guy, neither when it comes to training nor fortitude. I'd run away from him; they'd arrived and run toward.

"What happens now?"

"I'll send somebody out to grab the DNA," Grimaldi said. "There might be fingerprints, too. That could help. And he left a couple of things sitting around, that he didn't take the time to grab when he had to clear out quickly. Some empty fast food wrappers and a couple of other small things. I'll have someone go over the place."

"I don't figure we need to go to Laurel Hill now," Rafe added. "The camp won't be his. Not if he was in Nashville until two days ago, and he's been here since. Lawrence County can handle the camp."

Grimaldi nodded. "You two go on home together. You—" She gave Rafe a look, "should be resting."

"By now, I'm sure this guy has figured out that Rafe isn't dying," I said. "He must have recognized me. And if I'm here, and not in the hospital with my dying husband, Rafe must be OK."

Grimaldi nodded. "He could still use some rest. There's nothing anybody can do right now that isn't being done. Lance is gone again. We have people watching Rodney and Kyle. If they go anywhere, they'll be followed. I'll take care of this crime scene. Lawrence County will handle the tent. Unless something else comes up, we can do without you for a couple hours."

Rafe looked like he wanted to argue, but he also looked like he was in some pain. He'd bounded out of the car and into the house like nothing was bothering him, but I hadn't missed the wince and the hand he'd held against his ribs for a second as he came back out.

"Come on, Rafe," I told him. "Come home with me and make sure the mansion is safe. He probably won't go there, but it's not like it hasn't happened before, and I'd hate to walk in and find him hanging out in the parlor, now that Pearl isn't around to protect the place."

Rafe nodded. A little grudgingly, but he did it. "You'll let me know if something happens, right?"

"Of course," Grimaldi said. "Anything breaks, you'll be the first to know."

I tugged on his hand. "Come on. You can drive, if you want."

"I do want." He turned to the car and then back to Grimaldi. "You staying?"

"Until the crime scene techs get here. Just in case this guy's waiting around, and decides to come back for the rest of his stuff once we're gone."

"Want me to stay with you?"

"No," Grimaldi said. "I've got a gun and a badge, and I don't think he's going to take a shot at me in broad daylight. Go on home and get some rest." She went to sit in the Chevy while Rafe and I got into the Cadillac and, once again, headed for Sweetwater.

Twenty-One

I changed Carrie, and fed her. And then I left her with Rafe, both of them stretched out on the sofa, and went to the kitchen to put something together for lunch. Five minutes later, when I came back in with a tray, they were both asleep. Rafe had a big hand on Carrie's back, keeping her snug against his chest, and she was dead to the world, her little pink pacifier working and her lashes—both of their lashes, if it came to that—sooty against golden skin.

I covered them both with a blanket, and then I sat down on the other end of the sofa and ate my lunch. I didn't want to go too far, just in case Rafe moved and I had to keep Carrie from falling.

That didn't happen, though. They both stayed asleep for the next hour and a half. And Carrie woke first. As soon as she started twitching, Rafe's eyes popped open. He blinked a couple of times, and looked adorably shocked to realize that he'd been sleeping on the sofa. The smile he gave me was more than a little sheepish. "Morning."

"Afternoon," I told him. "Getting close to three."

"Man." He stretched, as best he could without dislodging Carrie. She was making noises now, and I moved to take her away from him so he could sit up. "I was out."

"Like a light," I confirmed. "I went ahead and ate. Are you hungry?"

"I could eat." He sat up—not without a grimace as his ribs

protested—and twisted his head this way and that. "Getting old."

"Not noticeably." I gave him Carrie back. "Hang on to her for another couple of minutes. I'll take her upstairs and change her when I've brought your food."

"No problem." He leaned back, carefully, hanging on to the baby. I got up and went to the kitchen to reheat the tomato soup and make another grilled cheese sandwich, since the first one had gotten soggy.

That done, and delivered, I took Carrie from him, and dealt with her. By the time I got back downstairs, he had polished off the soup and sandwich, and was trying—very carefully—to stretch out some of the stiffness, not all of which was from sleeping on the couch. "Any news?"

"If you're wondering if your phone rang," I answered, "the answer's no."

"Nothing new, then." He reached for it anyway. "I'm gonna check in."

"Knock yourself out." I put Carrie on the floor to give her some tummy time on the rug. Any day now, she'd be turning over and pushing up, and after that, it was full speed ahead toward college.

Rafe took the phone and wandered off down the hall, probably in search of a bathroom.

"Anything?" I asked him when he wandered back in a few minutes later, phone in hand.

He shook his head. "Tammy waited for the CSI techs and got them working. Then she met up with Mendoza before he turned around and went back to Nashville. He still has a murder and a crime scene to deal with in that jurisdiction."

Of course he did.

"Kyle Scoggins is still hanging out at his parents' house. Rodney Clark is still hanging out in his apartment. Clay's in his apartment, waiting to hear from Rodney."

"Did he report in?"

He nodded. "That's the report. He's waiting to hear from Rodney. Apparently Rodney has no other way of getting in touch with Lance than the phone number that's disconnected. So Rodney's waiting for Lance to get in touch with him, and then he'll get in touch with Clay and Kyle. That's how they left it."

"So we're waiting."

"Pretty much," Rafe said, with barely concealed impatience. He's not good at waiting.

"Sit down." I nodded to the sofa. "Let's talk about this. See if we can come up with anything."

He looked reluctant, but he sat.

"So Lance—for lack of another name—killed Jennifer on, probably, Tuesday night, and came down here. Without the Tannerite. Maybe—we think—because he didn't have room for it in the car."

Rafe nodded.

"There might have been more, and he loaded up as much as he could, but he still had to leave what you found yesterday."

Rafe nodded. "Or what was in the garage was all there was, and he didn't take any of it. No way to know."

"Then, Thursday night, Lance told Rodney to go get the Tannerite in Nashville. Probably because he didn't want to risk being caught there himself, with the dead body."

Rafe nodded.

"But when Rodney and Kyle and Clay didn't come back with the Tannerite, he figured something was wrong, and disconnected his phone."

Rafe nodded.

"He hasn't been to Kyle's parents' house or Rodney's apartment, since they've been under surveillance. We think he might have spent the past couple of days at the house on Fulton. Or at least he was there today. So he's sticking close to

Columbia. Which tallies with what Clayton said. Something's happening tomorrow, and it's happening here."

Rafe nodded.

"Will he still go ahead, even if he doesn't have all the explosive?"

"Depends on what it is he's trying to do," Rafe said. "If the explosive he has is enough to do what he wants to do, then yeah. He'll go ahead. He's still here. That sounds like he's planning to go ahead."

"Will he try to get his hands on more Tannerite?"

"He might." Rafe reached for his phone. "I should make sure somebody sent a notice to all the outlets within an hour's drive or so."

Grimaldi would have already done that, if I knew her. Or Bob. It didn't come as a surprise when Rafe lifted his eyes from the screen and told me, "Already done."

"So we can hope Lance will be stupid and will get caught trying to buy more. Although I doubt he's that stupid."

"Me, too," Rafe agreed. "But it won't do no harm to hope."

No, it wouldn't.

"Do you have any idea what he's planning to blow up?"

He shook his head. "We don't even know for sure that the Tannerite is part of whatever's happening tomorrow. The Tannerite might just be for target practice. It's a helluva lot of Tannerite to practice with, but maybe he got a good deal on it. Or maybe the target practice was for something else, and that's what's happening tomorrow."

"A mass shooting?"

He shrugged. Not because a mass shooting isn't a big deal, because of course it is, but because he didn't know the answer.

"Where would you go if you wanted to shoot a bunch of people and you wanted attention? That's what these people are after, right?"

Rafe nodded. "It's usually a church, or a school. Maybe a

concert or outdoor festival."

"If Alexandra is out for spring break this week," I said, "Maury County schools might be, too. So there might not be any school tomorrow."

It would be nice not to have to worry about that, at least, so I pulled out my phone to look it up while I kept talking. "Mule Days won't take place for another month, or that might be a possibility. Lots of people here for Mule Days. But not until April." And Southern Baptists don't congregate on Fridays. "Are there any concerts going on tomorrow?"

"Not sure," Rafe said, also using his phone to look things up, "but I'm trying to find out. The crowd ain't likely to be big enough to interest a mass shooter, though. Not here. And not when he could drive an hour up to Nashville and find a lot more targets."

"So it's something he can't find there. Something specific to here. Something at the courthouse? A trial? Or hearing? Some guy who thinks he got a raw deal? Or someone Lance thinks got a raw deal?"

Rafe contemplated me—and the idea—for a second before he went from research to dialing. I listened with half an ear while I kept scrolling. "Todd Satterfield," Rafe said into the phone, and added a belated, "please."

My eyebrows rose, but I didn't comment.

"Satterfield? Collier. Is there anything going on at the courthouse tomorrow that might interest a shooter?"

That was straight to the point, anyway. And interesting that he'd call my ex-boyfriend for the information. Although it was going straight to the source, since Todd is an assistant DA and would have that info at his fingertips.

"No school this week," I informed him while he waited for Todd to respond. "So at least we don't have to worry about anyone opening fire into a crowd of students."

He nodded, and then turned his attention back to the phone

when Todd came back on. After about half a minute, he said, "Appreciate it."

Todd said something else, and Rafe told him, "I don't think so. Don't sound like anything that would interest this guy. But talk to your dad about it. He knows what's going on."

He hung up.

"Nothing going on at the courthouse?" I said.

He shook his head. "Nothing that sounds like it'd be related. And you said school's closed?"

"For spring break. So we don't have to worry about anything happening there." And it was a relief. Nobody likes to contemplate children in harm's way. "Any concerts?"

"Nothing I could find." He leaned back, with a sound that could have been frustration, or pain, or both. "For all we know, he's going after a private event. A family reunion. Or a wedding. Maybe his girlfriend dumped him for a black guy, and now they're getting married, and he's planning to shoot up the wedding. It could be as simple as that."

And as hard to pin down. "I'll call Aunt Regina," I said. My father's sister, she writes the society column for the *Sweetwater Reporter*. "She might have some idea if anything like that is going on. At least in Sweetwater, but maybe in Columbia, too."

He nodded. "There's just no way to police everything."

I shook my head, in the process of dialing. There wasn't. We could blanket a church on one side of town with SWAT and police, and all along, Lance could be across town targeting a McDonalds or a meeting of the Daughters of the Confederacy. And there wasn't enough manpower to target everything at the same time.

Aunt Regina picked up, and I told her what I needed and why. She said she'd get back to me, and I hung up. "Can you think of anything else?"

He shook his head.

I contemplated him for a minute, and then I told him, as

cheerfully as I could, "Tell you what. If you've rested and you feel OK, why don't we give Carrie a few more minutes on the floor, and then we load up the car and go visit your grandmother and Audrey? I'm sure Mrs. J heard that you got shot, and although everyone must have told her you're OK, I'm sure she'd appreciate seeing you for herself."

That did it. He nodded. "Gimme a couple minutes. I think I need a shower to wake up."

"No problem," I told him. "We have all night."

Audrey lives in a little Victorian cottage behind a white picket fence near the Albertsons and Sheriff Satterfield, in the old part of Sweetwater near the square.

The mansion is older, of course, and at one time, everything around it was fields. But the town grew up in the years after the war—that'd be the War Against Northern Aggression for you Yankees—and consists of a lot of Victorian and turn-of-the-(last)-century houses, and the ubiquitous Craftsman Bungalows and cottages that cropped up after WWI. You can see the progression of the architectural styles from the late Victorian town square, radiating through the war years, through the mid-century ranches and out to the more recent subdivisions of McMansions, where Dix and Catherine live with their families.

But Audrey lives in town, and now, so does Mrs. Jenkins.

When we knocked on the door, it was Darcy who answered.

"Oh." I blinked at her. "I didn't expect to see you."

"I've been grocery shopping," Darcy said.

"Audrey isn't sick, is she?" I peered over her shoulder into the interior of the house.

She shook her head. "Just Aunt Tondalia. And it isn't bad. I don't think you ought to bring the baby in, though. Just to be safe."

Maybe not. "Maybe we'll just stay outside," I told Rafe. "You go in and see your grandmother."

He glanced at Carrie and nodded. "I won't be long."

"Take your time," I told him. "The weather's nice. We'll just wait here."

I pulled Darcy outside with me, while Rafe went inside and shut the door.

"What's going on?" my sister asked.

"Nothing. I went to the house on Fulton earlier. Someone was inside, but I chased him off."

"Who?"

"I didn't see him. We're thinking maybe it's the guy who blew it up. Or who gave Rodney and Kyle the explosive to blow it up."

"You live an interesting life, Savannah," Darcy said.

I guess I did. "It isn't boring, anyway."

"No offense," Darcy said, "but I think I'd prefer things to be a bit more boring myself."

There was something to be said for that. However, she was dating a cop, so her life wasn't likely to be much calmer than mine. Although Patrick Nolan didn't seem inclined to take quite as many chances as Rafe, so maybe not.

"How's Nolan?"

"Getting off work soon," Darcy said. "We're going to grab some dinner."

"Nice that he's not working late again."

I'd never had that. Rafe's schedule was always erratic. A year ago, when he came off undercover work and started working for the TBI as an instructor, his schedule was supposed to become normal—pipe and slippers at the door at five o'clock, or so we'd joked—but that hadn't panned out. He'd mostly come home every night, so that was an improvement over the times when he hadn't, but it still wasn't a nine-to-five job. At this point, I didn't think it ever would be. He just wasn't wired that way.

"He's going back in the morning," Darcy said, about Nolan.

"But he has the weekend off. We're thinking about driving down to Alabama tomorrow night, to where my parents are buried. It's been a while since I was there."

Her adoptive parents, she was talking about. She'd grown up in Mobile, then moved to Birmingham after she got married, and then to Columbia, and to work at Martin and McCall, after getting divorced.

"That'll be nice," I said. "To show him where you grew up."

"I hope so," Darcy answered. "You don't need me for anything, do you?"

I said I didn't. "Go have some fun. We'll talk about the house on Fulton after you get back. Although the little bit I saw of it yesterday," before I hightailed it out of there, "didn't look like it would be impossible to fix."

Darcy made a non-committal sort of noise. "Will you stay in touch with my mother and Aunt Tondalia? We'll be back Sunday night, but until then?"

"Of course," I said. "I'm sure Mother's staying in touch with Audrey, too. But we'll take care of them."

"I'm going to go home and get ready for Patrick. I'll let you know when we're leaving. If we do."

I wished her a good trip and watched her walk through the yard to the street and get into her blue Honda and drive away. And then I waited until Rafe came out, and took my husband to dinner at the Wayside Inn since I didn't feel like cooking again.

The phone rang at ten minutes after four, and startled me out of sleep. It took me a second to realize what it was—that for the second night in a row, we'd been woken up in the middle of the night, and not by the baby wanting food—and then I groaned and buried my face in the pillow.

Rafe, meanwhile, reached over and picked it up. "Yeah?"

I listened to the faint quacking on the other end of the line for a few seconds before— "I'm on my way."

Unlike last night, nobody told him not to bother. It must be serious.

"What's going on?" I sat up in bed.

He stepped into the pair of jeans he'd left on the floor when he took me to bed earlier, and kept talking while he pulled them up over naked skin. "The cop keeping Rodney Clark under surveillance is dead."

I blinked. "How?"

"Double pop to the head," Rafe said grimly, tucking himself away before pulling up the zipper. He bent to grab the shirt he'd had on from the floor, and got halfway before he stopped, drawing in a sharp breath.

"I'll get it." I slid out of bed and bent to grab the shirt.

"Any other time, darlin', that woulda kept me here."

Naturally. I was naked.

I shook out the shirt and held it out for him. "What happened?"

"Dunno yet." He shoved his arms through the sleeves and stepped away to do up the buttons. "Thanks."

"No problem." I snagged the comforter from the bed and wrapped it around me. "What do you know?"

"Not much more than you do. Felicia Robinson's dead—"

The world tilted for a second, and I held up a hand. "Wait. Did you say Felicia Robinson?"

He nodded. "Afraid so."

"Oh, God."

He headed toward the door, and I added, "Wait for me."

"Darlin'…"

"Don't you darling me," I grabbed a pair of panties and began to drag them on. "She called me yesterday, wanting to know how you were. I told her you were at death's door, because that's what I was supposed to tell anyone who asked. She probably begged Grimaldi to give her this job, so she could do something to catch the guys who shot you. And instead she was the one who got shot!"

His face changed. "Darlin'…"

"No. Don't you dare leave me, Rafe. I have to go with you."

I grabbed a dress out of the closet at random and pulled it over my head. Easier than putting on both pants and a shirt. And then realized I'd need a bra. Under normal circumstances, maybe I wouldn't take the time—not in this situation—but with Carrie nursing, there was no way I could risk going without. "Wait for me!"

"I'll get the car," Rafe said.

"No! Don't you do that, either. You were shot outside this house two nights ago." And now someone had shot Felicia, at least if I understood the double pop reference right. "You're not going out there alone again."

He sighed. "So what do you want me to do, darlin'?"

"I want you to wait," I said, shoving my feet into shoes. "I want you to give me a damn—darn—damn minute to pick Carrie up and get her into her car seat without waking her. I want to go with you, and I want you to let me!"

"I'll be downstairs."

He headed out. I heard his boots going down the stairs as I hurried across the hall into Carrie's room and grabbed her, as gently as I could, to try to get her up out of her bed and into the car seat while not waking her before she'd wake up on her own.

Twenty-Two

The parking lot in Rodney's apartment complex was a zoo. Law enforcement everywhere, stringing crime scene tape and peering at the ground. Someone—probably Grimaldi—had brought in two big lights on wheels, so the lot was as brightly lit as if it were high noon. Something—either the lights or the activity—had woken the neighbors, many of whom were leaning over the railings. About half of them were in pajamas, while the other half were fully dressed.

Grimaldi stood, hands on hips, in the middle of the activity, keeping an eye on all the moving parts. Rafe pulled one of the strings of yellow tape up high enough that I could scoot myself and Carrie underneath, and we walked up to her.

She looked at me, and Carrie, and then at him. "Really?"

"It's not his fault," I said. "I spoke to Felicia yesterday morning. She couldn't stand me, but she thought enough of Rafe to want to make sure he was all right. When I told her he wasn't—because that's what we agreed that I was going to tell anyone who asked—she was upset. I was the one who told her Rodney and Kyle were suspects. I told her to talk to you about getting involved."

And now she was dead. And it was hard not to feel guilty.

"This was a girl you told me was coming on to your husband," Grimaldi reminded me.

"Yes, but I didn't want her dead. I wasn't even worried about it. It was just annoying to watch."

"Well, now you won't have to anymore," Grimaldi told me, rather cold-bloodedly, before she turned to Rafe. "What it looks like, is she was sitting over there." She pointed to a small, red economy car over in the corner of the lot. It was surrounded by cops and crime scene techs, and on one side, the big lights reflected on shattered glass strewn across the ground.

"We figure he walked up from the side, so she wouldn't notice him in the rearview mirror. Or maybe she noticed and just didn't think anything of it. Hell, maybe she was asleep."

"She wouldn't be asleep," I said. "She thought too much of Rafe for that."

They both gave me a look. Grimaldi's was fulminating. I deduced she was probably dealing with some guilt of her own, and the look was less about me and more about that. She was the one who had assigned this job to Felicia. She probably felt worse than I did.

"He put a pistol to the window," she continued after a moment, "and pulled the trigger. She died instantly. If she were asleep, she wouldn't even know it was coming, so you'll excuse me if I'm hoping for that."

I nodded. I could excuse that. Now I was hoping for it, too.

"At that point, he went upstairs and knocked on Rodney's door. Rodney came out, and they got in Rodney's car and left."

"Did someone see that?"

"Tenant in 203." She gestured to a middle-aged lady in checkered pants and a T-shirt who was talking to a uniformed police officer. "She's got a job that gets her up early, so she heard the shot, but thought it was a backfire. Then she heard footsteps outside the door, and running down the stairs, and got to the window in time to see Rodney and someone else run out of the lot and down the street to the Charger. She could see it from her window. Felicia wouldn't have been able to from where she was sitting."

So to recap, which I did in the silence of my own mind:

Lance had driven here in Rodney's car and parked on the street. It was before four ^AM^, so not a lot of traffic. He shot Felicia, who didn't notice him coming, maybe because she was asleep. Then he went upstairs, got Rodney out of bed, and the two of them left, again in the Charger.

"Nobody knows where they went from here," Grimaldi said. "We're pulling footage from the traffic cameras in the area, but it's going to take time."

"Kyle…" I began. God, was there a dead cop outside the Scoggins's house, too?

Grimaldi shook her head. "Nothing happened there. I've talked to the officer on duty. He's fine, and so is everyone else."

"Are you sure Kyle's inside his house?"

"The officer knocked on the door," Grimaldi said, "and woke them up. They weren't happy. But he's there. And hasn't heard from Rodney or Lance. Or so he says. At this point, the officer's in the living room with them instead of outside."

"Clay?" Rafe asked. His voice was even, but I could feel the tension radiating from him.

"Sitting tight. The officer on duty outside his place is fine. I've spoken to him."

Rafe nodded, and some of his tension dissipated. Some of mine did, too. Clayton was safe. Lance and Rodney hadn't figured out who he was and what he was doing, and gone to kill him. Or killed the person watching him, for that matter.

"You have someone watching Clayton?"

"If we put surveillance on Rodney and Kyle and not Clayton," Grimaldi said, "that'd be a dead giveaway that we know he isn't really involved, don't you think?"

Yes, of course. "Why didn't you give Felicia that job?" Something safe and simple, that wouldn't have put her in the crosshairs of this nutcase.

"Then somebody else woulda been dead," Rafe told me.

And of course he was right. Although it wouldn't have been

someone I felt somewhat responsible for.

Although whether it was Felicia or someone else didn't really matter. Not in the scheme of things.

I drew in a breath and let it out while I tried to let that knowledge settle over me. Felicia was dead, and there was nothing I could do. Other than put the blame squarely where it belonged: on the guy who had shot her. "What happens now?"

"Now I have to go notify her mother," Grimaldi said.

"Can't you let her wake up first?"

At the same time, Rafe said, "I'll go with you."

Grimaldi nodded. And turned to me. "By the time we get over there, it'll be pretty close to morning, anyway."

"But she's going to be waking up every morning for the rest of her life knowing that her daughter's dead." I glanced down at Carrie, still snoozing in the carrier. "Can't you let her have this last one before she knows?"

It was Rafe who answered, with a hand at the small of my back. "There are rules, darlin'. You don't drag out the time before notification. People have a right to know as soon as possible. And she mighta heard that someone's gone down. She might already be awake and worried."

I guess. Although if it were my daughter, I wouldn't want to know at all. But of course that was impossible, too. "Can I come?"

"Not to talk to her," Grimaldi said. "This is one of the hardest things that woman will ever have to deal with. She doesn't need an audience while we tell her that her daughter's gone and her world's never going to be the same."

Of course. "I'll stay in the car. I just don't want to go back home by myself." It was better to keep moving than sitting still and having to think.

Rafe gave me a nudge. "Text me the address," he told Grimaldi. "We'll meet you there."

She nodded. We headed back under the crime scene tape

and back to the Cadillac.

Felicia's mother lived in half a duplex a block or two away from Kyle Scoggins's house, and not too far from the house on Fulton. It was still dark when we got there, and the house was dark, too. Both sides of it.

Rafe pulled up to the curb on the other side of the street and looked at it. He didn't say anything, but I could feel him bracing himself.

I put a hand on his leg, and he looked at me like he'd forgotten I was there. For a second, he probably had. "Sorry, darlin'."

"There's nothing to be sorry for," I said. And changed it to, "You haven't done anything to be sorry for. You were nothing but nice to Felicia—probably made that girl's weekend last week—and I don't think anybody foresaw that this would happen."

He shook his head. "There was no reason for it. Somebody had to sit outside of Rodney's place, and she got the short straw. But it was simple surveillance. No reason to think something like this would happen."

Grimaldi's official SUV came to a stop behind us, and he twitched his hand out of mine. "Sit tight, darlin'. We'll be back."

"Good luck," I told him. "I love you."

He nodded. And opened the door and got out. Behind us, Grimaldi did the same, and the two of them crossed the street together. I watched as they knocked on the door, and knocked again, and then I watched as the door was opened a crack—probably with the chain on. Then the door opened wide, and a middle-aged black woman in a fuzzy, blue bathrobe stood there, her hair sticking out every which way. I still watched as her knees buckled, and in slow motion she started to crumple to the floor. Her keening cry was shrill enough that I could hear it through the closed windows.

Rafe caught her before she fell, and—like she weighed nothing—lifted her in his arms. Grimaldi shut the door behind them, and that's when I leaned my head back against the seat and started to cry, too.

Rafe came out ten minutes later, and crossed to the car. "Tammy's gonna stay with her until her sister can get here," he told me as he slid behind the wheel.

I nodded, but before I could say anything, he shut the door, leaned his elbows on the steering wheel, and put his face in his hands. "Fuck," he said, his voice muffled.

Or at least that's what I thought he said. And since there was nothing I could say in response to that, I just put my hand on his back and ran it in circles.

It seemed to do the trick, because after a minute, he straightened. "Sorry."

I shook my head. "Don't be. I'm sure that wasn't fun."

"Not even a little bit." He turned the key in the ignition. "Hardest part of the job, having to tell some woman that her little girl ain't never coming back."

He pulled the car away from the curb and added, "Or her little boy or her husband or his wife or whoever."

"I'm sure." We sat in silence for a few minutes, while he navigated away from the duplex and toward one of the main roads through Columbia. "Where are we going?"

"Home, I guess. Or we could stop at Yvonne's for something."

Beulah's Meat'n Three, I assumed, and not Yvonne's house in Damascus. Damascus was in the other direction. But Beulah's opened early, so the staff was probably already there.

I probed inward. "I could eat."

In fact, something to fill that hollow sensation in my stomach would be nice. Not that I thought food would really do it. But it might make me feel better for the few minutes before I realized it wasn't going to work.

Neither of us spoke as he mingled with the early morning traffic flowing into Columbia, and then back out the other side, where it was much less crowded on the road going out of town.

I'm sure he kept an eye out for Rodney's Charger as he navigated traffic. I did, too. "Do you think they left town?"

I didn't have to specify who I meant. "Could've," Rafe said.

"Maybe we don't have to worry about whatever was supposed to happen today." That would be nice.

Rafe grunted. It sounded like dissent.

"They're involved in two murders now," I pointed out. "And they have to know we're looking for them. The safest thing they can do is leave."

"Not sure they're worried about being safe," Rafe said, which was probably true.

When we reached Beulah's, the *OPEN* sign was blinking on and off in the window. The sun was starting to rise over the treetops behind the small, cinderblock building, outlining the budding branches in vivid orange, and the parking lot had a half dozen cars in it. None of them was Rodney's Dodge Charger.

Rafe shook his head. "I don't think we have to worry about'em being here."

Not after last time he'd thrown them out.

It was too early for Yvonne herself, too, but Maureen waved at us from a few tables away. "Sit anywhere you like. I'll be with you in a minute."

We grabbed a booth by the window, and since Carrie was starting to stir, and it was getting close to her usual start-time anyway, I took her into the ladies room and changed her diaper. By the time I got out, Rafe had already ordered himself a cup of coffee and me a cup of tea, and was scanning the menu, trying to decide what he wanted.

"You need energy," I told him. "It's going to be a long day."

"You got that right." He closed the menu, and Maureen materialized next to him. "You ready, hon?"

He nodded. "I'll take three eggs over well, with home fries, sausage, and wheat toast. You, darlin'?"

"Griddle cakes," I said. "No butter and light on the syrup."

The corner of Mo's mouth quirked, but she nodded.

"What's the point of having pancakes if you don't want the butter and syrup?" my husband wanted to know.

"It's not that I don't want them. Just that they'll go right to my hips." And then Mother would lecture me about maintaining my figure, so my husband wouldn't go somewhere else for his jollies.

"Your hips are fine," he told me. To Mo, he added, "Give her butter and syrup. Whipped cream, too, if you got it. And throw in some chocolate sprinkles."

Mo grinned. "Yessir."

She sashayed away, beehive swaying, snapping her gum.

"I'm going to get fat," I told Rafe.

"You're nursing. You gotta keep your calorie intake up."

Well… maybe. "Thank you."

He grinned. It didn't have its usual potency, but I gave him points for trying. "No problem. More to hold on to."

"Don't let Mother hear you say that," I told him, but I didn't quibble anymore about the food. If he wanted more to hold on to, I could certainly oblige. And if feeding me, and arguing with me about the food I ate, made him feel better about this morning, I was happy to oblige with that too.

Especially if I got pancakes out of it.

The pancakes were great, whipped cream, sprinkles, and all, and although I didn't have much appetite—and all I had to do was think about Felicia Robinson to lose what little appetite I had—I managed to make a respectable dent in them. Rafe polished off eggs and sausage and toast and home fries like nothing was wrong, but then he had a lot of muscle to maintain, not to mention a full day ahead of him. I didn't make the mistake of thinking his appetite had anything to do with his mental state.

"What happens now?" I asked him, when Mo had dropped the check on the table, and we were gathering our things—including Carrie—to go up to the front and pay.

"Now I take you home. And then I get a shower and put on clean clothes and go back to work. Those two bastards are out there somewhere, and we gotta find them."

Yes, they did. Now more than ever.

Rafe was just pulling out his wallet to pay for breakfast when his phone buzzed.

"I'll get it," I told him, plucking the wallet from his hand and opening it. "Get the phone."

I fished out enough money to pay the bill—Rafe still prefers cash to credit or debit cards, since it's impossible to track someone through cash—and handed it to Maureen, who was handling hostess-, waitress-, and cashier-duties this early in the day. She made change, and I gave her a five for the tip. "Thanks."

She smiled as she tucked it away. "We'll see you next time, hon."

I told her to tell Yvonne hi, and was just about to turn away when I caught sight of a poster pinned to the front of the cashier's station.

Friday, it said, with today's date. *Dedication of the bauta to commemorate the victims of the 1946 race riots. Join us in The Bottom/Mink Slide, 10 ᴬᴹ, to hear Mordecai Lawson speak.*

I glanced at Rafe, but he was still on the phone, half turned away, scanning the parking lot.

I reached out and grabbed the poster. "Mind if I take this?"

Maureen looked at it. "Not at all, hon. It's almost over anyway, ain't it?"

Was it?

I glanced at my watch. It was just past eight. So no, not almost over. But getting close to starting. People were probably beginning to congregate. Wherever The Bottom/Mink Slide was. I'd lived here in Sweetwater my whole life—minus the few years I'd spent in Charleston and Nashville—and I had no idea.

"Do you know where this is?" I asked Mo, who was close to Mother's age. Not old enough to remember the race riots, but perhaps more up on the old place names than I was.

She scanned the poster. "Mink Slide? That's what the whites used to call the black business district in Columbia a hundred years ago. Not sure about The Bottoms, but it could be the same thing. Or a business in Mink Slide."

Maybe so. I shot another glance at Rafe, who was still talking. "Do you know where it is?"

"South of downtown," Maureen said vaguely.

"What about the dedication? Know anything about that?"

She shook her head. "Nothing more than it says. Mordecai Lawson's from Memphis, I think. Important during the Civil Rights era."

So after the Columbia Race Riots—everyone involved in them was probably dead by now—but a big shot in the African-American community.

"This is a black thing, right?"

"Yes," Maureen said, giving me a pitying sort of look, like she suspected that while I might look bright, looks could be deceiving.

Rafe sounded like he was in the process of finishing up his phone call, so I kept a tight grip on the poster and took Carrie's car seat in my other hand. "Thank you," I told Maureen politely, and took the couple of steps toward Rafe, just as he lowered the phone and dropped it in his pocket.

"We gotta go, darlin'." He pushed the door open.

"I know," I said. "Listen, Rafe..."

But he talked over me. "Let me take the baby. We gotta

hustle."

"Who was that on the phone?"

"Tammy," Rafe said, as he legged it across the parking lot toward the Cadillac. He's six feet three inches, so quite a lot taller than me, and his legs are correspondingly long. I had to scramble to keep up.

"What happened?"

"They found Rodney's car."

So this was good news, not more bad. "Where?"

"In the parking lot at Laurel Hill," Rafe said, unlocking the car doors remotely and reaching for the back door to put Carrie inside.

I skidded to a stop next to him. "Laurel Hill?"

He nodded. "I gotta get down there. If they're in the park, it's gonna take a lot of manpower to root them out."

"Or you could just put a guard in the parking lot and wait for them to get hungry and come out on their own," I suggested. "Why set yourselves up as targets? It's not like they're going to want to be in there forever. Rodney, at least, isn't used to roughing it. He'll want his pizza delivery and his HBO in a few days."

Rafe gave me a look as he shut the back door.

"Well, he will." I lifted the poster. "Listen—"

"We don't have much time, darlin'." He moved me out of his way. Literally, physically, moved me, so he could open the door for me. "I gotta get home, get the SWAT gear, and get down to Lawrence County."

"I'm not sure that's a good idea," I told him, even as I let myself be maneuvered into the seat. "If you'd just listen to me for a second—"

But the car door shut behind me before I could finish my sentence. When he opened the driver's side door and slid behind the wheel, I decided I'd just bide my time and let him drive. This dedication wasn't scheduled to take place for an hour and a half, at least, and I could be wrong to focus on it, anyway, if Rodney's Charger was in Lawrence County.

"How big is Laurel Hill?"

"Not sure," Rafe said. He pulled the nose of the car up to the edge of the parking lot, hung there for a second, and then gunned the engine. We shot across the road and into the southbound lane between two cars, the second of which gave us an irate toot of the horn.

I let out the breath I'd been holding while I'd waited to see if we'd get creamed, and took another one. "You've spent a lot of time walking around there. How long do you think someone could, reasonably, stay hidden?"

"If we didn't know they were there, maybe a couple weeks. In this situation? We'll find'em by tomorrow."

He glanced at me and added, "We'll have'em in custody in a couple hours if they're heading for that camp the park service found yesterday."

"I thought we decided that had to be somebody else's. If Lance had been sleeping in the house on Fulton."

"Not sure we decided that, darlin'. As I recall, we thought it mightn't be, if he'd been in the house. But there's no saying the camp couldn't be his and they're there now."

"Well, what do you think they're planning to do there? It's not like there's anything going on in the park that it'll be fun for them to blow up."

"There's still that hypothetical family reunion we talked about yesterday." He zoomed down the road like the hounds of hell were on his heels. "Although, after last night, they mighta given up on that."

"If they've given up on whatever they were planning, wouldn't they be gone? And off to somewhere where it would be easier to disappear? I mean, Laurel Hill isn't exactly the Appalachian Trail. You can't get lost in Laurel Hill for very long. You said so yourself."

Rafe sighed. "So what are you saying, darlin'?"

The driveway to the mansion was coming up ahead, and he slowed down to take the turn. Good thing, too, because at the speed he was going, we would have ended up halfway across the field if he hadn't.

"Drive around to the back," I told him.

He shot me a look, but didn't ask why. It was probably obvious. If Rodney and Lance weren't in Laurel Hill, they could be anywhere else, including here. And while I didn't think they were, I didn't want to take any chances. Unlike the other night, Rafe wasn't wearing Kevlar today.

He pulled around the house and parked the Cadillac in front of the garage. ""I'll go open the door."

"I'll get Carrie," I told him. "But I really do need you to listen to me, Rafe."

"Come upstairs and talk to me while I change. Tammy'll be here in five minutes."

He was already gone. By the time the car door slammed, he was at the back door, fumbling for his key.

I sighed, and went to get Carrie out of the back seat.

Twenty-Three

I trailed him through the kitchen, down the hallway, and up the stairs. And then I planted myself on the bed, determined to get him to listen to me.

Here's the problem, though. He was taking his clothes off, and that's always distracting. And he was naked underneath, having gone commando this morning because it was too much time and trouble to dig out a pair of underwear, so that was distracting, too.

By the time the black cargo pants were fastened and the black T-shirt was going down over all those lovely muscles, I was ready. "So here's the thing…"

He held up a finger in a 'just a minute' gesture. "I gotta brush my teeth."

And he walked out of the room and into the bathroom.

I gritted my teeth, since this was getting ridiculous, and stalked after him. And planted myself in the doorway of the bathroom while he put toothpaste on his brush and stuck it under the water spray and then into his mouth. "Listen to me. This is important."

"I'm listening," he told me, or something like it, around the brush. Although with all that noise going on inside his head, I wasn't sure how much he'd be able to process. So there went another thirty seconds while he gave his teeth a quicker than usual swipe after breakfast.

"Now," I told him when he'd spat and was in the process of

wiping his mouth. "One minute. Sit on the edge of the tub."

He glanced from me to it and back. "I'll stand."

"Fine. Just don't try to get out of here until I've finished talking. If Grimaldi shows up, it won't hurt her to wait sixty seconds."

"Then start talking," Rafe said. "You're wasting time."

I took a breath, and used it to order my thoughts. It wasn't enough, but better than nothing. "I don't think Rodney and Lance are in Laurel Hill. I think the car parked down there is a ruse. I think they're trying to lure you down there so you won't be here."

He arched a brow, but didn't try to interrupt me, so I kept going. "They probably drove there in Rodney's car, parked it, and then came back, maybe in Jennifer Vonderaa's car. You still haven't found that, right?"

He shook his head. He was leaning against the edge of the sink, and his arms were folded across his chest—nice arms, nice chest—but at least it seemed like he was actually listening.

"There's nothing for them to blow up in Laurel Hill," I said. "And probably not a lot of people on a weekday morning, either. And Clayton was specific about something happening on Friday."

"Could be Friday night. Might be more people tonight."

"Sure. But it doesn't make any sense. If they want to make a splash, making it in a small wildlife area in the middle of nowhere isn't very impressive. You have to admit that."

Apparently he didn't, because all he did was arch a brow.

"While you were on the phone with Grimaldi, I saw this poster hanging on the hostess stand at Beulah's. This morning at ten, there's a dedication of a monument to the people who died during the Columbia race riots in 1946. Some big-shot Civil Rights leader from Memphis is the speaker. It's going to take place somewhere called The Bottoms or Mink Slide in Columbia. I'm not sure whether The Bottoms is just another name for Mink Slide, or whether it's a place—a business or something—in Mink Slide. But Mo told me Mink Slide is what the white population called the black business district back then. That's where the riots started."

Rafe's posture didn't change, but his eyes sharpened. "So there's an event at ten commemorating black history."

I nodded. "I was thinking—"

"I know what you're thinking, darlin'." He dropped a quick kiss on my lips before he moved me out of his way. "That the piece of paper you were hanging onto all the way home? Let me see it."

It was on the bed next to Carrie's seat—the baby was cooing and playing with her toes—and Rafe grabbed it and scanned it.

"If Lance wants to start a race war in Columbia," I told him, from the doorway of the bedroom this time, "this sounds like a good time and place to kick it off."

"No kidding." He looked pensive for a moment. "Any idea where this place is?"

"None. But Google is your friend." I pulled out my phone and typed. While I was scanning the results, there was the sound of an engine and the beep of a horn outside. "That must be Grimaldi."

"I'll go," Rafe said and turned toward the door.

I moved out of the way so he could get past me. "Don't leave with her."

"I won't. But I'm thinking maybe we'll let the sheriffs handle Laurel Hill, and the PD can handle Columbia."

That sounded like an excellent division of labor to me. Of course, he had to talk Grimaldi into it first.

He disappeared down the stairs while I finished my Googling. I grabbed the car seat and followed. By the time I got to the foyer, Grimaldi had, very reluctantly, left the car, and was standing just inside the door looking at the flier Rafe had given her.

"The riots took place just southeast of the town square," I told them both. "The black population called it The Bottoms, the area at the bottom of the hill along East 8th Street. The white population called it Mink Slide. There's already a historical marker on that block, outside the A.J. Morton Funeral Home. I don't know why I've never noticed it."

"I don't imagine you would have been there," Grimaldi said distractedly, reading the flier. "East 8th is a wasteland. There's nothing there but some boarded-up buildings and a couple of churches. Maybe a barber shop or two. And several empty lots. Nothing you'd be interested in."

Maybe not. But I should have known about the historical marker, at least. It was for history that had taken place less than thirty minutes from where I grew up, and within the last hundred years.

"Mordecai Lawson's a Civil Rights era activist," Rafe told her. "And a big deal in Memphis. I ran across him during the time I was working there."

During the years he'd spent trying to infiltrate Hector Gonzales's criminal organization, which had fingers in every major city in the southeast. "He wasn't involved in anything shady, was he?"

"No, darlin'. Upstanding citizen. Lawyer. Judge."

"If he were to be killed…"

"It wouldn't be good," Rafe said.

Grimaldi lowered the flier. "This makes enough sense that we're going to go with it. I'll call Bob and tell him that he and the other sheriffs can handle Laurel Hill. And to let him know what we're thinking might be going on here."

"If he knows that, I don't think he'll agree to go to Laurel Hill," I said.

"The sheriffs of Lawrence, Lewis, and Giles are sitting around with nothing to do," Rafe added. "Between them and the park service, they can cover Laurel Hill. And Bob can stay here and—"

He closed his mouth when his phone went off. Grimaldi's did, too. They both grabbed for them, and both their faces turned to ultra-grim at the same time.

"What?" I asked, looking from one to the other.

"Explosion at the park ranger station in Laurel Hill," Rafe said.

"Oh, no." Were we wrong about this? "Did anybody die?"

Grimaldi was already dialing. "Depends on how many rangers were there. Or anyone else." She put the phone to her ear. "Bob."

She turned away while she listened to whatever Bob Satterfield had to say.

"I don't think I'm wrong about this," I told Rafe, softly.

He shook his head. "Somebody's at Laurel Hill, though. If this was an ammonal explosion, somebody had to be there to set it off."

True. "Maybe it's Rodney. Maybe Lance killed Felicia and he and Rodney took off in Rodney's car early this morning. But Lance got out after a few blocks while Rodney went down to Laurel Hill. Or maybe they both went down there, and Lance helped Rodney get the Tannerite set up, and then Lance came back to Columbia in Jennifer's car."

"Possible," Rafe admitted.

"Then at eight-thirty, Rodney set off the explosion. Everyone from four counties converges on Laurel Hill. Rodney has fun picking off first responders." Just as I had thought when we were standing on Fulton Street three nights ago, and outside Rodney's apartment building this morning. If someone wanted to take out a lot of law enforcement, it would have been a golden opportunity.

Rafe looked grim, maybe at visions of the carnage that could ensue. But he was also keeping an eye on the bigger picture. "By ten o'clock, ain't no law enforcement left in Columbia.

SWAT and everyone else that can be spared has gone to Laurel Hill. And Lance can do whatever he wants."

"It makes sense, doesn't it?"

He nodded. "Got any proof?"

None whatsoever. "I'm not saying that you should ignore Laurel Hill, you know. Someone's down there, and it's probably Rodney. Somebody needs to go down there and catch him. And he's been practicing his shooting, so it could be dangerous. But blowing up the ranger station in a small wildlife area isn't going to start that race war they want. Blowing up, or taking out, the crowd that's gathered to commemorate the 1946 race riots might."

Rafe nodded. "We better get up to Columbia and have a look around."

"When you say we," I began, and he shook his head.

"Not you, darlin'. You and Carrie stay here."

"I wasn't going to mingle with the crowd," I protested. "But I can help look around, at least. If he has a rifle, he'll be somewhere at a distance, right? I can look around at a distance and not be in the line of fire."

He hesitated. Long enough that Grimaldi finished her phone call and turned back to us. "Bob's taking his team to Laurel Hill."

So there went any backup from the sheriff's department for Columbia. All the more reason to let me look around.

"What about the SWAT team?" Rafe asked. Since he was on the SWAT team, and already dressed in team colors, I guess he was afraid he'd be ordered down to Laurel Hill, too, now that we knew that somebody was down there and might start shooting.

"Bob thinks the SWAT team will stand out against the grass," Grimaldi said, with a twitch of her lips.

"So we're not going?"

She shook her head. "I told him to handle it. We'll handle

Columbia."

"Let's go, then." Rafe turned toward the door.

I opened my mouth to tell him that I wanted to come, too, and then I changed my mind and closed it again. "Good luck," I told them instead, as they both stepped through the door and onto the porch. "Let me know how it goes."

Rafe's eyes narrowed, but he didn't say anything. I smiled sweetly, before I closed and locked the door behind them, and watched them walk away.

I was out the back door before Grimaldi's SUV had cleared the driveway. Two minutes later, Carrie and I were clearing the driveway, too, and on our way up the highway toward Columbia.

I made sure I stayed far enough behind them that they wouldn't notice me in the rearview mirror. Once we got into Columbia proper, I did catch a glimpse of the SUV at the top of Main Street, taking a right to circle City Hall, but that was just as I was taking a left onto West 8th, so I didn't think they'd seen me.

I parked outside the library, and lifted Carrie's stroller out of the trunk of the car. After fitting the car seat into it—it was the newfangled kind, where the car seat did double duty as stroller with the addition of wheels—we set off down the street in the direction of Main, and of East 8th, on the other side of the main drag.

By now, it was past nine-fifteen, getting closer to nine-thirty, and a little crowd had gathered down the street on East 8th. I padded in that direction, pushing Carrie and the stroller ahead of me. Just a young mother out for a walk with her baby. Nothing to see here.

There were maybe fifteen people gathered, so not a big crowd yet. And the crowd might not get much bigger, since it was in the middle of the workday. Most of the folks here were older, probably retired, and most of them were black. I nodded and smiled in both directions as I pushed Carrie down the street past them. "Excuse us. Sorry. Coming through."

The funeral home I'd mentioned earlier, with the historical marker, turned out to be a boarded-up brick building, sitting well back from the sidewalk and positioned next to an alley. Up the alley and a little west, I could just see the top of the clock tower on City Hall over the roofs of the buildings fronting the square.

The monument itself was wrapped in a sheet, up on the grass not too far from the marker. On the other side of the alley was a paved parking lot, where a tent had been erected over thirty or forty folding chairs and a wooden podium. A black woman in her fifties was fiddling with a microphone, and there were a few more people in the seats. The crowd in the street was slowly seeping in that direction.

There was no sign of Mordecai Lawson yet. I gave the clock tower at City Hall another hard look—anyone who climbed up there would have a straight shot at the crowd down here—and dug in my pocket for the phone.

I dialed Rafe as I pushed the stroller up the alley, still nodding and smiling at anyone I passed. "You need to get somebody up to the top of the clock tower on City Hall and make sure it's empty."

"'Scuse me?"

"The clock tower," I said. "There's a straight sight line down to the monument on East 8th. Anyone who was up there would be able to pick off Mordecai Lawson without any problem."

There was a slight pause. "I thought you were gonna stay home, Savannah."

"Don't worry about it. There's nothing going on yet. Maybe a dozen people, and a woman who's setting up a microphone. There's a podium and the bauta. That's it. No media or anything. And no sign of Lance, or of Jennifer's car."

"Get away from there."

"I'm getting," I said. "I'm already on my way up to 7th. But I don't think anything's going to happen until the ceremony starts."

He didn't answer that, and I added, "So will you get someone up to check the clock tower? I think someone with some experience could make that shot. If they were crazy enough to climb City Hall to do it."

"I don't think he's that crazy," Rafe said, "but I'll tell Tammy. She'll get someone up to check."

"Thank you." I stopped at the mouth of the alley on 7th and looked around, catching my breath. It's a climb from 8th up to City Hall. Probably why the locals had called East 8th The Bottoms back then. It was at the bottom of the hill. "Nothing going on on 7th."

"Then go home," Rafe said.

"It's still early."

He didn't say anything, and I added, "I'm not being careless, Rafe. Not with Carrie." Nor with myself, for that matter. "I'm just walking around downtown Columbia. There are plenty of other people here."

And if somebody started shooting, we'd all be targets. But for now, I was going on the assumption that only the crowd on East 8th was in danger, and not until the ceremony started.

"You know," I told Rafe, "you could cancel the ceremony. Just call whoever arranged it, and tell them it's off. That there have been threats and they can't proceed."

"Tammy's already tried to get approval for that. The mayor's inclined to think this is a long shot, and the danger's at Laurel Hill."

"Maybe I could go down there on the sly and tell them—"

"No!" He took a breath and said it again, more calmly. "No, darlin'. I don't want you anywhere near there. And we don't know that anything's going on. It's just a hunch. There haven't been any threats to the ceremony. There's been a definite threat in Laurel Hill."

Yes. There was no arguing with that.

"Any news from down there?"

"Not yet. It takes a while to get there. I don't imagine they'll catch up to Rodney for a couple hours, at least."

"Unless he's set up close enough to take pot shots at the parking area."

He didn't respond to that. "I'll let you know when I hear something."

"What about the SWAT team?"

"Ready to go," Rafe said, "as soon as we know where we're going."

"And somebody's checking the clock tower?" I glanced at it again, just across the square from me now. There was no movement up there, and everything looked peaceful.

"I promise, darlin'. Now will you please take yourself and our daughter outta there?"

"I'm not in any danger. Nothing's going on."

"If there's a sniper with a gun anywhere around the town square," Rafe said, "I want you miles away from there. Not a block up from where we think his target is."

"Just let me know if he's in the clock tower. I'm going to buy a cup of coffee and try to look inconspicuous."

I dropped the phone back into my pocket and wheeled Carrie into the coffee shop on the corner. By the time I came out again, my phone was ringing.

"Clock tower's empty," my husband said.

"Good." I looked around for somewhere else Lance might be holed up.

"You about ready to head on home now?"

"Soon. I just want one more look around. I mean, he has to be somewhere."

"A good sniper can take out a target from a couple miles away," Rafe told me. "He could be halfway between here and

Sweetwater."

Not quite. Not only is Sweetwater farther away than that, but there are hills between. If he wanted a clear shot at The Bottoms, there were only so many places he could get that. And even as I stood there, another complication presented itself, rolling past in a plain gray van.

"Damn," I said, and didn't even think to apologize for it.

"What?" Rafe said in my ear.

"Audrey just drove past me with your grandmother. What do you want to bet they're headed to the ceremony?"

As the van rolled down the hill, the turn signal came on, indicating a right turn onto East 8th. "Yep. Looks like it."

Rafe said something unprintable.

"I'll try to catch them before they get out of the car," I said. "Although if I tell them what's going on, you know they're going to want to tell everyone else. And by then, Mordecai Lawson might have arrived, and—"

"Don't go anywhere near them," Rafe said. I could hear from the background that he was moving. "Stay where you are."

"It's your grandmother." And Mother's best friend. "I can't let them walk over there. If I can catch them before they leave the car…"

I dropped the phone into my pocket without taking the time to turn it off, and threw the coffee cup. It hit the gutter with a splat, and coffee flew everywhere. I grabbed the stroller handle with both hands and took off down the hill.

When I puffed around the corner—I've never been in great shape, and after giving birth a few months ago, I was in worse shape now than ever before—the van was parked halfway down the block, and Audrey was in the process of helping her aunt down to the sidewalk.

"Audrey!" I pulled to a stop next to them, panting.

She turned to me, surprised. "Savannah? What are you

doing here?"

"You have to go home," I said, breathlessly.

"Oh, we can't." She glanced down at Mrs. Jenkins. "Aunt Tondalia wants to see Mr. Lawson."

"She can see Mr. Lawson some other time. It isn't safe for you to be here."

Audrey looked at me. Mrs. Jenkins did, too, but I wasn't sure how much she understood.

"What's going on?" Audrey wanted to know. It sounded like she was taking me seriously, anyway, so that was good.

I looked around, to make sure no one else was close enough to hear me. "Something bad is going on. You have to leave."

"Not until I say hello to Mordecai," Mrs. J told me.

Say hello to? "You know Mr. Lawson?"

"Knew him back in the old days," Mrs. J said. "I marched from Selma to Montgomery with Mordecai in 1965."

Had she really?

"Then you definitely need to see him," Audrey said, patting her aunt's hand.

All the more reason to get her out of there, as far as I was concerned. If Lance was here and opened fire, and Mordecai Lawson was shot, I didn't think that experience would be good for Mrs. Jenkins. Her son had been shot right in front of their house the year before Rafe was born, and Mrs. Jenkins wasn't over it, thirty-one years later. I doubted she'd ever be. The last thing she needed was to witness another shooting, and of an old friend, too.

But as I tried to shoo them back into the van, a sleek, black stretch limo glided around the corner, and I realized it was too late. That had to be Mordecai Lawson's entourage, and if he was here, there was no way to convince Mrs. J to leave.

Maybe I could just keep them here instead, safely behind the van—

The limo rolled silently past us, and in its wake, a black-clad figure skidded around the corner. I tensed—my first thought was that it was Lance, ready to blow someone away. It only took a second for me to recognize Rafe, though.

He took in the street at a glance, found us, and headed in our direction. Meanwhile, up ahead, the few people still on the street parted for the limo, which glided to a stop in front of the bauta. The front door opened and a chauffeur in full uniform stepped out. He slapped a cap on his head and walked five or six feet backwards until he could swing the door to the back open.

The crowd surged back around the limo while Mrs. Jenkins tried to tug her arm out of Audrey's grasp. Rafe skidded to a stop next to the van just as a tall, skinny, old black man unfolded himself from the back of the limo and rose to a full height of close to six and a half feet. Someone in the crowd started clapping, and others joined in.

He headed for the tent, entering from the back and inclining his head left and right as he proceeded toward the front. The people who hadn't yet found seats disbursed themselves into the rows on the left and the right, and by the time Mordecai Lawson had climbed the single step onto the wooden podium and turned to the crowd, he was being cheered by thirty or forty people.

"Friends." His voice was rich and resonant through the microphone, as he gestured expansively with big hands at the end of long arms. "Friends, be seated."

And that's when the first shot rang through the air, so loud it hurt my ears. It hit the wooden platform, and for the second time inside a week, I watched something blow up.

Twenty-Four

"Down!"

Rafe pitched the word so everyone in a block radius could hear him, but he shoved me down with one hand, and wrapped the other arm around both his grandmother and his cousin at the same time, sweeping them down next to me.

"Stay," he added, for our benefit only.

"Keep your head down!" I told him, although I'm not sure he heard me. I couldn't hear me. My ears were still ringing, and besides, there was a whole lot of other noise. Screaming, crying, sobbing, from the other side of the street, interspersed with the staccato burst of a rifle.

I raised my head far enough to be able to peer through the window of the van and out the window on the other side. "He's on top of one of the church towers."

Rafe nodded, eyes already on it.

The church down on the corner, beyond the boarded-up funeral home, beyond the bauta and the podium and the limousine and the crowd, had a square tower on each corner, and a gabled, pointed roof in-between. Each tower was considerably taller than the top of the gable, and one tower was taller than the other. The ground rose in the back, so the front of the church was a solid story higher than the back of the church, too. The tallest tower was probably three stories tall, while the shorter one might have been two and a half. The gunman was on top of that one. If I squinted, I could see the slight movement as he jiggled the rifle to sight again.

Rafe's body tensed, like he was planning to move, and I grabbed the sleeve of his jacket—the one with SWAT in iridescent letters across the back—and spoke fast. "There's a one-story addition on the back of the church. Sort of a saltbox roof. And the ground's higher back there. Should be easy to get onto." I'd been looking at the architecture of the church when I'd walked up the alley earlier. Not for this purpose, although now it came in handy. "You need to move along the bottom of the roof so he doesn't see you, and then you have to climb around the tower once you get there. You can't go along the peak, or he'll see you."

He nodded. "You gotta let go, Savannah."

Of course I did. Because of course he had to do this. Even though he was hurt, and even though I desperately wanted to make sure he wouldn't get hurt again.

"Be careful."

"Always." He flashed me a grin before he moved away. I watched, heart in my throat, as he headed up the street, long legs eating up the distance.

I waited for the shots, but they didn't come. Maybe Lance was already breaking down and trying to make his escape, or maybe he just wasn't focused on anything outside the small area under the tent.

Nothing much was happening there. A few people were gathered around Mordecai Lawson, who had been thrown several feet through the air, and was flat on his back on the pavement. I assumed he was bleeding, because the lady who'd been setting up the microphone earlier looked like she was applying pressure to what might have been his leg, but at least that meant he wasn't dead, so silver lining there.

The rest of the people were huddled against the wall of the building, or trying to squeeze themselves under the flimsy folding chairs. A few were moaning or sobbing softly, but it was hard to be sure whether they were hurt or just scared. I distinctly heard a woman's voice praying, while another was having hysterics, and who could blame her?

"You OK?" I asked Audrey. Carrie was still crying from the rough handling, and I fumbled for her pacifier, dug it out from behind her back—that might have been part of the reason she was crying—and popped it in her mouth. She hiccupped a couple of times and then quieted.

"We're fine," Audrey said, her voice thin. She was hanging on to Mrs. Jenkins with everything she had. Mrs. J was practically hyperventilating, and I leaned closer to her. "It's OK, Mrs. Jenkins. We're fine. And Rafe will be fine, too. He knows what he's doing."

She didn't answer, and I wasn't sure she heard me. I wasn't sure she knew who I was, or who Rafe was. I had no idea if she knew where she was.

But she was safe and unharmed, and we could deal with the rest later.

I raised my head and peered through the car again. But it was hard to see clearly, and the shooting seemed to have stopped, so I told Audrey, "Stay with Carrie," and scooted around the back of the car.

There was no movement from the tower, and no sign of anyone up there. I could hear sirens coming closer, and the rumble of a big engine. Other black-clad shapes started pouring around the corner and down the alley—or maybe not pouring, but they came, and there were more than a few of them. A huge, armored SWAT vehicle rumbled around the corner up ahead. I heard noises behind me, too, and turned in time to see another, smaller SWAT truck turn the corner from Main Street.

Then the sound of the ambulance rose to a shriek, and it careened into South 8th from up ahead.

A tall guy skidded to a stop next to me. "Savannah!"

It was Patrick Nolan, Darcy's boyfriend, looking rather

impressive in SWAT black.

"She's not here," I told him, since I was sure he would be worried about Darcy. If I was here, she might be, as well. "Audrey and Mrs. J are over there."

I waved to the other side of the van.

"Hurt?"

I shook my head. "Rafe went after the guy. He was on top of the church tower. I don't know where he is now. Either of them."

"I'll go," Nolan said, and took off. Another figure in black followed, up the alley and behind the old funeral home. Since no shots rang out to stop them, I followed, too. Carrie was safe with Audrey and Mrs. Jenkins, Audrey would take care of her if she needed anything, and I needed to know if my husband was safe.

The area behind the old building was high with last year's weeds. I fought my way through, as brambles and burrs clung to my coat and tried to slow me down, and came out next to the side of the church. A much bigger building, it stretched farther back than the small funeral home. A very narrow strip of ground separated them, probably wide enough for someone to squeeze through, but nothing more. No one was in it right now. I could see through to the street, in time to catch another ambulance pull up next to the first.

Nolan was already on the roof, making his way along the steep side like a crab. His companion—I thought it might be Tamara Grimaldi—was boosting herself up. And behind her, another black-clad figure—this one much smaller—was peering up at the roof with what I could only describe as loathing. Lupe Vasquez, Nolan's patrol partner, is about a foot shorter than he is.

"Vasquez!"

She turned to me, and I waved. She came jogging, the stuff on her belt jingled. "You OK?"

"We were down the street when the shooting started. Rafe's grandmother knew Mr. Lawson back in the day, so she wanted to see him. She and her niece and my daughter are hiding behind the gray van down there."

"Hurt?"

I shook my head. "Mrs. Jenkins is shook up. I'm sure Audrey is, too. But nobody got shot. Do you know who did?"

"Not yet. We were already on our way when the shooting starting. Rafe took off like a shot after he talked to you, and the rest of us didn't even try to keep up. Although we got here as fast as we could. And brought the vehicles."

I nodded. "Mordecai Lawson arrived. He walked up on the podium and greeted the crowd. The first shot hit the podium itself. There must have been Tannerite under it, because it blew. Lawson went flying. And then I think Lance started shooting at other people, but there was so much noise and activity it was hard to know for sure..."

And speaking of Lance—

There was the sound of a scuffle up the roof, and I took a couple of steps sideways for a better view.

And there he was, my husband, with a scratch on his cheek that was oozing blood, and the shadow of a black eye starting to come up—not to mention several broken ribs under his clothes that I couldn't see—hauling the handcuffed villain along the peak of the roof.

"Careful," I heard him say, "so I don't accidentally let go. It's a long way down."

Lance must have thought that sounded better than what was happening, though, because he put up quite a fight. I held my breath as I watched him wiggle like an eel on a hook, trying to upset Rafe's balance. But then Nolan was there, and Grimaldi, and between them, they managed to wrestle him down the gable, and onto the one-story addition, and from there onto the ground. Lupe Vasquez stood ready to receive him, and so, by now, did several other SWAT officers.

Rafe grinned down at me. "Hi, darlin'."

"Hi," I said, my heart beating hard against my ribs. "You got hurt again."

"Just a little. He got hurt more."

He turned to Vasquez. "Come on up here. I gotta job for you."

Vasquez eyed the edge of the roof, and Rafe turned to Nolan. "Give your partner a boost. I need her to climb the tower and get this POS's stuff down."

Nolan grabbed Vasquez by the waist and basically threw her up on the roof. He was stronger than he looked. Rafe caught her, and the two of them started making their way back toward the front of the building and the two towers. "Be careful," I called after them.

Vasquez gave me a thumb up, with the hand she wasn't using to keep her balance. Rafe just winked, but I could hear his standard reply in my head. *"Always."*

"Only two fatalities," he told me later. "Not that those two don't matter. And not that those two are all he's responsible for."

No. There was Jennifer Vonderaa, and Felicia Robinson. And the single individual Rodney killed in Laurel Hill before sheriff's deputies took him down. And the injuries, both in Columbia and Laurel Hill, including Mordecai Lawson's broken leg. But still, two fatalities today wasn't bad. Not under the circumstances.

He could have killed everyone on East 8th street, most likely. I had no idea why he hadn't.

In Laurel Hill, the explosion had taken out a chunk of the wall and a chunk of the ceiling, but nobody had been in that part of the building when it blew, so nobody had gotten killed. We—or Rafe and Grimaldi and Bob—ascribed that to the

Tannerite they'd had to leave behind in Jennifer Vonderaa's house. Not getting their hands on that had meant that both explosions had been less powerful than Lance had wanted them to be. If they'd been able to add the rest of the Tannerite, Mordecai Lawson would probably be dead, and so would several park rangers.

There had been injuries in Laurel Hill, of course. Rangers hit by flying debris and the like. Cuts and bruises and a concussion. But nothing serious. And one fatality, a sheriff's deputy from Lawrence County. After shooting him, Rodney had been so shaken by what he'd done that catching him had been no problem.

"We found the little coward sniveling over a broken leg at the bottom of Finnie Peak," Bob Satterfield said disgustedly.

It was later that afternoon, and we were all gathered at Beulah's, halfway between Columbia and Sweetwater. Bob had brought Cletus Johnson, who had taken a seat practically as far away from Rafe as he could get, while still being at the same table.

After Rafe hauled her up on the roof, Lupe Vasquez had skinned up the church tower as easily as a monkey. She's both small and light, and in order to qualify for the SWAT team, obviously in good shape as well. She'd brought down Lance's weapon, and the backpack with his extra ammunition and other stuff. He was behind bars along with Rodney, and neither of them were likely to get out anytime soon, in spite of the surprisingly low number of casualties we'd just been talking about.

Mordecai Lawson was all right. He'd broken his leg, and in a man his age, that wasn't great, but the EMTs seemed to think he'd be all right. There were two fatalities, both of them older women, and a few other injuries, but nothing like it could have been. None of us could explain it, and Lance had declined to give us his version, so we just had to chalk it up to luck or fate or maybe just bad eyesight on Lance's part.

"What will happen to the two of them?" I asked. "Or three. Is Kyle being arrested, too?"

"Kyle looks like he's gonna get off with community service and a slap on the wrist," Rafe said. "He was more than happy to roll over on both Rodney and Lance in exchange for a reduced sentence."

"There isn't a whole lot we can charge him with, anyway," Grimaldi added. "He wasn't part of planning what happened this morning. Lance did that, and Kyle doesn't think he told Rodney anything about it until today. If he did, Rodney didn't tell Kyle."

"Or so Kyle says."

They both nodded. "We can't prove he's lying," Grimaldi said. "There are no text messages or anything like that implicating Kyle in the planning. Or any text messages, period, between him and Lance's burner phone. Anything like that seems to have gone through Rodney, and none of the messages between Kyle and Rodney mention anything specific about today."

"What about my house? They vandalized my house. Twice! Is he just going to get away with that?"

"Again, not much we can do," Grimaldi said. "You can sue for damages in civil court. But Kyle doesn't have much money, and since he's of age, his parents aren't responsible…"

I made a face. "So we just have to hope the insurance company will come through."

"Yes and no. Turns out Rodney and Kyle didn't vandalize your house on Sunday night."

"So who vandalized my house? And how do you know?"

"Remember that couple that came through the open house?" Rafe said. "The guy who tried to buy the place at auction, and his wife?"

My eyes widened. "You're kidding. They did it?"

"Their son," Grimaldi said. "Dusty Tremayne. We finally had a chance to make it through all the doorbell cameras in the area. It wasn't a priority, sorry."

I waved the apology away, since that was certainly understandable, with everything that had gone on this week. "One of the doorbell cameras caught him?"

"Cutting through the yard on the next street with a crowbar in his hand," Grimaldi nodded. "Going toward your house, and then coming back twenty minutes later. And even better—"

"Yes?"

"The camera caught the SUV parked across the street. And the person driving."

"Her? Or him?"

"Her," Grimaldi said. "Richelle. Dusty's mother. She sat there for twenty minutes with the windows rolled down and her head out, listening."

"Can you charge her with anything?"

"Depends on how much damage was done," Grimaldi said. "Over a thousand dollars? Over ten thousand? Over sixty?"

"Not over sixty. Probably over ten."

"Class C felony," Grimaldi said, "punishable by three to fifteen years in prison and a fine of up to ten thousand dollars."

That wouldn't cover the damage, and I might not get it anyway, but it would help. And the satisfaction would be considerable. Especially if it involved jail time.

"And you can take 'em to court," Rafe said. "Or Darcy can, since it's her house. Civil case. Ask for damages. Your brother or sister would litigate for you."

They probably would. Especially Catherine. She likes nailing people's ears to the wall.

"Are you going to arrest them? The Tremaynes?"

"When we're finished here," Grimaldi said. "You can come and watch if you want."

I smiled. "Can I invite Darcy and Charlotte to come along?"

"The more, the merrier," Grimaldi said. She lifted her glass of Pepsi. "To a job well done."

I clinked mine against it. "I'll drink to that."

So would everyone else, it seemed. Glasses were raised up and down the table. Yvonne, who didn't have a drink, but who was standing at the other end of the long table with her hand on Cletus Johnson's extra-broad shoulder, raised her voice instead. "Hip-hip—"

"Hooray!" we all chorused.

Yvonne bent to say something in Cletus's ear. Bob and Grimaldi knocked their glasses together, and so did Nolan and Lupe Vasquez, on the opposite side of the table. Rafe joined in with his own glass. I glanced down at my baby, who was taking in the scene with her eyes wide—big and blue and surrounded by those long, dark lashes.

Her world was safe once more. We had struck a blow for decency, and equality, and justice, and taken two people off the streets who would have taken that away from her if they could. We'd made the world a better, safer place today for someone like Carrie.

And then I fished my phone out of my bag to contact my sister and my best friend to put them on notice that the person who had destroyed our house was about to be arrested and we'd been invited to watch her humiliation.

It had been a good day so far, and it was about to get even better.

# # #

About the Author

New York Times and *USA Today* bestselling author Jenna Bennett (Jennie Bentley) writes the Do It Yourself home renovation mysteries for Berkley Prime Crime and the Savannah Martin real estate mysteries for her own gratification. She also writes a variety of romance for a change of pace.

For more information, please visit Jenna's website:
www.JennaBennett.com